When The Well Runs Dry

M J Dees

Published by M J Dees, 2018.

WHEN THE WELL RUNS DRY

First edition. August 12, 2018.

Copyright © 2018 M J Dees.

ISBN: 978-1386598251

Written by M J Dees.

Get M J Dees' first novel FOR FREE

Sign up for the no-spam newsletter and get LIVING WITH SACI for free.
You will find details at the end of WHEN THE WELL RUNS DRY.

When The Well Runs Dry

In a country divided by civil war, one city stands above the chaos.

Since the system collapsed, citizens are struggling to survive. Marauders are destroying what little is left. However, not everyone is ready to surrender.

The Alder and her loyal supporters find themselves caught in a life or death struggle to save, not only themselves, but also those around them. The future of the nation is at stake.

When The Well Runs Dry is the first book in M J Dees' dystopian series set in a future where resources have all but run out.

Read this book while there is still a future in which to read it.

Part One

December 31

It has been a long time since there have been fireworks. I remember when I was young, and I went to see the fireworks on the Thames for the millennium. They said there would be a river of fire. No-one was sure what happened to that. You probably wonder why I'm writing you this letter after all these years. I'm wondering that myself. I'm wondering how you will read it given that I've no means of posting it and no way of knowing where you are even if I did.

January 2

2°C, but at least it's sunny. I ventured out to take some cuttings from the fruit trees for grafting in the spring, but I've been looking through the seeds I've saved to make a plan of what to plant where and when. The plan more or less makes itself as I follow a strict rotation, although there is a little bit of annual variation because of the beds being different in size.

This is more of a diary than a letter, and it has more chance of someone discovering it than me ever posting it. Its chances of you discovering it are slim to non-existent, but I console myself with the hope that you might still be alive and that one day it might find its way into your hands and you may read it. But to what end? What do I hope to achieve? Maybe it will give me the opportunity to say all the things I should have said when we were together before everything became so messy.

I think there is also an element of vanity. I would like others to know how I survived for so long where so many others failed. Maybe they didn't fail. I have no way of knowing what is happening in the next valley, let alone elsewhere.

Take my water filtration system as an example. It is still one of my proudest achievements and yet it was one of the earliest necessities. As you know, I had been collecting rainwater for years to water the garden during dry spells, but the collapse of the water infrastructure meant I had to find a way of purifying this water myself. At first, I boiled the water, and I still do, but it became clear that this would require an awful lot of fuel. In one of my old books, I found a diagram of what they described as a slow sand filter. It required a barrel, but I had hoarded plenty of those over the years. Old containers from the days when they shipped fruit juice all over the place. I made a carbon filter from leftover charcoal and PVC pipe. I even fitted a recirculation system that, with the aid of a small solar panel and a battery, can run all day every day. It was easy to see what would happen back then and I could hoard all the things I would need. I remember you complaining about all the junk I was collecting, but I promise you I've made use of every single thing. Both solar panels and batteries were cheap and easy to get back then before the collapse. I shudder to think what I would do if I needed to replace one now.

January 3

It's warmer today. 5°C. There are more clouds in the sky, I expect they are keeping the heat in a bit. It has been mild enough today to do a bit of weeding, mainly chickweed and wild onions.

Do you remember Mary Poppins? She's still going strong. As is Mr Benn. Do you remember how you cried when we gave away her first doelings? I'm afraid I don't give them away anymore. There's no-one to give them to or to trade with. Both Mary Poppins and Mr Benn are getting on now. I think they'll both have to retire soon, so I'll select a doe and a buck to replace them. Mr Benn hasn't got any less cantankerous than you'll remember and he's smelly these days. I have to keep him away from the girls to stop the milk tasting bad. Poppins' current friend is Nanny McPhee, they are good friends and keep each other amused. I have a whole area dedicated to grasses, which is more than enough for the few goats I have.

I have the stove on pretty much constantly at the moment, which means I have a constant supply of boiling water which I store to supplement my homemade filtration system which I told you about yesterday. I think the way I have organised the house and land would impress you. It might not have many of the luxuries you used to enjoy, but with the state of things now, it's about as comfortable as expected.

I worry about the smoke from the chimney attracting undesirables, but I guess if they were going to raid me, it would have already happened by now. My land is remote, that was one reason for choosing it, as you know, but it's not remote enough to avoid those who would rather take than create. And you know more than anyone, the horrors of which people are capable.

I keep the milk outside. That's my refrigerator. In the summer, it is more challenging, but the stream is always cool, even in the height of summer as it runs from the hills behind the valley.

My storage techniques get better each year, and I am sure my range of pickles would impress you. The vinegar I make myself from the apples. You may be interested that I managed to make my sugar and grow enough beets for this purpose every year. I still keep the bees but the sugar helps with pickling and preserving which keeps these winters interesting.

I am not vegetarian anymore, you won't be surprised to hear. Once I ran out of people to trade with, I didn't want to waste the excess goat and chicken, so I've been honing my butchery skills too. At my age, I'm not that worried about my cholesterol.

January 4

The sun has been trying to poke its head through the clouds all day today, and on a couple of occasions, it succeeded. The thermometer registered a maximum of 6°C today.

I've been painting a pretty picture of the state of our settlement so far, but there are some things with which you would not be happy. Do you remember the composting toilet? How much you hated it. Well since the collapse of the state sewage system, the composting toilet has become the only method for processing my solids. I continue to wee on the compost heap; I know that always disgusted you but it is very good for the compost. I have a separate heap where I put all the animal waste, and to this, I add the human waste on the occasions I need to empty the toilet which is not often. The bacteria seem to be working very well in there, and it doesn't smell.

Last night I dreamt about you. It wasn't a good dream. I dreamt of the last time I saw you. I think about it a lot. It still hurts. I'm not sure I'm ready to deal with it yet. Perhaps this is what this diary is about. I remember in the days when you used to have a psychologist. In the days when everyone had a psychologist. She told you to keep a journal. I remember you used to write down all of your dreams. Some of them were weird. Maybe this diary is something like that, it isn't really for you, it's for me.

It will please you to know that the chickens are doing well. I see little in the way of wildlife these days. Only the odd bird. Even they aren't as plentiful as they used to be. I now grow enough cereals in the summer to provide the birds with enough straw to provide a deep litter right through the winter, and it all goes on the compost heap in the spring.

One thing you might not know is that I make my oil now. Years ago, when it was still safe to make the trip into town, I picked up a small press relatively cheap. It's worth its weight in gold now. I use the oil for cooking, but I also use it as a base for soaps and use oil lamps too. Each year I've grown enough sunflowers to keep me in oil with enough seeds left over for the next crop.

Today I harvested some parsnips and some Jerusalem artichokes. I know you never liked the latter. You always said they made me fart. They do. It's true. I still imagine you complaining every time I eat them.

I spent the afternoon checking the tools. It's a good time of the year to make minor repairs before it gets too busy in the garden.

I think tomorrow that I might start some cabbage seeds and some early lettuce. Every day seems milder than the last. However, I plan to add an extra layer of mulch around the root crops. It won't be long before I can sow the beets, carrots, radishes, cress, bok choy, and garden peas into the soil so I must clear the beds. It will be time to plant the dill and parsley into the herb garden too.

I've already used too much lamp oil tonight.

January 5

Another day like yesterday. Mild, with the sun trying to peek through the clouds. It's allowed me to get all my outdoor tasks done.

You'll be pleased to hear I don't smoke anymore, although I still spend the evenings with my pipe, even though I don't smoke it. It gives me something to do with my hands. And my mouth. When I'm not writing this diary, I take great pleasure in reading the books I've accumulated over the years. Books I never found time to read because of other distractions like television or the Internet. Now that those things are no longer here, there is no excuse to avoid all the literature I had been putting off for so long. Sometimes I have a few books on the go at the same time. I'm struggling through Hemingway's *For Whom the Bell Tolls*.

I drink though. I make a variety of wines from the fruits available around the property. My favourite is the elderflower champagne in the spring and the elderberry wine in the winter, a glass of which is beside me as I write.

I am very pleased with my brewing attempts, but one of my finest achievements is my soap. You would detest the stuff, but I am proud of it. Because of the lengths to which I had to go to make it.

It all starts with ash. And for this, I burn some beech which I can find in the wood. I burn it in a hot fire so that the ashes are nice and white. Then I have a large bucket with a small hole in the bottom. I create a filter using gravel and straw and almost fill the bucket with the ash. I boil some rainwater and add this to the bucket followed by cold rainwater. Then I add more ashes and more rainwater. I leave it to stand overnight and collect all the 'lye' that comes out of the bottom. The next day I pour this solution through the bucket again and collect it once more. The lye I can use to make soap and the ashes I dig into the garden. To check the lye is the correct strength I float an egg in it and if it is too weak I boil it down, and if it is too strong, I add more water. I have to be very careful not to get any on my hands or clothes because lye is a caustic soda. When the egg floats, there needs to be between two centimetres to an inch visible on the surface. Too much visible and it is too strong, not enough, and it is too weak.

When I butcher a goat, I put all the fat into a large pan and melt it down to render it into lard. At first, I just mixed the lye and grease with water and boiled it down, leaving the result to set into bars. It took a bit of practice to get the mixture right, but it was as simple as that. Then I discovered a recipe in one of the old books I bought to use goats' milk and oats. I always make this in the winter when it's freezing because I need to turn the goat's milk to slush. While it is out in the cold, I melt some lard and sunflower oil in a pan. Then I add the lye to the milk. The chemical reaction creates a surprising amount of heat. So much heat that it caramelises the sugar in the milk and makes it go yellow. I have to add the lye slowly to avoid it exploding. Once it is mixed, I add the lard and oil mixture and once that is mixed I add the oatmeal and stir stir stir stir. This takes a while, so I have a nice glass of elderberry wine beside me to keep me company. I keep stirring until the consistency has become more like a pudding and the action of stirring leaves a visible line on the surface. Once it has reached this stage, I pour the mixture into a variety of moulds made from old plastic containers - you know me, I throw nothing away. When they stopped collecting the rubbish and recycling, I started re-using all the things I would have thrown away.

Even after the soap has set, I still need to wait at least a month before I can use it because there is a chemical reaction still taking place within each bar called saponification which is what gives the soap its lather. It doesn't matter as I make more soap than I can use in a year. I even use the non-oatmeal version when washing the dishes or doing the laundry. Well, I don't have any alternatives.

January 6

You're probably wondering why I haven't mentioned Molly. I don't see her as often as I used to. You'd hardly recognise her, she's lost so much weight. The only reason she's come to see me today is that it's been raining all day. I had to stop feeding her. There was nothing left to feed her. I give her the occasional piece of goat or chicken when there is some, but most of the time she has to make do with whatever she can find in the fields. She's turned into quite a good hunter. I know that seems hard to believe when you think back to that fat, lazy moggy that used to hang around you all the time. But I guess that necessity is the mother of invention. Molly has reinvented herself into a lean, mean, hunting machine. Although you wouldn't think it to look at her now. I'm struggling to write this diary because Molly feels she's not getting enough attention and keeps lying on top of it.

On rainy days like these, I tidy the house or tackle the mending pile. I've taken up knitting again. There was a jumper my mother made which was beyond repair, so I've unpicked it and am trying to knit a new jumper from a pattern I found in your old arts and crafts stuff. I'll let you know how it turns out.

Tidying the house today, I found a box of old photos. They brought back a lot of memories. Mainly of our arguments but there were good memories too. Like the day we had a party for the King's coronation. I know the party was meant to be ironic, but everyone had such a good time. I wonder what happened to everyone in the photos. We lost touch with all of them over the years as communication became more difficult. I hope some of them survived. However, it seems unlikely now.

I still get the occasional pack of stray dogs up here. Molly comes to see me when they are around. I don't shoo them away anymore. The risk of rabies is too great. The goat and chicken pens are too sturdy and high for dogs, though they cause the poor animals some distress. Those are sleepless nights until the pack gets bored and moves on. I have everything too well secured for them to do any damage. Trampled vegetables are about the worst of it. I don't see many foxes either. I think people ate most of them not long after the collapse. The chicken coops are fox-proof. Mr Roy always wakes me up in the morning. He's the current cockerel. I have to keep him separate from the girls for obvious reasons.

Talking of Molly, I heard her making a terrible din last night. If I didn't know better, I'd have said there was another cat around, but I haven't seen another cat since we got Molly.

I also took the Christmas decorations down today. Yes, I still bother with Christmas, although it is becoming more and more tedious doing everything just for myself.

January 7

Cloudy today but no rain. Thermometer gave a maximum of 7°C, so it's warming up. Molly has gone off hunting. Won't see her again until it rains.

January 8

Cloudy again. Maximum of 9°C. Getting mild. I forgot to tell you that my old smartphone still works. Can you believe it? There is no Internet or network coverage, but I still use it to play music with my old Bluetooth speaker, I charge them both off old car batteries, which I charge from an old car alternator, connected to a Pelton wheel in the stream. I still have all my old vinyl albums too, but I don't play them often because they run down the batteries too quickly, I use the batteries for electric light when the lamp oil is in short supply.

I have all the Beatles on that old smartphone. Lots of jazz, Belle and Sebastian. I wonder how long it will last.

January 9

Saw a bit of the sun today. Maximum 8°C. I've been thinking you might not know how bad things got after you left. I just assume that things got bad everywhere. The first I knew was when Mark from the village stumbled out of the woods in a blind panic. It took me a good half hour and a cup of mint tea to calm him down enough for him to tell me what had happened but he never calmed down altogether. He was always on edge, looking down the valley as if he expected something to come out of the woods at any minute. After a while, he told me his story. How the men arrived in trucks and went house to house, stealing everything and killing whoever was inside. Mark was in his garden. He hid behind the compost bins and could see through his French doors, his wife, Sophia, first raped and then murdered but he was too scared to do anything about it. He waited until the men moved to his neighbour's house then jumped the back fence and followed the river upstream until he came to the wood. I fed him and tried to persuade him to stay with me but he was too scared, and I also think a little ashamed. He was convinced that at any moment the men would appear at the edge of the wood. When he had finished eating, he left. Climbed the hill behind the house and I never saw him again. I climbed the hill too and watched the village burn, waiting for them to come but they never did. I've often climbed the hill since but I've seen no sign of life. No smoke. I assume that gangs like these were everywhere, and that few escaped their rage. Maybe a few like me survived. Hidden away in the hills. I like to hope that you escaped and that one day you might return. I know it's a dream and more unlikely than the possibility of that gang of murderers returning one day to take me and everything for which I've worked. But without hope. I have nothing except a cat, a few goats and some chickens. Sometimes, I connect the old radio and scan the dials, but all I get is static. I doubt you'd recognise me now. I've lost some weight. My whiskers are grey. I wonder if I would recognise you?

January 10

Next month I will need to plant my spring cereals so today I took advantage of the good weather we have had to prepare the fields. With a horse, I could cultivate a much larger area, but it would be one more thing to take care of and I grow enough for my needs.

It might surprise you to hear I have made patchwork quilts. They are not very good, but they make use of some old clothes, and they are a way of making new blankets. My clothes are a little worse for wear. I can mend and darn but I can't make new clothes, apart from the knitting I told you about. That is very hit and miss.

January 11

Although it is mild in the day, the minimum temperature last night was still only 2°C. I sleep near the stove which I leave burning through the night, and I sleep in my clothes beneath a few blankets, old and new. There is no gas anymore and therefore no central heating.

If the sun comes out during the day, then it warms the water in the black pipes I have coiled on the roof but more often than not, it is cloudy like today, and I boil water for a wash.

I don't have the benefit of weather forecasts anymore, but I've learned to get a feel for what the weather is doing. It still feels mild now, but I perceive that this mild weather will not last and that we have another cold spell on its way. This has a bearing on which plants and seeds I dare plant outside at the moment. I think I'll wait a week before planting any but the hardiest of varieties.

Today as well as checking all the canes and making small repairs to the trellis, I weeded the asparagus and strawberry beds and renewed the mulch.

I sieved the third compost bays, returning the large matter to the first bays and setting the small matter aside ready for me to dig into the beds. Having freed up the third bays, I turned the second bays into the third bays and the first bays into the second bays, freeing up the first bays for the next batches of food and garden waste.

I also emptied the composting toilet into the first bay I use for that kind of waste. It wasn't as bad as you might imagine. The way the compost toilet works means that the waste has already decomposed well by the time it is ready for me to remove. The capacity of the toilet is much greater than the small amount of waste I produce.

We were fortunate in the years leading up to the collapse to prepare well, I know that you thought I was mad but I accumulated many things that are now proving useful. I wonder how those who didn't believe the collapse was coming are managing, I wonder how you are managing.

I miss rice and pasta, I could attempt to grow it or make it, but it always seemed more hassle than it's worth, I don't even bake bread anymore because of the effort to grind the wheat into flour. So, for most of the year, I eat a lot of potatoes. I have butter from the goats and plenty of herbs, but I am fed up with them. Most meals involve potatoes with seasonal veg unless it is goat or chicken killing time.

You know the thing about people is that they are addicted to the way they live their lives, and they refuse to believe anything that might interfere with them living the lives they want to live. I've seen it repeated over and over again. First, they denied the climate would change, then they denied the resources would run out. You know, right until the end, the people in the village refused to accept the inevitable. I saw Mark the day before it happened. I was there down in the village. There had been warnings and reports of similar attacks in other valleys. Then a man came. He was raving. He kept saying: "They're coming." Repeating it over and over again. He wouldn't stop. We gave him some food and drink and tried to get him to sit down, but he wolfed down everything we gave him as quickly as he could and left the village. Mark's wife, Sophia was there. We did not understand what was about to happen. We tried to tell people what the man had said, but everyone dismissed him as mad. Even Mark and Sophia convinced themselves that everything would be OK. I tried to persuade them to come to my house for a few days, just in case, but they refused. No-one wanted to accept the inevitable that was staring them in the face. I went after the man, thinking he might head toward my place but I never saw him again. The next time I saw Mark, he was raving just like the man had been, but he knew I believed him.

You remember all those DVD box sets you used to say were cluttering up the place. Well, when the batteries are holding a good charge, I turn on the old TV and watch some DVDs. I've been watching old box set, I think it's the violence in some series that starts me thinking about *them.* I remember you laughing at me and saying why do I insist on getting everything on DVD when it's all in the cloud and I said: "What happens when there is no cloud?" and you said there would always be a cloud, I guess that was the scientist in you. Ever the optimist, believing that science will find the silver bullet to solve all of our resource shortages.

January 12

A day of cold rain. I now wish I hadn't stayed up so late last night as I have plenty of time to write my diary today. I've cleaned the house. Done some mending. Molly is here again today. She is very affectionate.

And my collection of DVDs, you'll remember me collecting lots of books. Hoarding I think you called it. Since we lost the Internet, these books have been of huge value. One that has been very useful is

The Complete Book of Butchering, Smoking, Curing and Sausage Making by Philip Hasheider. It is by reading this book I learned to butcher the goats. Because I had this book long before the collapse, I could accumulate all the tools I needed.

Being a scientist, you would appreciate the detail of the techniques I have learned when I butcher a goat. I first tie its legs, lay it on my butchering table. I say butchering table, it's the old kitchen table, but it does the job. I slit the goat's jugular vein with a knife, draping its head over the edge of the table so I can collect the blood in a large bowl I have. When the blood has finished flowing, I turn the goat onto its back so I can skin it. I'm getting much better at this, I was terrible at first, I'll be honest, at first, the whole procedure filled me with horror, but once I became practised, I felt much more detached from the process, and the quality of my butchering improved. To separate the skin and fleece from the body, I use my hand, rather than a knife, so I don't cut or bruise the carcass. Once I have removed the skin, I remove the feet. The hind feet I remove at the joint nearest to the hoof. This leaves the backside tendon anchored, which I can use to suspend the carcass. I slice along the leg bone for about three inches separating tissue holding the tendon to the leg bone. These slits allow me to insert hooks that will hold the carcass. I can then hang the carcass on the hooks and remove the head. Before the collapse, I would never have been able to do this because of health and safety, but now nobody gives a damn.

I can now remove the pelt by severing it from the anus and sliding it off before washing the carcass to remove any dirt or anything that has stuck to it. Placing a bucket under the carcass to catch the intestines and blood, I begin by cutting the anus, loosening it from the pelvis. I cut as close around the pelvic and tail bones as I can until it is free to pull out. I then tie the anus shut with string so that any faecal contents do not spill out. Once tied, I let it slide down into the body cavity.

To open the belly, I start with my knife tip at a point just below the junction where the outer skin of the two hind legs intersects. I pull the skin towards me as I make a cut long enough to insert my first and second fingers to help guide the knifepoint. Once the body cavity is open, with my free hand, I grasp the tied end of the anus I let slide into the cavity earlier and slowly pull the intestines and organs towards me. Gravity helps pull these from the body, and the bladder and kidneys drop as I sever the uterus.

When I have removed all the viscera, I split the breastbone with a saw, wash both the inside and the outside of the carcass with cool water and remove any traces of blood, dirt, tissue, and other foreign matter. I prefer to do this on cool days, as the fat becomes firm.

Everything I learned about butchering, I learned from this book including all the equipment I needed. It has some graphic photos, which you would hate. You know, for a scientist you were always squeamish about these things. You weren't a biologist, I suppose.

It is very sad for me butchering a goat. I have huge respect for the animal and am grateful for its life that I have taken. It did not give it to me. Before the collapse, it was possible for me to live a vegetarian lifestyle. Even vegan for a while. I suppose there might be ways for me to live a vegan lifestyle now but with everything else that I've had to give up, I'm not ready to give up milk and butter and cheese. I could survive without the protein, but life is complicated enough right now without more sacrifices. For the moment, I will transfer that sacrifice to the goats. I don't know why I'm apologising to you. You always ate meat, and I imagine you still do, you loved it so much.

January 13

More rain today. And it's getting colder. Maximum of 5°C today. As you can see, I keep track of dates, days, hours, and years. However, I don't observe weekends anymore. If it's good weather, then I work outside. If it's raining, like today, then I work inside. January involves lots of preparation for the spring and summer months when the outside jobs occupy almost all of my time. The more I can achieve now, the easier it will be when things grow.

I haven't finished telling you about the goats, I leave the goat hanging until rigour sets in. I used to refrigerate and freeze things, I ran a fridge and a freezer off the batteries that the Pelton wheel charges. But one day the fridge stopped working and then, less than a week later the freezer stopped working, and I just didn't have the expertise to fix them. Since then I've had to smoke the meat. I can't salt it because I don't have enough salt, so smoking is the only option.

January 15

It's stopped raining and warmed up a bit, so I could get outside today. Although it's stopped raining, Molly has decided to hang around which is unusual.

I didn't finish explaining how I smoke the goat meat. First, I rub the meat with oil and herbs. Then I place the goat in my homemade barrel smoker on low heat for three hours. I don't trust my meat curing ability, so I eat the cooked meat as quickly as possible leading to periods of feast whenever I butcher a goat. It's a busy time because I have to make soap with the fat. This is one reason for doing these sorts of tasks in winter. It also is one of the less abundant times of the year regarding produce from the garden.

January 16

Raining again today and Molly is hanging around for an unprecedented third consecutive day. I've never seen her so affectionate. I dreamt about you last night, I dreamt that you were in the village when they attacked, I dreamt that I was there too, but I was helpless to save you.

I think it's a good job that I'm a bit of an introvert. All this time isolated from society might be difficult to deal with. I sometimes miss contact with other humans, I miss my visits to the village and the White Harte where I could catch up on the gossip with the locals, I haven't been back to the village since the day Mark came and went. I often climb the hill to see whether I can spot any signs of life but I dare not go into the village myself. It still feels like too much of a risk. I miss many of the things we used to take for granted before the collapse, I miss being able to jump in a car and visit people hundreds of miles away in a matter of hours. I miss fridges, gas cookers and electric light. I have the light I run off the batteries, but it's not the same as the light we used to get from the mains power. I miss the news, the television and the radio. The thought I can only watch programmes that have already been made and that there aren't, and may never be, any new television programmes makes me sad. There may not be new books. It's so difficult at the moment to imagine a civilised society developing out of the barbarism in which we find ourselves. You always had an incredible faith in humanity, but the events we have witnessed here in the village and that are occurring all over the country bears witness to the true nature of humanity. The greed, selfishness and tribalism that made humanity so dominant on this planet. That allowed it to cover every corner of the world and destroy the precious resources on which our lives depend. The only planet we have. It just reveals how stupid our species can be. That we believed the lies of the people to whom we were stupid enough to hand our power. The same people who sold our future for personal gain. Where are these people now? Their wealth is useless, and money holds no value now. The only things of value are food, water, shelter, heat. The comfort of other individuals lucky enough to have someone still. I hope you have found someone and that you are somewhere where you can look after each other. Even the bag of silver coins I have hidden under the floorboards is useless to me now.

Last night I overdid it a little with the elderberry wine and have had a dull headache the whole of today, I can't take the drink like I used to when I was younger. I also allowed myself to look through the old photographs again, which is why I feel so melancholy today, I found a photo of you with your mother. You both looked so happy.

I've no idea what she would have made of the situation today. She was another one who never believed that the collapse would ever happen. There was this universal belief that something would happen, that someone would do something, that *they* would do something. But *they* never did anything, there was no magical solution and when we lost the power and the water we were on our own, fending for ourselves, helping each other as best we could. Trading what we could for whatever we could get. It wasn't long before the money became useless. I used to trade whatever I could produce. Vegetables, goats, chickens, eggs, even some of my homemade soap, wine, seedlings. I enjoyed my trips to the village, trading whatever I could. There was a real sense of community, and it enabled me to get my hands on valuable products like salt and sometimes sugar. In those days, I could still find important things in the market like seeds, tools, flour with which I used to bake my bread. It was sometimes possible to trade what I had for small amounts of useful stuff like baking powder, bicarbonate of soda, borax. I never realised what had real value until after the collapse. If I was having a good day, I might afford a real luxury item like a packet of coffee or a packet of beans. Supply of these things was always unreliable, but they appeared less and less until the valley itself produced everything that appeared in the market. When outsiders stopped visiting the village on market days, we knew that something was wrong and the day the madman came through the village, he confirmed our fears. Until that day, I had always enjoyed visits to the White Harte. The pub was an even more important part of the community than it had been before and the whole village would gather to exchange stories. It brewed its own beer, and they grew the barley lower down the valley. The beer became less and less hoppy as the hops became more and more expensive to buy from the south. On the day the madman came I didn't stay at the pub but went home and prepared for the inevitable that many of us realised was coming. I still don't understand why they came no further than the village and why they have not returned. A lot of time has passed since Mark stumbled up to my house and explained what they had done to the village and everyone in it. I've been thinking a lot about whether I should go down to the village and see what I can find. Finding the corpses of villagers in the burnt-out remains of their homes fills me with fear, but there is always the thought that even though I have seen no signs of activity from here, there might be someone down there still alive and struggling to survive.

For many weeks after what had happened, I daren't light the stove in case the smoke gave me away. I slept badly for weeks and kept a knife by the bed. Eventually, I plucked up the courage to relight the stove and climbed the hill to see whether anyone was coming, but no-one came. Over the months I have become less worried, but there is always the fear in the back of my mind that one day they will come back.

January 17

More rain again today, on and off. Molly slept with me last night and had started following me around. I'm not sure what's got into the old girl.

Today, I washed all my plant pots. It helps to control pests and diseases, giving them a good wash every year. I boil up a load of water on the stove, put all the pots and trays in the bath, and scrub them with a brush and some of my homemade soap. It's important to clean all the pots and trays because little bugs and bacteria can gather in the cracks and crevices and cause all kinds of problems for young seedlings.

I also cleaned out the inside of the greenhouse and polytunnel and used a little bit of repair tape to cover two small tears in the polytunnel. Once I'd done this, I added some compost I'd sieved last week to the beds in the polytunnel and then washed the empty bags.

All day I've been thinking about the village and what it might be like down there. The thought has frequently occurred to me, and I'm not proud of it, that there might be things in the village that would be useful to me. I know that whatever I might find does not belong to me, but with the owners dead they will not make use of them anymore, and I don't think they would have begrudged me the use of them.

I have resolved to go down to the village on the next dry day and see what I can find. I'll take some bags to bring back anything which might be of use. I'll also take a knife for self-defence, though I'm not sure what use it will be if there is anyone there who is not pleased to see me.

I'll go via the fields. The same way that Mark fled after seeing Sophia raped and murdered. I've resolved to go to his house to see what I can find.

January 18

Today was the day. It was cloudy but no rain. As soon as I got up, I had two boiled eggs and a cup of tea before grabbing the bag I had already prepared and headed off through the fields towards the village.

The fields, which used to be full of crops or grazing cattle, now grow weeds and long grass. The overgrown hedges made it easy to move unnoticed towards the village.

I knew that I must have been retracing the steps that Mark must have taken last year, only in reverse, and I emerged at the foot of his garden. The garden was a mess as if someone had ransacked it, and now all the vegetable beds were covered with weeds. The door of the chicken coop was wide open, and I made a guilty mental note that the wire on the walls and door might be useful for repairs to my coop.

Skirting the edge of the garden, I made my way towards the house which had been gutted by fire. I crept up onto the patio towards the hole in the wall where the French doors had been. The windows were broken, and the frames charred by the fire. I didn't see her at first when I looked into the darkness of the smoke-blackened room. But when my eyes had grown accustomed to the darkness, I saw her, a black corpse lying in the centre of the room. At first, I turned away, looking instead at the low clouds which hid the hilltops but then as if drawn by some macabre curiosity, and I looked again. The body was unrecognisable, but I knew from what Mark had told me, it was her.

I stayed for a moment and thought of Mark and Sophia. Nothing I could do would help either of them now and, taking a deep breath, I walked slowly around the side of the house where the wooden gate lay open. Moving to the front of the house, I stopped at the gate, peering out towards the village main street. All the houses I could see had received the same treatment as Mark's. Most of the roofs were missing along with the windows, and smoke had stained the walls around every opening.

I walked through the overgrown front garden and into the street, looking both ways along the road before walking along it in the direction of the square where the market traders used to gather. Bodies littered the road and many of the gardens. They had been partially eaten by what I assumed had been a combination of wild dogs and birds. I gave each of them a wide berth and, although I was sure there was no-one in the village, I reached for the knife inside my bag.

As I approached the White Harte, on the corner of the square, it became clear that they had burned it, too. They had spared nothing and no-one. I decided not to go into the pub just yet, but continued into the square, debris and half-eaten rotting corpses littered everywhere. A terrible stench of rot filled the air. I felt unable to see any more for now and retraced my steps to the pub, I only needed to look through the window of the lounge to see that fire had destroyed everything inside, I could make out some charred corpses beneath burned joists and rubble that had collapsed on top of them. It was then that a thought occurred to me. The White Harte had a cellar. Perhaps some things or someone had survived in there. Clutching the knife, I entered the pub, crossing the lounge and heading for the bar, behind which I knew was an entrance to the cellar. There was a lot of debris, and the thought occurred to me that what remained of the upstairs floor might not be safe. There was a reasonable amount of debris littering the floor behind the bar which I kicked aside trying to find the trapdoor. That the entrance to the cellar was not clear was proof that no-one had hidden there. I found the wooden door and cleared away the debris to find the latch which I opened, pulling the door up and peering into the darkness below.

"Hello?" I shouted with just a little optimism, but there was no reply.

I tried to peer into the darkness, but it was useless, I promised myself that next time I would bring candles. I could swear I could hear something in the darkness, but I couldn't be sure, so I left it and rushed back the way I had come.

January 19

My plans to return to the village today were confounded when I awoke to discover the entire valley covered in a thick blanket of fog. I could barely see the tree line of the wood from the house, so I did not fancy a trip into that graveyard of a village unable to see what's around the corner. They stole everything from the village that was of value and burned the rest, but there might still be things like Mark's chicken shed which are of no value to them yet very useful to me.

The fog made everything wet, so I confined myself to the house with Molly who was very upset about me leaving yesterday. She is still very affectionate again today. I wonder how long this new found friendship will last. She must be cold.

I keep thinking about the half-eaten, half-decomposed corpses that litter the village. The thought has occurred to me that there might be all manner of disease in that village and to bring anything back from it could be a big mistake. Is there anything in the pub's basement of real use to me? I also thought of the butcher where I used to take my excess chickens and goats. I expect that when they came, they took anything metal out of the butcher's shop. Not because they wanted to do legitimate butchering of their own but because the metal would be worth something to trade or to sell for silver. I would like to see for myself.

January 20

When I looked out the window this morning, I was hoping for more fog or rain, but the sun peeping through the clouds greeted me. It seems I had no excuse to postpone my return to the village.

I packed a bag with some tools, a beeswax candle and one of the lighters I have hoarded, I have quite a few and hoped that maybe I would find more today.

I left straight after breakfast. This time I was less careful and headed straight for the road, which ends, or starts, depending on your point of view, at the edge of the wood which forms the boundary of my property. I allowed the old entrance to grow over with bushes so that any intruders would imagine that the owners had abandoned the property long ago. So far it has worked.

Replacing the section of removable fence, which serves as my actual entrance, was easier said than done as it had become overgrown during the months I hadn't used it. I'm not as strong as I used to be and struggle with any work which is very physical. Once I'd got it looking as natural as possible, I headed off down the road, which is only a track this far up the valley.

Although I was less cautious than the first visit, I was still nervous as I turned each corner on the way to the village, but when I reached the first houses, the street looked as I had left it. As if nobody or nothing had been through the village and why would they?

I headed straight to the pub, and straight behind the bar, and lifted the trapdoor of the cellar. Lighting my beeswax candle, I climbed the stairs into the dark basement and shone the light around. The shelves were empty. They must have taken everything. I stepped down onto the stone floor and heard a noise behind me. I swung around and shone the light but just heard a scurrying. Probably a rat. Then a box fell off the shelf, there was a scratching noise, and a black shape flashed across the room and out through a gap in what must be the street entrance to the cellar. It looked like a cat, but I couldn't be sure.

I shone the light on the shelves, but it looked like they had stripped everything out. Even the piping, which had led to the bar upstairs, had gone. The box, which had fallen, was empty and damp, and the cellar itself had a foul smell. I climbed back up the stairs, extinguished the candle and resolved to head straight to the butcher's shop on the other side of the square hoping *they* had left behind some equipment.

In the square, I chose a route, which kept me as far away from each of the rotting corpses as possible. Until, on reaching the far side of the square, I could see that fire had gutted the butcher's shop, along with every building on the road. I headed for the entrance and peered inside.

The shop itself was black with smoke damage, but the floor above looked intact, so I ventured inside, eager to get to the back room where they had done the butchering. In my haste, I crossed the centre of the room but froze when I heard a splintering of wood and the floor shift. I only froze for a moment before realising that the centre of the floor was the worst place to be. I made a move for the edge of the room but, as I did, the entire floor gave way, and I fell along with the floor into the room below and landed with a splash in two feet of water. The floor fell around me, and a chunk of floor tile hit me on the head, cutting me and sending a dribble of blood down my forehead and nose. I was soaked, and from the smell of the water, I assumed the water was filthy and did not want to touch my wound for fear of infection.

A little light entered through the newly made hole, and I could see that they must have used this as a cool room. The stench was probably rotting animal flesh. In the dull light, I could make out a door and waded over to it only to find it locked. Looking around the room, I could see that, in one corner, there stood a set of shelves. Perhaps if I could move these to the centre of the room, I might climb out. Pots of what might have been herbs were covering the shelves, even tubs of salt but this awful stench in the room made me fearful of disease, and I daren't take any of the pots or tubs with me. Instead, I cleared them off into the water and pulled at the shelf. They had fixed it to the wall but not so much that I couldn't pull it loose. Moving the shelf took more effort, and I was glad I had worn gloves, which protected me from the metal corners of the shelving. I pulled the shelves across the floor, through the water, until I felt something brush against my leg. I kicked at it thinking it might be the remains of some butchered animal or perhaps a dead rat. But as I kicked whatever it was, was connected to something much larger and, in giving it a bigger shove with my foot, I could see that what I was kicking was a human corpse.

At first, I pulled away in horror but, when I had time to calm down, I took the beeswax candle and lighter out of my now wet bag. I kept it dry in the case you gave me for one of my birthdays, I forget when. After two tries, I lit it. They say that it is possible to get used to anything, and I had already seen enough corpses in the village, including Sophia's, not to be shocked at every new corpse I encountered. However, this had taken me by surprise. I shone the light over the water and could just about make out two adult corpses and the corpse of a child. It was the first time I had seen a dead child, and I just wanted to get out of the water we were sharing as quickly as possible. I realised the bodies belonged to the butcher, his wife and his daughter. They must have hidden down here when *they* came and been unable to escape. Had they died of starvation? Perhaps the smoke from the fire had asphyxiated them. I hoped it was the latter because a pang of guilt was gnawing away at me telling me that had I come to the village sooner I might have found them and been able to help them. How many others might have hidden in their basements only to find themselves trapped? The question is now academic, as no one could have survived this length of time unless they had enough provisions, which is unlikely given the lack of everything at the moment.

I put out the candle, placed it back in its case, and dropped it back in my bag with the lighter. Then I pulled the shelves into the centre of the room, kicking the corpses of the butcher and his family out of the way as I went. The shelf wobbled as I climbed and I was worried that it might topple over, dumping me into the water along with the rotting remains. It stayed upright, and I could stand on the top shelf and reach what remained of the floor. The floor was made of tiles, and this made it difficult to find anything to grab. On the side furthest from the street, most of the floor had fallen away exposing the joists, which I was just about able to grab onto to pull myself up and crawl to the edge of the room where a part of the floor remained. I pulled myself up, which was no mean feat for a man of my age, and sat with my back against the wall, hoping the remaining floor would not give way. I edged around the wall until I reached the door leading through to the room where they would have prepared the joints of meat. With my back pressed up against the wall, I stood up and edged around into the back room. There was no sign of any equipment, and fire had gutted the room. I had no confidence in the floor so, sticking to the edge of the room I made my way to the back door which I could see was wide open. When I reached the door, I could see the cause of the butcher's fate. The entire staircase had collapsed on top of the stairs to the basement, making it impossible to open the basement door. I wonder how many other villagers met a similar end. I had had enough for today though and came back as fast as I could to wash all the filthy water off my clothes and skin.

January 21

All night I have been thinking about the possibility that others might be trapped in basements. If someone has hoarded enough provisions, they might still be alive.

I decided I would check every building in the village and got up early to get a good start. It was cloudy, but it did not look as though it would rain so, after breakfast, I headed back to the village for the third time and this time I went from house to house checking for basements, calling to see if there were any survivors. The thought has also occurred to me that someone hiding in a basement might have already escaped and left down the valley. Had all the villages in the valley met the same fate? Was I now the only person living in the valley?

They had burned every house. *They* had spared none. In some houses I found charred corpses, others were empty, but in all of them, *they* had emptied the kitchens of pots and pans. *They* had been very thorough. Then I noticed for the first time that they had even taken all the cabling that used to span the telegraph and electricity poles. The electricity never went as far as my property, which could be a reason *they* stopped.

Every house brought fresh hope and fresh disappointment. Some houses had collapsed altogether and were now just piles of rubble. *They* had even burned the church. I had a quick look. It was now just a stone shell.

They must have had big trucks to transport everything they had stolen. And there must have been a fair few of them to strip the village in its entirety. And when they run out of villages, what then? How can they feed themselves if there is no-one left to grow food?

I became more and more angry with each house I visited. I thought how typical this was of humanity. They had populated the world by taking advantage of each other, and now they had reached a saturation point, they continued to take advantage of each other as they followed the path of their demise.

I checked every house from one end of the village to the other and saw no signs of life. At the very foot of the village, I could see far down the valley but saw no signs of smoke or activity. All was silent save for a few birds calling and the occasional bark of some wild dogs.

On my way home, I stopped at the top of the village from where I could see smoke from my stove, rising through the trees. Only a little, but perceptible. If they came back, the smoke would give me away, though there was very little I could do about that.

January 22

It was cold today. There had been a frost overnight. In the three visits I had made to the village, I had not returned with Mark's chicken coop, so I did that today. I have a trolley which I use to wheel large objects around the property, so I took that down with me so I could wheel the dismantled coop back again. It took a bit of taking apart and barely fit on the trolley but once I got it all on it was a simple task. At the end of the track, I had to take each piece off the trolley and walk it through the wood, but then it was home, and I could relax. I was shattered. Still am. I'm too old for this level of physical work.

Molly has not left the house for a while now, and I'm getting worried about her. She isn't hunting, so I've been giving her some goat and milk which I know isn't good for her, but I'm worried she will waste away if she has nothing. She has been vomiting, and she seems exhausted.

I have been thinking a lot about how we got ourselves to this stage. How we ignored all the warning signs. Year after year, we elected leaders who told us there was no need to worry. We believed the adverts telling us we needed more and more stuff to be happy. Then, when our resources started to run out, instead of blaming ourselves for consuming too much, we blamed our leaders and elected other leaders who told us that everything would be OK. So addicted were we to our lifestyles, that we allowed our leaders to take any measures necessary to preserve our lifestyles even if those measures made the situation worse. Even when the system started to collapse, we did not look towards ourselves for the blame but placed the blame on the leaders who, so desperate for power, had done anything to secure our votes, said anything they thought we wanted to hear no matter how mad the path down which they were leading us. We lived in denial right to the end, maintaining an unfounded faith in those in power to provide some miraculous solution to allow us to return to living the life to which we had become addicted.

When I say *we* I don't mean *us*, I mean *they*. There were some of us that could see the end on its way long before it arrived and tried to prepare for the inevitable. Most people tried to adapt as best they could, but none of our preparations could cope with those prepared to kill to take what they wanted. Once the rule of law had broken down, we found ourselves back in the violent tribal world of thousands of years ago.

You always had an incredible faith in humanity and science. How disappointed you must have been when both failed us. I pleaded with you not to go, but you were always very stubborn and convinced you could make a difference. I had tried. For a while, people listened to me. I united the regions for a while, but corruption destroyed everything as it always does and they forced me into my almost hermit-like existence.

January 23

Another cold day today after a heavy frost last night. Molly is sleeping with me and barely leaves my side, except to vomit which I encourage her to do away from the bed, so that is easier to clear up. She is eating well though so I'm not too worried.

I have been wondering whether I should take any measures to make my property, or myself, safer. The trouble is that I'm not sure what I can do that will make any difference. It's too cold to stop using the stove, and if they see the smoke and get as far as the top of the track, then the woods will hardly stop them. I've already hidden my silver, but I wonder whether it is safe enough. Under a loose floorboard seems such an obvious hiding place.

January 24

The strange thing is that I want somebody to come. I just don't want *them* to come. I have to admit that it can get very lonely here with only an odd cat, some goats and a bunch of chickens to keep me company, I sometimes daydream about you coming home. You can even bring him with you. I'm sure I'd get used to him.

It warmed up again today, and I saw a little bit of sun. I planted more onions, leeks, broccoli, cabbage, and cauliflower into trays in the greenhouse. From now on I'll be planting every couple of weeks to create a succession of crops.

I did a little more weeding and planted more cabbage, early lettuce, and broccoli in the polytunnel. In the garden, I planted more beets, carrots, radishes, cress, bok choy, and garden peas in rows of compost.

This afternoon I finished the last of the pruning of the fruit trees then planted some pepper, tomato and aubergine in pots and set them on the windowsill. If it doesn't rain tomorrow, I hope to plant some nasturtiums and maybe more carrots, broccoli, lettuce, spinach, cilantro, parsley, and Asian greens. I also have to mulch the peas to extend the harvest, sow pumpkins and winter squash into the garden. I have to start cucumbers and watermelons in pots and plant heat-tolerant chicory, lettuce, and Swiss chard in the shade so they'll stay cool when the weather warms.

I harvested some carrots, radishes and brussels sprouts today which I had for dinner with some goat, and potatoes flavoured with my homemade chutney, and more of the lovely elderberry wine.

It was nice to do a good day's work in the garden after the distractions of the village over the last few days.

January 25

They are on their way, I know this because I saw a drone today, I heard it first while I was mulching the peas, so I rushed to the tree line and hid behind a tree before it came into view.

I don't think it saw me, but it got a good look at the property and everything in it, and it would have seen the smoke rising from the chimney. There is still a lot of frost at night, so I still have the stove on pretty much all the time. If *they* will come, they will come whether or not I am producing smoke. Besides, they got a good look at the goats and chickens, and I'm sure they'd come just for those.

I had just planted some cucurbits into pots before mulching the peas, but now, after seeing the drone, I abandoned any jobs and started thinking of a plan that would leave me alive once *they* had gone. I have no idea how long it will take them to get here. They might be on their way here right now as far as I know. The first thing I did was to create a kind of emergency bag, like the bag your mother had when she was due to give birth to you. Something I can leave by the back door and grab as soon as I know they are here and with which I can flee over the hill to relative safety until they are gone. The first thing that I put into it was the bag of silver. Then I added a hunting knife, a waterproof jacket, a jumper, some lighters from my hoard, some dried goat meat, a bar of my soap, a pair of binoculars, a woolly hat and gloves. It was already heavy because of the silver.

I think I've worked out what's up with Molly. The reason she is hanging around, eating a lot and vomiting is that she's pregnant. Probably something to do with the cat I saw in the village. I noticed that her nipples are bigger than usual and, although I can't be sure,

I could swear that her belly is bigger. I keep bowls of goat meat and milk out for her all the time, and she grazes on it whenever she wants.

January 26

The fact I am writing this at all is something to celebrate. I was checking the goats when I heard trucks coming up the track. It was freezing this morning, it's even colder now, but it was still freezing this morning. I opened the doors to the goat pens and the chicken coops and encouraged the inhabitants to escape before rushing into the house to grab my bag. I thought *they* would take every chicken or goat so giving them a chance to escape would give me a chance to recover them if I returned. My bag, I slung on my back and I grabbed Molly and wrapped the confused moggy in a blanket. Almost as an afterthought, I stuffed some dried goats meat in my pocket, grabbed a handful of dry kindling and stuffed that in another pocket. Then, afraid to stay any longer I left through the back door and started heading up the hill through the wood just as the sound of the trucks pulling to a halt at the end of the track echoed through the wood.

I climbed the hill as fast as I could which, at my age, is not quick, taking care to keep a tight hold on Molly who was struggling. I daren't imagine what *they* would do with Molly had I left her.

By the time I reached the summit of the hill, I could hear voices by the house, shouting orders. I was confident they couldn't see me as I couldn't see them unless they had some infrared technology which I thought unlikely. I decided not to hang around and to put as much distance between them and us as possible for the moment. I began crossing the moor, which spread out on the other side of the hill.

Before long, I was further away from my house than I had been for years but with no real idea of where to go. It was cold, but the sun was poking through the clouds, though its rays didn't seem to warm at all. I kept walking until I was out of sight of the brow of the hill. I rested for ten minutes, knowing that *they* would be busy ransacking my house but I didn't stay for long as I couldn't be sure *they* hadn't sent someone out to find me.

It was becoming difficult to hold on to Molly who was becoming agitated so I continued walking until I reached a ridge with some bushes in which I could shelter from the wind but from which I could see the brow of the hill at the top of the valley. This way, if they sent anyone after us, I would see them with plenty of notice.

By this time, Molly was becoming annoying, so I let her go for a while. She wandered around but didn't wander very far and as soon as I offered her some dry goat meat, she came back and sat on my lap while I kept a vigil with my binoculars. Nobody came over the hill but smoke rising from the burning house billowed up.

January 27

As I sat in the bushes on the ridge watching the smoke rising in the distance, it became colder and colder but I daren't return, and I daren't light a fire. Molly snuggled close under the blanket. It started to get dark, and I crept back across the moor to the brow of the hill and listened. I could hear the crackling of the fire, which was destroying my house, but I couldn't hear any voices. I descended through the wood, taking care to make as little noise as possible and looking all around in case any of *them* were still around. When I was close to the tree line, I kept hidden behind the trees as I skirted the clearing looking for any signs of movement, which was difficult in the dark. Having negotiated one side of the clearing, I made my way through the wood towards the track, stopping well from the entrance where anyone might spot me. I found a place from where I could see the top of the track and saw that the trucks had left. Deep tracks in the mud bore witness.

Feeling certain they had gone, I headed straight for the smouldering house where I had to put Molly down and take stock of the situation. The house was gutted and still smoking. They didn't take the chicken coop, but they took the chickens, and by the look of the blood on the floor, they killed them first. The goats met the same fate, and the fencing had gone with them. The tool shed was still standing, but the tools had gone. It started to rain, so I picked up Molly and took her into the tool shed to shelter for the rest of the night.

It has been raining all day today, so we have been keeping each other company in the shed, looking outside now and again at the soggy ruins of what used to make up our lives. I have enough goats meat in my bag to look after the pair of us for now. Tomorrow, I must check out the damage and work out how we go on from here.

I can see from here that some things I cannot repair. The water purification system, for example. It's funny, I don't feel as angry or as devastated as I thought I would feel. I am angry that *they* have ruined everything I took so long to establish. But I also feel a strange sense of pragmatism that I just have to get on and make the most of what I have left.

January 28

The rain stopped, and I picked through the rubble to see whether I could salvage anything from the ruins of the house. I could still get water from the river, but I could not be sure what bacteria lurked within, so I needed a pot to boil up some water before I could drink. I had taken a lighter so could start a fire but I had to find something in which to boil the water. In the rush of leaving the house yesterday, I hadn't thought to take any pots, and *they* had stolen the entire contents of the kitchen before they set fire to it. The only thing I could find that would hold water and withstand fire was the enamel bath, which, if I set it at an angle would hold some water. I had no issues getting it downstairs as it had fallen through the floor during the fire, but I had to drag it all the way to the stream to wash it, which was no small task regardless of my age, and then washing it was difficult with little in the way of equipment. The trucks they brought must have been large as they had taken just about everything including the Pelton wheel and the batteries. They even took the broken fridge and freezer. Perhaps they could fix them. The problem, having washed the enamel bath as best I could, was how to stand it at an angle with a fire beneath one end. The answer came in the form of rocks which I gathered from around the property to construct a base on which I could stand the bath at an angle with a gap underneath large enough for a fire. Do you remember the border I have for one of the vegetable beds, made from the bottoms of plastic two-litre drink bottles? I washed out two of these and used them to fill the bath. I used the kindling I'd stuffed in my coat pocket and found some dry wood in the wood pile which remained only partially damaged. This way I could boil water in the bath and make some mint tea by picking fresh leaves from the garden.

I have to admit I am feeling a lot less pragmatic than yesterday and a lot more pessimistic about maintaining my life here.

January 29

It rained all day today, and I spent all day in the shed with Molly thinking about what I need to do to rebuild my life. It feels like this time I have lost everything. It felt like that when you left, but it feels even more so now. I have no pans to cook anything, no tools to tend my garden. I have to boil water in an old bath. I sleep in a shed.

I don't know how long I can go on surviving like this, I sometimes wonder whether I should have confronted them when they came and let them kill me.

They left the compost toilet untouched. They didn't even take the porcelain bowl.

I have a bar of soap, but it is too cold to strip off in the river. I saved this diary, I don't know why. Perhaps I still harbour the hope that one day you will come back and read it. Even if I am not here.

January 30

Something amazing happened today. In fact, two amazing things happened. I was walking through the woods and found two stray chickens. I caught them and took them to the chicken coop. On the way, a chicken under each arm I caught sight of a goat. A doe. I hurried to the coop, locked up the chickens and was about to go back for the doe when I realised I had no fence to keep her in. The chicken coop was composed of three smaller coops with space for layers, broilers and cocks. If I kept the goat at one end and the chickens at the other, with an empty compartment in between, what could go wrong?

I got some dead branches and swept out the chicken coop as best I could and then went to get the doe. It was not an easy task, but I gained its confidence and got it back down the hill and, with only a little struggle, into the coop.

I'm now saving all the goats meat for Molly. I'm on a vegetarian, raw food diet, eating whatever I can harvest. Jerusalem artichokes, parsnips and carrots.

Maybe these small miracles are the start of something new. Maybe I can find a way.

January 31

Raining again today. Another day in the shed, and another miracle happened. Miracle in my world, not in anyone else's. Both chickens had laid an egg this morning. During a break in the showers, I boiled up some water in the bath and the eggs with it. I stuck some Jerusalem artichoke, parsnips and carrots in too, not forgetting to take some boiling water out before the veg went in so I could make a mint tea. It's funny how smells evoke images. I haven't washed in a while, and I smell of smoke, amongst other things, I caught a whiff of myself, and it took me back to my childhood at scout camp.

I don't think I will stay here. I've lost the seeds that were in my seed bank, so I only have what is already in the ground, two chickens and a goat. All the careful planning I had put into surviving the collapse *they* destroyed in one stroke. There's always the possibility that there might be seeds in the sheds in some gardens in the village. *They* seemed to burn the houses and take the tools, but they don't seem to burn sheds, and I very much doubt that they are bothered about growing their food. If it's not raining tomorrow, I'll go on another scouting expedition, and this time I'll be more thorough.

By this time I should have started a lot of seeds in pots and the garden. I still have what's in the polytunnel and greenhouse, but that's not going to see me right through the year.

Out of everything I've lost this week I think I miss my books and my music the most. The days seem to drag now, and I wonder whether it is worth it to exist at all cost. What do I have to live for now, anyway? I have a sense of responsibility to Molly and her unborn kittens and maybe to the chickens and the goat. I don't have the means to butcher them now, anyway.

Two eggs are just not enough to lift my spirits anymore, and I am feeling more and more despondent about my prospects of survival.

February 1

Another wet day but at least it is warming up now. The nights have been cold without the stove. I've been wearing the same clothes for quite a while now. During a lull in the showers, I tried to have a quick wash by the river. I shivered as I undressed and got dressed again while I was still wet, not having any towels anymore.

I had boiled eggs and milk. They seem like a luxury now. Perhaps too much of a luxury given that the limited ability of the garden to feed now has to be shared between the chickens, the goat and me. Molly enjoyed having more milk. I'm now rationing the remaining dried goat's meat, assuming that it will need to last beyond her pregnancy until she can catch meat again. Never having had a pregnant cat, I've no idea how long all of this will take. On nice days, she's been going out, but she begs me for food, and I doubt I have enough to last.

I've postponed my trip to the village until tomorrow if tomorrow is dry. Not having a stove to dry myself, I don't want to risk pneumonia.

I saw trout in the river when I was washing, I'd forgotten about the trout, I never ate fish, and so trout was not on my radar. Now, with the supply of Jerusalem artichokes, parsnips and carrots getting very low, the thought of trout has become appealing. The only problem is that I have no rods or tackle and wouldn't know how to use them if I did. If I had just a roll of fishing line and a hook, I might work out a way of catching one other than leaping into the river and trying to grab one with my bare hands. An alternative might be to fashion a hook from some rose thorns and a line from my shoelace. When it stops raining, I might try.

February 2

More rain today but at least it is getting milder, so the nights are less unpleasant. Molly is becoming very annoying with her demands for food. At this rate, the goat meat will not last for very long.

I dreamt about you again last night, I wonder where you are, how you are getting on and whether he is looking after you.

I feel lonelier than I used to and think often about how different everything could have been.

February 3

It stopped raining today, so as soon as I had boiled two eggs and milk the goat, I headed down into the village which looked unchanged except that some bodies which lay in the road had been run over by trucks and were now lumps of pulp.

As fast as I could, I went from garden to garden visiting all the sheds I could. *They* had broken into most of them already. I was looking for old biscuit tins, the standard receptacle for seeds. It surprised me how much I found. At first, I kept the tins, but so many of the sheds contained tins of seeds that, before long I could pick which tins I kept and filled these with the seeds from the inferior tins. It wasn't just tins and packets of seeds I added to my loot, I found an enamel mug and an old tin plate and some sheds contained receptacles of useful things like comfrey fertiliser, which I could come back for later. I found a patch of comfrey as well and took some to plant on my land. I didn't find any pots, pans or utensils, despite checking the kitchens of some houses. *They* were so thorough when they came, their job was so professional that I imagine they must do this looting on an almost daily basis.

I was very pleased with what I had collected. I need to sort through it all but, assuming that most of the seeds are still viable, I should have enough to keep my garden going though I have to admit I am no longer enthused at the prospect.

February 4

Rain again today. Heavy for most of the day, so I spent most of the day in the shed, sorting the seeds into a planting plan and re-planning the garden in a notebook I found in one shed yesterday.

It was a good hoard of seeds, I only wish that *they* had left some tools behind. I will fashion tools out of sticks and twigs. I feel like a bit of a cave dweller. Albeit living in a prefabricated shed. I planned my garden like the garden I had planned before, with the same crop rotation. Only this time I adjusted the sizes of the beds in relation to my new stock of seeds. My biggest loss has been my seed potatoes. The potatoes I used to complain about all the time. I had stored my seed potatoes in the house, so they had gone up in smoke. Sometimes I have violent daydreams about what I might do if I got my hands on the bastards that did this to my property.

February 5

I got to work implementing my new plan today. First, I planted onions, leeks, lettuce, tomatoes and garlic in the greenhouse along with some marigold seeds, which I will plant out along with the tomatoes when they are ready. Some spinach and radishes in the polytunnel. Some lettuces cabbages and onions that I'd planted in seed trays look like they might be ready to plant out soon. I planted some spinach, turnip, and peas out into the garden and covered the pea bed with a sheet of clear plastic, which had survived the raid. I started pots of all the seeds I had potted in the house, lost in the fire. I put them all in the greenhouse. I also planted lettuce in one bed and added compost to the beds according to my new planting scheme.

Tomorrow I plan to plant some peppers and aubergine in pots in the greenhouse. If it doesn't rain, I'll plant some radishes, spinach, carrots, peas, beets, onions, sweet corn, cucumbers and cabbages into the beds.

I miss the potatoes now. I'm sure I'm not getting enough carbohydrates, and I can't seem to get rid of this permanent sensation of hunger that I have.

Molly disappeared for the day and came back looking very satisfied with herself. I'm sure she must have caught a mouse to supplement the goat's meat with which she's getting fed up.

I'm struggling to sleep now. The days and nights seem to go on forever. I keep wondering whether this price of survival is worth paying. I feel I need to look after Molly until she has her kittens. However, after that, I wonder whether there is any point struggling on like this.

February 6

Another rainy day, stuck in the shed, apart from a bit of planting in the greenhouse. I saw another drone today. It came very close to the shed, and this time I didn't hide. I stood in the shed's doorway and showed it the middle finger. I've decided that I will not run away and hide this time, I will stay and fight them. If they kill me, then it will be a blessing to end my suffering. Who knows how long it will take them to arrive. Maybe they will arrive tomorrow, in which case this could be the last entry I make in this diary. I know we had our differences in the past, but I want you to know that I love you more than anything, I always have done since the day you were born, and

I hope that you don't think badly of me, after everything that happened. I'm sorry, and I wish I had the opportunity to apologise in person and tell you how much I love you. I hope that this diary goes some way to make up for me not saying the things I should have said when you were still here.

To anyone who finds this diary. Please, I appeal to all that is good in you not to destroy this it but to deliver it to the person for whom it was written. I beg you to please try to find Dr Olivia Smith. Alternatively, she might go by the name of Dr Jones. Her husband was or is Ryan Jones, the politician. If you find her, please tell her that this is the diary of Dr James Smith, her father.

Part Two

"The rain felt like pinpricks on my face as I crossed the moor," Jack told his audience which comprised an old man, who looked like he might not be long for this world. "I was cold, soaked to the skin, and faint with exhaustion. I reached the edge of the moor at the head of a tree-lined valley and began to descend through the shelter of the trees, I reached a clearing in which there was the burnt-out shell of a house, a few disused chicken coops and a shed. You can't imagine my excitement at finding genuine shelter, even if it was just a shed. I burst in and collapsed on the floor and lay there for a very long time."

A cat leapt up into the lap of the old man, who stroked it without looking at it. He had his eyes fixed on Jack, even when he sipped on his ale. Jack felt a little intimidated by the stare but it flattered him that the old man was interested in his story, so he was about to continue when the old man interrupted him.

"For how long did you stay in that shed?" he asked.

"I slept the rest of the day," said Jack. "And through the night, I woke late the next day and, although it was still cold, the sun was shining, I wandered around the property and, though everything looked destroyed, there were clear signs of recent habitation. Someone had tended the garden, and there was a fire pit which had been used not such a long time before and over it, at an angle, perched a bath."

The old man had a little chuckle.

"I hung my clothes over the chicken coop, and by midday, they were dry. There was nothing for me there, nothing of use. So I moved on. I went back to the shed to collect my things. In the corner, I found this book." Jack took a pale blue battered notebook out of his satchel and set it on the scratched wooden table top. The old man eyed it with curiosity. Jack flicked through until he found the last page on which there was writing. "It's a diary. In the last entry, the author pleads with whoever finds it to deliver it to a woman, Olivia Smith."

"May I see?" asked the old man.

Jack pushed the diary across the table, and the old man took it and examined it.

"I don't know why. I suppose I thought there was room in my satchel and there would be no harm in taking it. Perhaps I thought it gave my wandering a hint of purpose. Whatever the reason, I took it with me and left the clearing, continuing downhill through the woods, the other side of which I found a track. It was a beautiful day if a little cold. Life-changing events always seem to happen on beautiful days, don't they? The outbreak of World War II, the attack on the Twin Towers, the collapse of human civilisation. This day was no different. There I was, happily enjoying the weather, unaware that my life was about to turn even more upside down than it already had. I think God must have a little joke. He says let's give them a nice day, lull them into a false sense of security, and then wham!"

"Do you believe in God?" the old man asked.

"No," Jack laughed. "I'm not one of those apocalypse types. God knows I've seen enough of those over the last few months. No, I think we brought this on ourselves. It was inevitable. Humans became successful by being greedy. The world, being a finite entity, would not support the exponential growth forever, and the secret of humanity's success became its downfall."

"What did you have to eat?"

"What?" Jack had already forgotten he was telling a story. "Oh yes, I had some dried meat in my bag, though it would not last forever. I found a little bit of dried meat in that shed I was telling you about."

"Goat?"

"Isn't it always these days?"

The old man took another sip of beer and looked around the pub. It was busy, but he was sure that no-one would disturb them where they were sat, almost in the fireplace.

"So I found this track and followed it down the valley, through a village which had burnt to the ground. Mutilated bodies lay rotting in the streets. I'd seen this kind of thing before on the other side of the moor. The marauders were part of the reason for leaving."

"Only part of the reason?"

"There was nothing left for me there. I would have perished had I stayed there. It was 'do or die'. So I did." Jack gulped his beer. It was bitter, and the head left a foamy moustache on top of his own. He wiped it away with the back of his hand and stroked his beard. "I walked straight through that village. I'd seen it before. They left nothing behind on those raids. I just kept walking. Right through the village and out of the other side. I just kept walking downhill until I came to another village and that village was the same. I knew that they would have destroyed everything until I reached the nearest town, and then I risked falling foul of whatever gang controlled the town. It never ceases to amaze me how these people destroyed the people who were putting food on their plates. All so they could sell their loot for silver."

Jack took a long drink and wiped his mouth on the sleeve of his worn tweed jacket.

"But what use is silver," he continues. "If there is no longer any food to buy with it."

The old man raised his eyebrows in agreement.

An unwanted tout, a tall, thin man, pulled up a stool, uninvited, and plonked his glass down on the table with a clunk.

"Evenin' gentlemen," the interloper chirped, betraying his origins as not from around these parts and making him even more unwelcome than he already was.

"We were in the middle of something," the old man scolded using all the weight of his seniority.

"Don't mind me guvnors, you just carry on," the tall, thin man replied in an outrageous parody of a cockney accent which had become fashionable.

"This is a private conversation," said the old man.

"Sorry, I'm sure," said the cockney with mock offence, picking up his glass and leaving.

"You were saying?" the old man turned back to Jack.

Jack needed a moment to gather himself.

"Yes. So I slept in a barn that night. Somewhere near the mouth of the valley just before it opens out into the plain. I had seen no one in days, but I didn't mind. I was apprehensive about meeting anyone not knowing whether they would be friendly or... well, you know the alternative."

The old man nodded.

"The trouble was that the next day it rained, so I stayed in the barn. It was empty apart from some rotting straw. No animals, no equipment. The surrounding farmland looked like it wasn't tended. Gangs had murdered the family. The night was so cold I'm not sure I slept a single minute, and even if it hadn't been so cold, I wouldn't have slept anyway because I could hear shouting and banging and the occasional shot being fired further down the valley. When the sun rose over the hills in the east, a white blanket of frost covered the entire valley. Tired of the barn and cold, I started walking right then and meet whatever fate awaited me."

The old man smiled. Jack, unaware he had made a joke, looked quizzical.

"I was just thinking how many people have become fatalistic these days," the old man explained. "You reminded me of the very moment I stopped running and face the music."

Jack relaxed. Satisfied that he was connecting with the old man. It was so rare to find someone who wasn't out to exploit you, and yet, in the back of his mind, Jack still wondered what this old man wanted. Why had he bought Jack a drink? There must be a price to pay somewhere along the line. Maybe he was gay, seeking young male company? Jack thought this unlikely, and he was ready to rebuff the old man's advances if that turned out to be the case.

"Well it was that morning that I found them, I don't think anyone else had been along. I think it was me who discovered them. The road from the valley meets the old dual carriageway near to the barn where I had slept, and before I had even reached the junction, I could see smoke. As I drew closer, I was taking great care not to be spotted by anyone at this stage, I saw the smoke was coming from trucks, some had collided, some on their side, and around the trucks lay a great deal of debris, but more disturbing, some bodies. I didn't go too close but circled trying to see what had happened and what remained. It was clear, after circling the site twice, and making a closer inspection of the vehicles, that everyone was dead. I scanned the surrounding fields, trying to ascertain..."

"You don't have to use fancy words with me," the old man interrupted.

"I was trying to find out," Jack corrected his vocabulary. "Whether there was anyone watching, waiting to ambush me, but it appeared, whatever had happened, everyone involved in the fight had either died or had fled. Growing more confident, I investigated... had a look around the trucks. The sun, rising over the eastern hills threw an orange light over the whole scene which made it all look unreal. Like some painting. The gang members, their brains splattered over the road, looked like martyrs in renaissance paintings. I looked in the back of one truck, and it was full of all kinds of things, metal and iron tools, dead chickens, pots and pans, stoves, fencing, a few vegetables, a fridge freezer and washing machine. It looked like they were on their way to the junkyard, and I'm sure they were. It was astonishing to think these people had killed each other over all this stuff which might be worth a fair sized bag of silver if sold to the right people, but the silver was useless if there was nothing to buy with it."

"Greed does terrible things," said the old man.

"Well that's the thing," said Jack. "I had nothing. Just what I could carry. And that was running short. Here was a truck of stuff, valuable stuff. With the keys in the ignition and no-one to stop me taking it."

The old man smiled.

"So, I pushed the dead body out of the cab, turned the key which was still in the ignition and turned that truck around and headed straight up that road I'd just come down. I drove right up to the end of the track, to that old burned-out house in the woods with the chicken coop. I unloaded the truck into the garden of the house as quickly as I could and then drove the truck back down the road as far as I dare. Back to the second village, I think. And I wrecked it. Jumped out and let it drive off the road watching it tumble down the side of the valley toward the river."

"Why didn't you just drive away in the truck?" asked the old man. "Why did you go back up the valley?"

"You know I wouldn't have got far before they picked me up. If not by the security forces, then by another gang. I wouldn't have sold the stuff. Not without being lynched. My one chance was to put the stuff to use. But you know, the thing was, I did not understand what to do."

"But you thought a truckload of scrap metal would help," The old man laughed.

"The day I slept there," said Jack. "I also found some biscuit tins stuffed with seed packets and, even though I didn't know the first thing about gardening, some seed packets had instructions about when and how to plant. And also, in this diary, I found a plan of what to plant where and the plan corresponded to the layout of the garden. I had noticed that there were no tools and assumed when I saw the contents of the truck that that's where all the tools had gone. I was just repatriati... I was just giving them back."

"How long did you think you had before they came looking for their loot?" asked the old man, smiling.

"I didn't think about that," Jack admitted. "I dumped the truck most of the way down the valley, and I guess I was just optimistic hoping that they wouldn't come right up the valley looking for me, I'd also hoped that the gangs had killed each other in the gunfight over the trucks and that there was no-one left to come after me."

The old man nodded. He knew all about unfounded optimism.

"I spent the rest of the day putting all the junk away. The fridge and washing machine I left where they were at the top of the track. I should have left them in the truck, but it was too late by then, I had some vegetables. Water, the means to grow my food. It felt good."

"For how long did that last?" asked the old man.

"It was a cold night," said Jack. "And the next day was miserable. A mix of sleet and snow. I spent the whole day wondering whether I'd made the right decision. And then, in the afternoon, in a gap between the rain and snow, the drone came. I hid in the shed. I'm not sure whether they saw anything which gave me away, but they could certainly see the fridge and washing machine at the top of the track. It was almost certain I would receive a visit in the next day or so, if not the next few hours. I armed myself with some knives and an axe and listened for the sound of vehicles coming up the track."

"Another beer?" asked the old man, getting up from his seat.

"That's very kind of you," said Jack. "Are you sure?"

The old man produced two silver coins from his pocket.

"Of course," he said, taking the empty glasses from the table. "You can't take it with you."

Jack watched the old man walk to the bar. He saw the mock cockney watching from the corner and tried not to meet his stare. There weren't many other people in the pub, and the mock cockney made him feel uncomfortable. Jack stared at the table until the old man returned.

"I know who you are," the mock cockney stood over Jack, leaning close to his ear. His ridiculous accent has gone. Jack, looked up and the tall, thin man stepped back and stared at him before turning around and leaving the pub.

The old man watched him go as he returned with the pints.

"What did he want?" the old man asked.

"He just told me he knew who I am."

"Does he?"

"How should I know?"

The old man handed Jack a pint.

"Thanks," said Jack, taking a swig.

The old man looked at the door out of which mock cockney had just left.

"We need to be careful," he said. "Better make this the last one."

"Why?"

"I'm surprised you have to ask me that," said the old man turning back to his drink before gazing at the large stone fireplace. "You know, the First English Civil War started here."

Jack raised his eyebrows. He didn't know.

"I wouldn't be surprised," the old man continued. "If the streets didn't look very much different then as they do now. I mean the poverty, the shit, the disease."

Jack shrugged. He hadn't thought about it like that. He had been very young when things made a drastic turn for the worst, so he hadn't experienced the halcyon days of the capitalist empire like the old man had. It was possible to get used to almost anything, and what you never had, you never missed.

"It's always been a bit of a shithole," Jack said.

"Ah, but even you have to admit that things are worse now than they have been for millennia. Tribal warfare. Mass killings. Mass starvation. And yet some things seem to withstand any circumstances." The old man picked up his pint. "Cheers."

Jack chinked glasses with the old man and took a large gulp. Experience had taught him that anything could happen at any moment to deprive him of the rest of his beer and the sooner he got it down him, the better.

"So," said the old man wiping his grey beard with the back of his hand. "Before I went to the bar, you were arming yourself with knives and listening for the sound of vehicles coming up the track."

"I don't understand why you want me to go over all this. You've already heard it from security."

"Let's just say I have a personal interest," the old man sipped his beer. "If you don't want to tell me, then don't."

"Sorry," said Jack, feeling ungrateful.

"It's OK," the old man smiled. "I know how you feel."

"It was the diary," said Jack. "There I was, my pockets full of knives, ready to defend myself against I don't know what. I was looking at the diary, and then I saw, between two of the pages, like a bookmark, there was a business card. It was for Dr Olivia Jones, I assumed this was the person to whom the author had requested the diary be delivered. It wasn't the name that caught my eye, it was the organisation she worked for. Homeland Security."

Jack looked for signs that the old man was impressed, but he wasn't. He didn't look in the slightest bit surprised.

"The card said that this woman was chief scientist in the food security branch of Homeland Security." Jack continued. "A woman like this would have connections. I wasn't safe where I was but if I could get to her and deliver this diary, then maybe this could earn me some favour. Get me into a Government compound or something like that."

The old man raised his eyebrows in approval of Jack's plan.

"I risked staying the night and leaving early the next morning. The next day was cloudy and mild. I carried what I could from my hoard. Mainly the knives, but I took the seeds and two pans, which I tied to my bag, some small tools, and the remains of the vegetables. I headed east, straight across the fields, I hadn't got very far when I heard the noise of a truck further down the valley. I hid behind a hedge, through which I had a view all the way down to the village where I had dumped the truck I had stolen. I could see the visitors stop at the bend in the road and heard shouting as they went to investigate the truck. As soon as they began pointing up the valley, I knew I had to get to a more sheltered position. Although hidden from them now, I was visible from the top of the track and so had to half run, half stoop across the fields to the far side of the valley, being careful to stay behind the hedge at all times. I was only halfway across the valley floor when I heard their truck restart. My best bet was to make it as far as the river and find a hiding place in the river bank until they had gone. If I started to ascend the hill on the eastern side of the valley, they would spot me easily. I ran as quickly as I could, stooping lower as the height of the hedge shrank the nearer I got to the river. All the time, the sound of the truck grew louder and louder, and I feared they would soon draw level and see me. As soon as I was close enough to the river, I leapt over the edge of the bank, hoping I wouldn't land straight in the water. As luck would have it, the bank made a shallow descent to the water's edge, and I was able to crouch out of sight of the track. I felt the morning dew soaking into my trousers, and the soft mud squeeze between my fingers as I listened to the truck pull to a standstill and the unintelligible shouts as they discovered the abandoned washing machine and fridge and made their way through the woods to search for the rest of their booty. I thought about trying to wade across the river there and then, but feared that one of them would have been left by the truck as a lookout and might spot me. So I stayed there, as still as I could, listening to the shouts, wafted on the wind, sometimes louder, sometimes quieter. The occasional clanking of metal betrayed the transfer of my hoard, their hoard, to their truck. I felt very uncomfortable but was too scared to move. It wasn't until I heard their truck start up again and drive down the track that I found the courage to poke my head over the edge of the river bank. They had gone, but I wasn't about to go back and see what they had taken. I was already soaked to the skin, so I lifted my bag above my head and waded across the river which is still not much more than a stream this far up the valley. Then began climbing the other side of the valley, shivering in my wet clothes. I walked as quickly as I could, trying to keep warm. About halfway up the hill, I reached a dry stone wall from where I had a good view of the valley and could see the truck descending all the way to the junction. I hurried up the remaining part of the hill until reaching the summit. I could see the whole of the valley from which I had just fled and, only a few paces further on, the beginnings of the next valley. I decided not to descend but to follow the ridge around the back of the valley where I knew it would join the moor."

"Where were you heading?" The old man asked.

"At that point, I just knew that if I headed for Leeds, there would be a garrison of the Homeland Security and maybe there I could use the diary to bluff my way into a little safety. I knew that Leeds was east of where I was, so I just needed to head towards the rising sun and away from the setting sun. It was cloudy, but I could see a brighter patch of cloud around what must have been the sun, so I skirted the top of the valley and headed east."

"When I was younger, I made many a hike across that moor," said the old man. "I remember one weekend, it was raining so much, and the wind was blowing so hard that it seemed that the rain was going upwards, under my waterproofs."

Jack smiled at the old man's reminiscence.

"When was that?" he asked.

"Oh, a long time ago, when I was a boy. Long before the collapse."

"What was it like before the collapse? Is it true what they say?"

"You were born before the collapse."

"Yeah, but I was too young to remember much."

"Well, what do they say?"

"That you could do anything you wanted. Go anywhere anytime you wanted. Eat anything you wanted whenever you wanted."

"It's true," the old man sighed. "As long you had enough money."

"Silver?"

"No, money. You must have seen the old banknotes."

"When I was young. And of course, I've seen pictures of them since."

"Pieces of paper about so big," the old man traced a small rectangle in the air between them.

"Yes, I never understood how people bought things with paper? Where's the value in that?"

"They weren't valuable in themselves. Their value lay in what they represented."

Jack look puzzled.

"Everybody agreed to use them so you could buy something worth ten kilos of silver without having to carry around the silver."

"Yes, I understand the theory behind it. We had them when I was growing up. They called them... something beginning with L. Leds, lets. Yes, I think that was it, lets."

"Lets. That's right. That's what replaced money for a while after the money lost its value."

"How did it lose its value?"

"The money was only good as long as people had confidence in the system. As soon as they lost their confidence, the money became worthless."

"But what happened? Why did the people lose confidence?"

"They discovered that the people they had chosen to be their leaders had been lying to them for years. They had always assumed they were lying to them, but when they discovered the extent of the deceit, they lost all faith in the systems that their governments had established to keep them in their places. The leaders who had promised them business-as-usual were no longer able to deliver on their promises. When people discovered they could no longer go where they wanted or buy what they wanted whenever they wanted, they felt betrayed, and they exhibited their disgust at this betrayal by refusing to participate in the system any longer. Of course, by that time it was too late, but it made the people feel better taking part in a system they felt a part of rather than something that their 'so-called' leaders had inflicted upon them."

"But it wasn't as simple as that, was it?" asked Jack.

"No, of course not. They could have maintained the illusion of a monetary system if they wanted to. It was more a problem of supply and demand. People were demanding all the things they'd always enjoyed, but they were becoming increasingly expensive to supply. Oil was becoming more and more difficult to extract, and as the price went up, so the cost of everything made with oil went up. Pesticides and fertilisers, transportation and packaging. Electricity. Hot water. Industry found it increasingly difficult to fulfil people's needs, so people turned more and more to local alternatives. There was a point when I thought it might be possible to make a transition to local interdependent systems, less reliant on oil."

"So why didn't it work?"

"It did for a while. Local communities started taking more and more responsibility for producing their food, generating their electricity, dealing with their waste. But the needs of nine billion people were just not sustainable. People were not willing to make the sacrifices needed to ensure that everyone had their fair share. They elected leaders who promised to maintain their lifestyles but the only way they could do that was by force and when that approach failed there was no alternative, and the goods stopped arriving and the economic system failed, and people refused to participate anymore."

"They just refused to participate?"

"Well, of course, it wasn't quite as simple as that. The measures the government had taken to try and save the financial system had alienated large sections of the population."

"What kind of measures?"

"Well the nationalisation of gold, the freezing of assets, the searching of homes to find out who was hoarding and then the exemptions for special groups like the monarchy, that was pretty much the last straw for them, and the chickens came home to roost."

"How do you mean?"

"The culture of violence which, for so long, had been directed outward towards those whose resources we were taking by force, turned inwards and those without the creativity, patience, work ethic or moral fibre to make things work with their neighbours began to take from their neighbours. When it is more lucrative for the police or members of the security forces to join in with the looters, then anarchy ensues."

"But here we are," said Jack. "Sitting in a bar, drinking beer. It's not complete anarchy."

"That's right." said the old man. "Some communities were clever enough to protect themselves. You know, during the first civil war this city was a walled city. It was besieged with the King's men camped outside. After the second civil war, it became a walled city again, and it looks after its own so that its own protect it from what's outside those walls. No doubt it's clever enough to profit from what's outside those walls, but it's clever enough to make sure it has everything it needs within the walls. Its geographical location helps, but it was its foresight which was its saviour."

Jack nodded in agreement while the old man drank his beer.

"Of course that does not mean it's not dangerous here within the walls, but it's less dangerous than outside, as you know."

Jack nodded some more.

"Did you encounter much in the way of trouble on the way here?"

"The first stage of the journey across the moors was fine. I followed the rising sun in the mornings and away from the setting sun in the afternoon. The sunsets were truly spectacular. It never ceases to amaze me how nature seems to produce such beauty on days that humanity is tearing itself apart. I slept in the shelter of bushes and didn't see anyone until after a couple of days when I knew I would have to turn south and head down one of the valleys towards Leeds. I skirted around the villages I passed, not wanting to risk contact with humans until I was so close to Leeds that I couldn't avoid it. My supplies were getting low and the long distances I was covering each day made me hungry. On top of this, I'd been drinking stream water wherever I could, and I must have picked a bad one cause I'd started to get the shits. I had no choice but to keep drinking the water. Otherwise, I would dehydrate, but I was stopping every five minutes to go for a poo behind a tree or a bush."

"Nice."

"I know. I must have stunk like a tramp."

"We all stink like tramps."

Jack conceded the point by taking another sip of beer.

"And did you manage to evade detection until Leeds?" asked the old man.

"More or less," said Jack. "People spotted me near a couple of villages but I was always too far away, and nobody bothered to come after me."

"Don't you think someone in one of the villages would have been willing to help you?"

"I wasn't willing to take the risk."

The old man knew that feeling of mistrust and didn't question his young companion.

"The combination of the shits and my constant hunger and weakness made that journey down Nidderdale seem to last forever," Jack continued. "But eventually I made it to a built-up area where it seemed that people were avoiding me. I had expected someone to pursue me but the first person I encountered turned on their heels and ran. Maybe I looked like the walking dead but, as I grew more confident in my safety the more people seemed to shrink away behind closed doors and dirty, torn net curtains. I had the address of the garrison, but I had no idea where it was. Silence met my door knocking attempts. Even the houses where I had spotted inhabitants at the window were refusing to open their doors. One resident, an old man, stayed at the window. He listened to me and then pointed in the direction I was going. Broken solar panels littered almost every rooftop, and black clouds hovered above, threatening rain. Someone had stolen all the road signs long ago. I reached a wide, gently flowing river crossed by a large stone bridge. The bridge seemed in good condition, and I made sure the coast was clear before running across as fast as I could and sheltering behind a small wall until I felt confident to continue, past an abandoned building site. Each new junction I came to I followed my instinct and took the road my hunch suggested. The roads became busier, and the people didn't shy away from me anymore. They didn't even seem to notice me. The sun was going down, and I felt spots of rain. I reached a square where the homeless masses were already bedding down for the night. I didn't ask anyone for directions there and carried on. On the next corner was a church. It was full of people singing. I passed a fire station, the doors were missing, and it seemed empty. On the corner of the next junction there was another church, again it was full."

"People need something to believe in," the old man chipped in.

"Their god doesn't fill their bellies."

"On the contrary, the communities help each other."

"OK," Jack was prepared to agree to disagree. "When I started walking back into the country, I realised that I had only walked through a small town or a large village and not Leeds at all. The road was badly potholed, but it must have been a main road in the past, so I was confident I was on the right route. I didn't want to enter the city at night, and the rain was starting to get heavier, so I decided to try to find shelter. I was also struggling to contain the contents of my bowels. The further I got from the town, the fewer people there were until I was on my own again. I spied a shed. At least it used to be a shed. It had half collapsed into a crumbling dry stone wall but still provided shelter. I crawled in out of the rain but straight away realised I would have to crawl out again and find somewhere to evacuate my bowels."

"You're quite a poet with these big words of yours," the old man laughed.

"There were some trees in the field," Jack continued. "So I picked one of them, squatting behind it with my trousers round my ankles. Almost straight away a torrent of pungent liquid cascaded from my arse into the roots. I wondered whether the tree was grateful for this deposit of fertiliser."

The old man almost choked on his pint.

"Have you ever considered being a writer," he chuckled. "You have a way with words."

Jack ignored the interjection.

"My arse was sore and, pulling up a clump of grass, I wiped it with care. Pulling up my trousers, I could see the stains on my boxer shorts. I hadn't had a decent wash in some days, and my clothes hadn't been washed for a much longer period, I must have looked like a tramp which is why nobody in the town had paid attention to me. I was hungry, thirsty and tired and if my plan to use the diary to get into the garrison failed, then I had no backup plan.

"The next morning the sun was trying to squeeze through the grey clouds which covered the sky. I grabbed my things and pressed on with a new found enthusiasm. I was sure to make it to the garrison before the day was out and they would decide my fate. What I hadn't counted on was the fact that soldiers guarded the city with large semi-automatic weapons. I could see the roadblock from some distance and rested while I contemplated my course of action. Marching up to the soldiers, waving the diary at them and demanding to be taken to the garrison seemed optimistic and yet I struggled to find a better alternative. I decided I would bite the bullet and go for it. What did I have to lose? I walked up to the two soldiers blocking the road. 'Stop. Who goes there?' One of them shouted. 'I'm on my way to the garrison to see Dr Olivia Jones,' I said with as much confidence as I could muster.

"The two soldiers eyed me up and down, wondering what this tramp could want with one of the most famous scientists in the country. 'What do you want with Dr Jones?' one soldier asked. 'I have something for her,' I said. 'What is it?' asked the guard. 'I'm afraid it's for her eyes only,' I said. 'How do we know it's not a bomb?' said the guard. 'You can search me,' I said, offering him my bag. He looked through the stuff in my bag, flicked through the diary a little and then returned my stuff to me. 'I see nothing there for Dr Jones,' he said. 'It's the diary' I said, pulling it back out of my bag and flicking through to the page where Dr Jones's father requests that the bearer is given safe passage. 'Her father requested I take it to her in person.' I showed him the page, and he read it carefully then said: 'Wait here.' He went to take the diary with him, but I wouldn't let go.

"The soldier walked into a tent, and a few moments later he returned and asked me to follow him, he led me to an armoured personnel carrier, told me to get in and then told the driver to take me 'to base', I hoped that was the garrison. They locked me in the back, which was devoid of windows, so I had no idea of where I was being driven, but it couldn't have been more than about five miles. When we stopped, I could hear the muffled sound of the driver talking to someone and the metallic clank of a gate being pulled open before the vehicle started moving again, this time for what must have been only a few hundred metres. It was the driver who opened the back door and beckoned me out into the sunlight.

"I stepped out into what looked like a car park within a walled compound. 'This way,' the driver said, gesticulating for me to follow him. I obeyed and was led into a nearby building with a waiting room in the reception. I was told to take a seat while the driver muttered something to the soldier behind the reception desk. The receptionist eyed me up and down, nodded to the driver who left, and then picked up a phone. He muttered a few words before replacing the receiver not interested in either me or what I was carrying. 'Do you think I might use the toilet?' I asked, and the receptionist nodded to a door which I walked to as quickly as I could without running. I couldn't remember the last time I had sat on a proper toilet. My boxer shorts were in such a poor state I binned them. I washed as best as I could and dried myself on the cotton towel then re-dressed before returning to the waiting room under the suspicious glances of the receptionist.

"After about half an hour, there were no clocks in the reception, an officer, I could tell by her uniform, came in through a door I was facing and approached me. 'Mr..." she said, extending a hand for me to shake. "Hughes, Jack Hughes," I said. 'Ah, a fellow countryman?' She asked, her strong accent betraying her Welsh upbringing. 'Fraid not,' I said. 'My great-grandfather was Welsh,' I said. 'Oh,' said the officer, disappointed. 'Did you know there used to be a singer called Jack Hughes?' I shook my head, the officer looked even more disappointed. Not a good start. 'Follow me.' I followed her through a door which led to a corridor and then through another door which led into a small room with a table and two chairs. She nodded for me to enter then followed me in, closing the door behind her. 'Please take a seat,' she said, and I followed the instruction, sitting on the far side of the table while she seated herself opposite me. 'I understand that you have something you wish to deliver to Dr Jones. May I see it?' I took out the diary and showed it to her. 'Thank you,' she said flicking through the pages. 'I'll make sure she gets it.' 'Oh no,' I said, taking the diary back. 'Her father was insistent I deliver it in person.' 'Her father?' the officer raised her eyebrows. 'When was this?' 'About a month ago.' 'Where?' 'Out West.' The officer thought about this for a moment, weighing up the information. 'Her father will be very upset if I don't deliver it in person,' I said.

"It was a gamble, but it seemed to be working. 'Yes, well,' the officer said. 'That will not be possible. Dr Jones is no longer at this facility.' 'Where is she?' 'That's classified.' 'But if you know where she is, tell me. It's very important I get this document to her.' The officer sighed. 'We have a transport going East tomorrow. I can put you on it, but it's at your own risk. We've had three transports attacked in the last month.' I nodded. 'OK then,' she said. 'I'll show you where you can sleep and eat, but we will have to confine you to those areas, all other areas of the base require additional clearance.' 'That's fine,' I said, delighted at the prospect of a bed and some food. Maybe I could have a shower too. The officer looked me up and down. 'Would you like me to arrange for some clean clothes?' 'Yes please,' I said. 'Very well then,' the officer rose from her chair and opened the door.

"I followed her back into the corridor where a soldier was waiting. 'Walker, here, will show you to your room, give you some clean clothes and will collect you and take you to the mess when it is time to eat.' 'Thank you,' I said. I followed Walker down the corridor, around the corner to another much longer one where, at the end, he let me through another door to yet a hall lined with doors on either side. He stopped at the first, unlocked it and opened the door. 'Here you are, sir,' He said, gesturing for me to step inside. I did as he suggested and found the room to be no larger than a boxroom with a bed, a sink and a shower box in the corner. On the bed was a towel and a set of clothes. 'They should fit,' said Walker. 'I will lock the door, you know, for security. I'll come and get you at meal time.' I thanked him and listened to him lock the door before stripping off and getting into the shower, I couldn't seem to get the water hot, but I was just thankful to have running water and a bar of very basic-looking soap. Having dried myself, I tried on the clothes, a khaki T-shirt, white starched hemp boxer shorts, khaki wool socks and a pair of camouflage trousers. Clean clothes felt good against my skin. I felt almost human again.

"Confined to the room, with no window to stare out of, the only window was a small one about two metres off the ground, I began reading the diary. It seemed like a mundane account of a gardener. I couldn't see why anyone would be interested in reading it or why it was so important that this Smith guy have it delivered to his daughter. From my point of view, reading it helped pass the time until Walker came back and unlocked the door to take me to eat. I followed him to the end of the corridor to a mess hall where many soldiers were collecting food given to them on tin trays, or already eating.

"A multitude of eyes followed me as Walker led me to the serving counter, I collected a tin tray and some cutlery and proceeded along the counter until I was facing a soldier in kitchen whites. He looked first to Walker who nodded, before spooning a large dollop of, what I can only describe as slop, onto my tray. 'Stew,' said Walker, 'It tastes better than it looks.' A little further along stood another soldier in kitchen whites. He dolloped a healthy serving of what looked like a form of mashed potato. Last on the serving counter were rows of tin cups, filled with water. I added one of these to my tray and followed Walker to a table that none of the other soldiers had yet occupied. 'Eat here,' said Walker. 'I'll be back for you later. Don't talk to anyone.' With that, he left me alone with my piles of slop. I didn't agree with Walker's assertion that the stew tasted better than it looked but this was my first proper meal for as long as I could remember, so I wasn't about to let the taste put me off. It didn't take me long to eat the lot, and as I did, I noticed other soldiers seemed to snigger at me. They pretended not to be looking when I glanced their way, but I was the butt of some joke or other. I tried to keep my head down and not attract attention. I didn't want to get on the wrong side of Walker or his superiors and miss the chance to get on that transport tomorrow. What I wanted didn't seem to come into it. A soldier sat down in front of me and said: 'I know who you are.' I couldn't be 100% sure but I think it was the same person as that man who came up to us earlier."

The old man looked at the door the mock cockney had left through but didn't seem too worried.

"Carry on," he said.

"Well, I tried to ignore him. I didn't want to get into trouble, but he wouldn't leave me alone. 'Aren't you going to ask how I know who you are? Come on, didn't your mother tell you it's rude to send people to Coventry?' I mean, Coventry. What the hell has Coventry got to do with anything?"

"It means ignoring someone. It dates back to the first civil war. Few people use it nowadays."

Jack acknowledged the trivia while taking the opportunity for another sip of beer.

"I tried to ignore him for as long as I could," Jack continued. "But he wouldn't give up. He kept asking me to guess how he knew me. Eventually, I said: 'Look, I don't mean to be rude. But I've been told not to talk to anyone. I don't want to get into trouble.' The man laughed. 'You're already in trouble matey. You're up to your neck in trouble, you're just too dumb to realise it.' 'What do you mean?' I asked. 'Why are you here?' the man asked. 'I don't think I should tell you that. Is this a test? You've been sent to test me, haven't you? Well, I'll not tell you anything. You should leave if you don't want me to be rude to you because I'm not talking to you.' The man laughed again. 'Look,' he said. 'It doesn't matter why you think you're here because that isn't the real reason you are here.' I looked at his smirking face for a while and then gave in. 'OK, so why am I here?' He laughed again. He was annoying me. 'You'll find out soon enough. You'll find out.' I dismissed him as mad and tried not to make eye contact.

"Walker saved me. He marched up to the table and scowled at the man. 'Off with you, Taylor,' he said, sending Taylor scurrying away to the nearest vacant place. 'Don't listen to a word he says,' Walker warned me. 'He's mad.' I nodded my understanding. 'Come on,' Walker continued. 'I'll tell you where to leave that.' I got up, took my tray and followed him to a hatch in the wall where he told me to deposit it. 'I will take you back to your room,' he said, and I followed him out of the mess hall back down the corridor to my tiny room where I was glad to lie on a real bed, no matter how lumpy the horse-hair mattress.

"Before long I had fallen asleep and did not wake until Walker unlocked the door and handed me a tray with a bowl of soup, a chunk of bread and a tin cup of water. 'I've saved you a trip to the mess hall,' Walker said. 'Get some rest, I'll be waking you early in the morning.' The soup was more of a watery stew made with the meat of an origin I could not pinpoint. The bread was hard. Despite sleeping for most of the afternoon, the weeks of sleeping rough had taken their toll, and I had no problem with falling asleep again and did not wake until Walker opened the door. 'Time to go,' said Walker. 'Get dressed.' There were two soldiers, even bigger than Walker, standing behind him in the corridor. As I got dressed, I realised that my old clothes and my bag with the diary inside were missing. 'Where's my stuff?' I asked. 'Sent for cleaning,' said Walker. 'But the diary?' 'Safe,' he said. I didn't know whether that meant it was safe or it was in the safe. 'Time to go,' he repeated and, judging by the look on the two lumps who stood behind him, it would not have been a good idea to argue.

"They led me outside to a waiting armoured personnel carrier, and Walker handed me a khaki jacket, for which I was grateful as it was cold. The back of the vehicle was already almost full of soldiers with the same attire as mine. They seemed to be trying to avoid my glances as I climbed in with them. One of the big guys with Walker slammed the back door shut, and moments later the engine started. 'Do you know where we are heading?' I asked the soldier next to me, but he ignored me. I looked around at my fellow passengers, but all of them were avoiding my stare. They maintained the silence for what seemed like an hour until the vehicle ground to a halt and a man I hadn't seen before opened the back door. He was holding a rifle. He gestured for us to get out and we all obeyed.

"As soon as I stepped out of the back of the APC, I could see that we were on a farm of some sort. I could see fields of crops, a barn and I could see that large security fences surrounded the property. The man with the rifle signalled for us to line up and I saw that there were some other men carrying rifles stationed a small distance from us. They ordered us to load the APC with sacks from the barn, and I wondered how we were all going to fit back in again with all these sacks of grain. My fears were answered as soon as the grain was loaded and the APC started up and drove towards the entrance gate leaving us all standing facing the man with the rifle. 'Excuse me,' I said. 'Shut up!' he bellowed. And gestured for us to walk towards a shed where more men with guns were waiting. As they passed the shed, a guard handed each man a mattock and led them towards a field that looked fallow.

"As I reached the shed, I tried to make eye contact with one man. 'Excuse me,' I said. 'Shut up!' came the shouted response. 'It's just that...' I persisted, but before I could finish, the man nearest me had hit me square in the mouth with the butt of his rifle, knocking me to the ground. 'We've got a talker,' he shouted to the man who seemed in charge, before bending down towards me. I could smell his foul breath as he spoke. 'Say one more word,' he said. 'And see what happens to the rest of your teeth.' I got up, took my mattock, and followed the rest of the men into the field.

"The rest of the morning they made us dig trenches. My hands were accustomed to manual work, but blisters were forming. At midday, we could sit at the edge of the field and were each handed a lump of stale bread, a chunk of mouldy cheese and a tin cup of water. When I thought the guards weren't watching, I turned to the person next to me. 'What's going on?' I asked. 'Shhh,' he warned me looking straight ahead. 'But I thought you were soldiers?' I asked. He laughed and then pretended he was just coughing. One guard looked over with suspicion. 'You'd better learn to keep your mouth shut,' my neighbour warned me, concentrating on eating his meal. I looked at the other men, they were all looking straight ahead at the ground in front of them, stuffing their meagre rations into their mouths. What the hell had I got myself into? I thought this book had been my passport to easy street and instead I'd jumped out of the frying pan and into the fire."

"It's not the book's fault," the old man commented.

"I know," said Jack. "But if I hadn't found the bloody thing, I'd have never have gone to Leeds."

"And you'd be doing what instead?" asked the old man.

"Who knows," said Jack. "Who knows what might have been. I wouldn't have been sitting here now that's for sure. But it doesn't change the fact that they worked us like dogs. We'd just had time to eat our mouldy food before they forced us back into the field to work until the sun went down. Then they marched us to a large shed where they gave us a similar stew of unidentifiable meat that I had eaten at the barracks and more of the stale bread. They gave us each given a towel, a block of soap and shown to the showers, which were cold. The showers were next to the dormitory where we all slept on bunk beds. They gave me a bottom bunk, thank God."

"I don't think he's listening."

"It didn't feel like it that night. Although, the strange thing is that, no matter how bad the food tasted, it was still better than what I'd been feeding myself the previous weeks. Something was reassuring about being looked after. Even though the work was hard, the food tasteless, the shower cold and the bed uncomfortable, it was still a bed and still food that we could rely on. We knew where the next meal was coming from."

"So why didn't you stay?" the old man joked.

"Because I hadn't chosen to be there," said Jack. "We were slaves, and there didn't seem to be anything we could do about it, and nobody was talking about it. I didn't know what to do. I showered and put my boxer shorts back on. My clothes were covered in mud. So I just hung them over the end of the bed hoping the mud would have dried by the morning. It was a chilly night, but the bed had a wool blanket on it. I got into bed because that's what everyone else was doing. I'd just got comfortable when a guard switched off the lights and bolted the door. My mouth still thronged from the blow that morning, and I just lay in the darkness contemplating my situation. It couldn't be much more than 7 pm, but I'd been up since 6 am, and the work had been physical. I didn't expect to have very much difficulty in falling asleep, and sure enough, before long I snored and rolled over to my side.

"The next thing I knew, I was being woken by bright lights and the sound of a gong. I sat up and saw that my fellow prisoners were pulling on their clothes, so I followed suit. With only one set of socks, I slipped into them and pulled on my mud-encrusted trousers, causing chunks of caked mud to fall to the floor. 'You'll clean that up later,' barked a guard. I didn't argue. I just followed the others out to the area where we had eaten the previous night, a row of trellis tables under a dirty green canvas awning.

"Breakfast was the lumpiest and least tasty porridge I'd ever had the misfortune to encounter. However, I knew that this would be the last thing before bread and cheese at midday and, guessing by the not yet risen sun, it was not long after six. I tried to keep up with the others who, I assumed, had been doing this for longer than I and knew when it was time to move and where to go. I also noticed that there were prisoners who had cooked the breakfast and were now clearing the bowls away, I followed the rest of them, back to the shed where another prisoner handed out the mattocks, I wondered why the prisoners hadn't used the mattocks in revolt, they made formidable weapons. Then I looked around at the number and distribution of guards and the high fences and realised any form of rebellion would be pointless. The odds were stacked against us. Almost too much so.

"Then I looked again, and I realised that the guards stationed around the fence were not looking at us at all. They were looking outwards, beyond the fence. The guards were not here to stop us from escaping, not all of them anyway.

"Neither was the fence. The guards and the fence were here to stop what was out there from coming in. The starving masses. It then occurred to me that I might have leapt from the fire into the frying pan but that I might not be as bad off as I imagined. But yes, I still did not want to stay. Under these circumstances. Without choice. I took my mattock and headed out into the field where we had stopped work the night before. It wasn't at all warm, but the sun was shining, and the heavy work of digging the trenches soon warmed us up. I know that parts for tractors and machinery are almost impossible to get now and the biodiesel to run them almost as scarce, but a decent horse and a man who knew how to operate a plough could have done this work in a fraction of the time, but I guess that even horses must be difficult to come by these days. I suppose this was how the Government forces sustained themselves, via a system of fortified farmsteads using slave labour.

"At least I was being fed, though I wasn't sure how long my socks would survive. I'd noticed two men washing theirs in the shower but couldn't imagine they'd have time to dry overnight. Maybe they had a secret supply of spares. My toilet situation was getting better regarding frequency. I think the cheese helped. The toilets on the farm were the giant pit variety over which someone had erected a platform so that the faeces fell into the pit and someone must then cover them over when it was full. This pit looked like it might be close to capacity. Throughout the morning, I mused on the pros and cons of escape.

"At that moment, the chances of success didn't seem very great and the prospects of what I might do if I survived an escape were as uncertain. I watched the sun rising in the sky trying to work out when it was midday and time for our mouldy bread and cheese. The morning seemed to last forever but then a guard blew a whistle, and we all rested by the side of what now felt like an enormous field and it was. It hadn't occurred to me before the scale of this farm. The guards must outweigh the prisoners to keep vigilance on a property of this magnitude. I wondered what the guards ate as I picked off two green furry lumps from both my bread and my cheese. I looked around at my colleagues. As usual, all of them were avoiding eye contact. Before we had finished our lunch, there was some kind of commotion on the far side of the farm. Guards were running and shouting at each other. Then shots were fired. Some guards were pointing their rifles through the fences and firing at something that must have been approaching. We couldn't see because the fence was on a brow of a hill and the guards were firing down at whatever was approaching, but before long we heard engines. Two guards pointed their rifles at us while the others ran to assist their colleagues, but none of our company looked like they had the slightest inclination of making a run for it.

"The sounds of the engines grew louder, and the firing of the guards became more rapid. We were all transfixed on what was about to unravel in front of us. A truck with metal plates welded onto the front of the cab, reared over the brow of the hill, crashing into the security fence, bringing the fence down and grinding to a halt in the soft mud of the nearest field. The fire from the guards was ferocious, but there was a similar quantity of fire being returned from the truck or somewhere not far behind. The excitement of the truck penetrating the fence had made me jump, but I could see now that my colleagues were becoming nervous and restless. I couldn't discern the source of their discomfort.

"Though a gunfight unsettles most people, this was a group for whom I had imagined it would take a great deal more to scare them than shots fired on the far side of a hillside. Their discomfort didn't seem to be triggered by the gunfire, it was more the presence of the truck that unsettled them. Could it be that whatever was in that truck was worse than the enslavement they had been experiencing here? I examined their faces, and they seemed terrified by whatever was in that truck. The only thing stopping them from fleeing were the two guards who looked as scared as the prisoners did. We all watched the gunfight develop on the far side of the hill.

"The more we watched, the more it looked like the intruders were getting the upper hand. My colleagues were becoming more nervous, and one of them made a run for it, but he hadn't moved more than a few metres before a rifle shot to the back brought him down. No-one went to his help. I looked at the guard who had fired the shot. He looked younger than me and more scared than the prisoner he had just murdered. We all sat where we were. I made sure I finished all my cheese and bread. I was not sure where my next meal would come from. We watched as, one by one, the guards on the other side of the field fell.

"Then we saw them, the people who had come, either from the truck, or whatever was behind the truck. They came over the brow of the hill wearing some kind of armour, and they shot the guards, one by one. They entered the compound. I looked at the faces of our own guards. They look petrified, and once the interlopers had entered the compound, they ran, rifles in hand. And once the guards ran, the prisoners ran but not away from the guards towards their freedom as you might expect but towards the guards, to the far side of the farm.

"Whatever had come through the fence was worse than slavery so, although I hesitated for a moment, I too ran after the others to the far side of the farm and, as I had just realised, some armoured personnel carriers. The guards ran straight to the vehicles and into the front, starting the engines almost straight away. Some of my fellow prisoners had reached the vehicles too and were yanking open the back doors trying to climb in. This didn't concern the guards much who reversed the APCs back, running over two prisoners.

"The other prisoners didn't pay much attention to their fallen colleagues either, running after as the APCs sped up away and over the fallen prisoners a second time. By the time I arrived, the APCs were already well on their way to the entrance gates which they just smashed through, ripping them off their hinges. We followed a little way behind and ran through the open gap turning left, away from the gun battle, which continued to the right.

"I don't know if the prisoners had any idea where they were heading or if they even cared. I followed them if they wanted me to. They cut across fields, stumbling in the mud, as did I, and none of us dared look back to see what was happening to our captors or whether we were being pursued. We were running downhill towards the bottom of what could be described as a valley. In the dip was a small woodland, and I followed the others into what felt like the relative safety of the trees. I had no idea what I would do now.

"The whole diary thing hadn't worked out very well, and I didn't have a Plan B. The others had stopped for a rest on some fallen trees in the centre of the woodland, and I joined them. They eyed me with suspicion as I sat on one of the tree trunks. We sat in silence for a while, catching our breaths. After a while, I broke the silence. 'What now?' I asked. All eyes turned to me. "You can do whatever you want, mate," one of them said. He was a skinny man with eyes, which seemed to bulge out of his head.

"The men seemed to know each other. I was the interloper as the newest addition to the pack. 'How do we know you're not one of them,' the man with bulgy eyes said. Did they imagine I was some kind of spy? 'Did you not see that guard hit me in the face,' I asked. 'That could have been all part of the deception,' said Bulgy Eyes. My goodness, what had happened to these people to make them so paranoid? 'Fine,' I said. 'You go your way, and I'll go mine.' 'That's what a spy would say,' said Bulgy Eyes. I could not win.

"They whispered among themselves, and I sat where I was, a mere spectator of their affairs. They moved as one, heading through the woodland, looking back to see whether I would follow. I sat where I was, watching them leave, I'd taken my chances alone before I could take my chances again, I watched them disappear into the trees, and almost all of them had gone when the last of the party stopped. He was the fattest of the group and had a kind face. He looked at me and beckoned before turning and following his colleagues into the wood. I rose and followed him. What else was I to do? I caught up with the group at the edge of the wood where they had stopped to survey the land.

"The sound of shooting from the farm had stopped, and I wondered whether they might now turn their attention to us. From the edge of the woodland, we could see that the edges of this shallow valley were lined with other farms, surrounded by large security fences and guarded by men with guns. We could see that some guards were taking an interest in what was happening at their neighbour's farm, but there were no obvious signs that they were concerned for themselves. I think the fact that the guards were distracted by what was happening on top of the hill gave the former prisoners confidence that they could travel along the floor of the valley undetected.

"They were following a small stream alongside which grew some trees so that the fugitives could move with reasonable assurance that no-one would not spot them. One by one, the men started dashing from tree to tree and, when all had left the wood, I began to follow them, dashing from tree to tree myself, imitating those I was following. Now and then, I observed whether the guards on the farms on the hillsides were taking an interest in us, but their attention seemed to be focussed on the activities on the hill from where we had just escaped. They did not seem to be interested in the movements of a bunch of fugitives even though, given their vantage points, they must have known where we were.

"I took care to follow the others at a small distance and, as much as possible, to keep out of sight of the guard towers which bordered the farms, not that they were interested. We were heading downstream and the further we went the marshier the land became. The trees began to thin, and we seemed to pass the extent of the fortified farms. We were approaching what appeared to be a large estuary. I guessed it must have been the Humber.

"My fellow fugitives appeared to be familiar with their surroundings and turned right to follow a track through the marsh long before they reached the water's edge. The path soon led to drier land, and they continued to follow it along the bank of the estuary. Although I was warm with the exercise, I realised I had left my jacket behind and began to worry about where we might spend the night. For now, the sun was on my back, but I knew that as soon as it fell below the horizon, the temperature would drop. Looking ahead, I saw that most of my fellow fugitives were in the same boat having abandoned their belongings in a rush to escape the farm. Soon I would need to do another poo. My bowels were much better than they had been because of all the cheese and I could just about get away with going twice a day, but all this movement was speeding up the process.

"The group stopped for a rest, and I could see that there was a settlement not far in the distance. I may have been getting paranoid, but I was sure that the group had been discussing me as I approached. They stopped talking and turned to look at me as I sat down. 'It's too late now anyway,' said the fat one with the kind face. 'He can just keep going. Find his own way,' said Bulgy Eyes. 'Are you talking about me?' I asked, stating the obvious, somewhat. 'This is where we part company,' said Bulgy eyes. 'What did I ever do to you?' I asked him. 'Nothing.' 'Exactly,' he said. 'You've done nothing for me so why should I do anything for you?' I had no answer to this, but I felt I had to say something so I said: 'We should all be helping each other.' This did not have the effect I had hoped for. 'Why should we?' he snarled. 'Why the fuck should we help each other? One more mouth to feed is one share less for me. We don't need you. You're extra baggage.' No-one else seemed willing to take part in the debate, they seemed indifferent whether or not I went.

"Fatty was the only one who looked uncomfortable. 'Let's put it to the vote,' I gambled. 'No, let's not,' said Bulgy Eyes. 'This isn't a fucking democracy.' I persisted. 'Who thinks I should go with you? Raise your hand now.' Only Fatty raised his hand and then only half-heartedly. 'Who thinks you shouldn't come,' said Bulgy Eyes and raised his own hand high into the air. None of the others even reacted but just stared in front of them. 'That's settled then,' said Bulgy Eyes. 'Bye-bye.' 'But it was one vote each,' I protested. 'Like I said,' said Bulgy Eyes. 'It's not a democracy. 'He got up to leave, and the others followed suit. They all headed off, except Fatty who lingered a while. 'We're going to Freetown,' he said when the others had left. 'There's a boat in the next village. Hang around the village, and I'll see if I can change their minds.' 'Thanks,' I said and watched him leave.

"I let them get a head start on me before setting off myself. With the muddy bank of the estuary on my left, I followed the others, at a much greater distance this time, and before long arrived at a reasonably sized village with an old Norman church. Or was it Anglo Saxon, I could never remember these things. As with most villages I'd passed through or near in the last few weeks, this one looked deserted, but it hadn't been raided because, as far as I could tell, none of the houses had been burnt down.

"The church door was closed, no worshippers here. I headed down in the estuary's direction thinking that's where any boats would be found. Freetown sounded like a good idea. I'd heard about it but wasn't sure it existed. I thought I'd like to see this mythical city guarded by its own residents. Find out whether it grew half of its food within the city walls and almost all of its fruit. It seemed too good to be true, and I'd heard a lot of stories since the collapse that had turned out to be false."

"Now you know," said the old man.

"Yes, now I know," said Jack. "Sometimes it's OK to dream I suppose."

"So how did you get on this boat?" asked the old man.

"That's the thing," said Jack. "When I reached the water, there was no boat. I trusted the fat guy but just assumed he must have been mistaken. Or maybe given false information by Bulgy Eyes in the knowledge he would pass it onto me. I sighed and watched the muddy water slip backwards and forwards at the edge of the estuary. The village appeared to be on the banks of a river that led into the estuary, and there was a harbour gate but no boats. I wondered whether the boats were moored further upstream and began to walk that way. The river was very straight as if they had canalised it back in the day when they used to do those things. On the other side was a disused factory. I guessed that past generations had built the canal to deliver and retrieve goods from this factory. The banks were overgrown with long grass, and despite the incredible straightness of the river, it was difficult to see whether there were any boats further upstream.

"There seemed to be a path trodden through the grass, and it looked like it had been freshly trod. I couldn't wait any longer, I had to go to the toilet, I waded through the long grass to what I considered the most secluded spot, pulled down my trousers and squatted. It was a blessed relief to evacuate my bowels, but the smell was terrible. I knew I was not alone only an instant before Bulgy Eyes and Fatty came wading through the grass towards me. 'Are you following us?' asked Bulgy Eyes, with less aggression than the last time we had met. They didn't seem that bothered by the fact I was squatting, mid poo, trying to hide my privates from view. 'No,' I said with no real intention of convincing them. 'Well you may as well come with us, now you're here," he said. I don't know what Fatty had said to him, but whatever it was it had worked.

"They stood there looking at me, waiting for my response. 'Do you mind if I finish first,' I said after a while. Bulgy Eyes snapped out of what had become some kind of trance. 'Oh, yes. Sorry. We'll just stand over here.' The group moved away to an appropriate distance to preserve my modesty, and as they walked away, I heard Bulgy Eyes say: "I wondered what the smell was.' They had thought I was just hiding and hadn't realised I was taking a dump."

The old man laughed.

"So what had caused Bulgy Eyes to change his mind?" he asked.

"I don't know," said Jack. "And I wasn't about to question him, I was just glad to have an option again and getting a lift to Freetown seemed like a good one, I tried to clean my arse with some long grass with limited results, gave up, pulled up my kegs and went to follow the others. They led me about another half mile up the river to a mooring and a small yacht. Bulgy Eyes shook hands with a grey-bearded man who I assumed to be the captain. They seemed to know each other and began negotiating some deal. Greybeard must have been convinced by Bulgy Eyes' argument because he waved us all onto the boat.

"We sat on the deck, trying to avoid getting in the way of anything which looked like it might be important. Once everyone was on board, Greybeard began preparing to leave. He did not want to hang around with a gang of fugitives. That was understandable. The captain had two mates helping him. They used long poles to move the yacht away from the bank and then down the river towards the open harbour gate, which I could see in the distance downstream.

"It took a while before they pushed the boat out into the open estuary, but once we were there, they pulled the poles on board and set to work hoisting the sails. With the assistance of the wind, the yacht picked up speed, and the captain steered a course downstream, towards the centre of the estuary. The yacht glided along with ease, and I looked at the distant bank becoming more distant by the minute. One of my fellow fugitives pointed ahead, and I turned to look at what he was pointing towards. It was the ruins of the Humber

Bridge. Once the largest bridge in the world, it still stood but only just. Most road sections were missing and what was left hung at acute angles from what supporting cables remained. They ruined it. A symbol for the decay that had set in right across the country. Right across the world, though it was becoming more and more difficult to know with any certainty what was happening in other parts of the globe. I looked up as we passed underneath, hoping loose sections of road would not choose this moment to separate from the surviving metal strands, which once suspended a mile of roadway from one bank to the other.

"We seemed to be in the centre of the channel now with the banks on either side appeared to be about the same distance away. There was very little other traffic on the estuary and the traffic that there was, seemed to keep its distance from us. I wasn't sure whether they feared us or whether we feared them. Although both banks were quite some distance away, I could see some wooden jetties, some of which had small boats moored to them. The sun was getting lower behind us now, and the light shimmered off the water, which rippled in the yacht's wake. I tried not to look at Bulgy Eyes in case he reconsidered and tried to throw me into the water, but I could see Fatty from the other side of the boat staring at me with a wry smile on his face, I wondered why he had been so keen to get me on board and how he had managed it. I looked the other way but could sense his eyes burning into the back of my neck. He was making me feel uncomfortable. I tried to ignore him and looked ahead at the expanse of water ahead which stretched out all the way to what must have been the North Sea. Then I noticed the wall. I don't know why I hadn't seen it before. Not far back from the jetties. On the first bit of solid ground, I guess, there was a huge wall. It made the fence surrounding the farm look insignificant, it was made of a variety of materials, wood, brick, concrete, corrugated iron, all cobbled together but all erected to a uniform height. It was difficult to see from a distance, but I guess it must have been about three metres high. But I don't know why I'm telling you all this, you know this already, don't you?"

"Not at all," said the old man. "I never tire of hearing first impressions of our great wall. It's not just for security. It also defends our city from flooding. With the combination of sea level rises and the storm surges we seem to get all the time these days, the city would be underwater like Atlantis if it wasn't for our huge wall."

"Well it is impressive," smiled Jack. "It seemed to stretch right along the foreshore all the way to the bridge."

"It does," said the old man. "It surrounds the whole city and some surrounding countryside."

"Yes, well I could see it was unbroken along the riverside until we reached the flood barrier."

"What was the flood barrier," the old man corrected. "It's now one of our main entrance gates. There is one at the marina too."

"Oh yes," Jack remembered, but the correction didn't seem that significant as the two gates were only a few hundred metres apart. "It is possible to enter by land, isn't it?"

"Of course," said the old man. "There're more gates than you realise. There's Boothferry gate, Willerby gate, Cottingham gate, Beverley gate and Holderness gate. Plus another gate on the river further up than you went."

"But who guards all those gates?" Jack asked.

"It's voluntary in most cases. Local groups who take it in turns to keep watch. The city has several garrisons of guards who maintain order, however. Nothing gets in or out without being checked."

Jack laughed to himself. He knew this to be the case from first-hand experience.

"Yes, well, you know that to be the case, don't you?"

Jack nodded.

"We have to be very careful to preserve what we have here." said the old man. "I hope they weren't too rough."

"Not at all," said Jack. "They were very thorough."

"You came through Myton gate didn't you?"

"I think so."

"Not Minerva gate into the marina?"

"No, I don't think so. We passed through this big rectangle and up the river."

"Yes, that's Myton Gate. And how did you get the diary back?"

"Well, that's the weird thing. We were all searched. They searched the boat. The captain seemed to spend an age talking to the guards, but when the search was over, they waved us through. I watched in amazement as this huge section of the wall that had continued through the water was hoisted high into the air to allow the captain's mates to punt us through and up the river. Vessels lined the banks, beyond that, warehouses teeming with activity even though the sun was going down, and dusk settling. We passed the boats, the warehouses, the bridges until we found a mooring.

"They led us off the boat and into a warehouse. Fatty took me aside from the others and handed me my bag that had been taken from me in Leeds and the diary was still inside. I asked him how he got it, but he just laughed. He said what I was looking for was here in Freetown, showed me through a door and then shut it behind me. I found myself on my own on the street, and it was getting dark, I know that inside the free city is safer than somewhere like Leeds but I knew the risks and didn't want to hang around in the street after dark.

"I followed the river as best as I could downstream where I knew the centre to be. If these Smiths were as important as I thought then finding some official looking building was the way to go. Workers were shutting up the warehouses which flanked the streets. There seemed to be a pub on almost every corner, and these were filling up. I tried to walk as if I knew where I was going so as not to alert the locals to how vulnerable I was.

"When I reached one bridge, a guard stopped me. I tried to walk on at first but he shouted for me to halt so I did as I was told and waited for him to approach. He inquired after my business, and I explained that I had something for Dr Jones, He realised straight away that I was not from the city, Free Towners speak like no others, and so I had to recount the story of having just arrived by boat and of having been searched at Myton Gate. He seemed to know the yacht that had brought me here and asked me if I knew where to find Dr Jones. I admitted that I didn't, and he told me I should go to the Guildhall and pointed me in the right direction. He advised me to speak to no-one on the way and wished me luck, shaking me by the hand. This last gesture surprised me as did his parting words, which were 'be careful, there are spies everywhere'. I did not understand why he wished me well or why anyone would want to spy on me but, not wanting to appear ignorant, I thanked him and headed in the direction he had pointed. It was in the direction I was already heading. He told me to continue to the next bridge and then turn right.

"I crossed the road to put as much distance as possible between myself and any guards that there might be at the next bridge, I avoided eye contact and quickened my pace to maintain the impression I knew where I was going. I needn't have been so cautious because the road curved to the right so that, by the time I reached the next bridge, the guard post next to the bridge was quite a distance.

"I turned right and saw some large stone buildings which looked official enough for one of them to be the Guildhall. It soon became clear which the Guildhall was. A large stone clock tower rose high above the building. The building itself was decorated with impressive stone columns. It was obvious where I had to go. The square it faces was quieter than the surrounding streets had been, but as I approached, there were guards at the front entrance. I took a deep breath and approached the three iron doors, each guarded by two sentries. I was still some distance away when the first sentry shouted at me asking my business.

"I waited until I was closer before replying but he shouted for me to halt before I had reached a distance which would have dispensed with the need to shout.

'What's your business?' the guard asked again, pointing his rifle at me.

'I have something for Dr Jones,' I said tapping my bag.

'What?' he demanded.

'A book,' I said. 'It's from her father.'

"The sentries looked at each other. It was at that point that you came round the corner. The guards seemed to know and respect you. You had a private conversation with one of them and then suggested we come to this pub to discuss the matter. That's it. I've told you my story. I've included every detail as you asked me. Too many details. You now know everything about me, and you still haven't told me anything about you. How are you going to help me deliver this diary to Dr Jones as her father requested?"

The old man finished the rest of his pint and set the empty glass down on the table with a clunk.

"I am her father," he said.

Part three

"I think it's time for another pint, don't you?" the old man said, getting to his feet.

"You've been very kind already," said Jack. "I can't remember the last time I had so much food and beer."

"Think nothing of it. You've had a rough time, and I have the silver."

Jack finished his pint and handed the old man the empty glass.

"Thanks," Jack said. He watched the old man walk to the bar and contemplated whether what the old man had said was true. He was old enough to be Dr Jones's father, and the guards had treated him as if he was Dr Jones's father.

The old man returned with two more pints, handed one to Jack and sat down.

"Cheers," said the old man, and they touched glasses.

"This is good," Jack said, nodding to his beer.

"Yes it is, isn't it? No matter what else we lose the ability to do, making beer is the one thing we'll always be good at."

"Apologies for asking this," Jack began. "You've been very kind to me. But how do I know that you are the person you say you are?"

"Does it matter? Does the diary matter?"

Jack shrugged.

"Be honest, Mr Hughes. Why did you bring me that diary?"

Jack looked at the battered pale blue cover of the diary, then back at the old man.

"The honest answer is that I thought the diary might give me access to somewhere more secure than a shed in a garden at the top of a valley."

"And did it?"

"Well, it got me here," Jack admitted.

"So does it matter if I'm Dr Jones's father, as long as you are where you want to be?"

"This city is more secure than where I was. That's true. But I still don't have the means to feed or house myself. In that respect, I'm worse off."

"You may be right. Your journey has proved yourself to be a resourceful young man, and I could do with the help of a resourceful young man."

Jack couldn't help feeling there was something sinister about the way the man spoke.

"I could offer you a position which would mean we would look after you as long as you were in the role."

"And what role would that be?" Jack asked.

"My helper. I know. It's vague, isn't it? You are right to be sceptical. I know I would be. But it's very difficult to be specific about a task when I'm not sure how to go about it myself."

Jack looked unconvinced.

"OK. First things first," said the old man. "Would you like me to prove that I wrote that diary?"

Jack nodded.

"OK. Well. You found it in a brown shed, near a chicken coop close to a burnt-out house, on a property surrounded by trees and a little stream, next to which was a bath stood over a fire where it had…"

"None of this proves you wrote the diary," Jack interrupted. "It only proves that you know where I found it."

"Fair point," admitted the old man. "OK then. What about the content of the diary? What if I showed you Molly, the pregnant cat?"

"That just proves you have a pregnant cat."

"Ah, but it also proves that I know there is a pregnant cat in the diary."

"Yes, but you could have read the diary after they had taken it from me in Leeds and before you gave it to your lackey, Fatty, to give back to me."

"Ah yes, Fatty. You are right. I could have done that. But why would I?"

"To convince me you are Dr Jones's father when, in fact, you are someone different."

"I suppose that would be a reason. But why on earth would I want to pretend to be Dr Jones's father?"

"To get close to Dr Jones."

"My goodness. You have thought this through, haven't you? I'm not sure there's any arguing with that theory. So how am I going to prove it to you?"

"Take me to Dr Jones."

"And why do you want to see Dr Jones?"

"I think she might offer me some security."

"Is that so? Interesting."

"And how do I know your intentions towards Dr Jones would be honourable?"

"Honourable?"

"How do I know you aren't trying to talk your way close to her to assassinate her?"

"With what? The diary? Do I look like an assassin?"

"They never do."

"Look," said Jack. "I've told you my story. And left no part out. It's time for you to tell me your story and convince me you wrote this diary."

"OK," said the old man. "You've read the diary, so I'll start where the diary ends. The day the second drone came. I was ready to fight to the death with whatever came up the track that day, and when a vehicle arrived, it wasn't a truck like before, it was an armoured personnel carrier. God knows what they thought when they came through the trees and saw this crazy old lunatic brandishing, I forget what it was now, a big stick or something. They did a very fine job of calming me down. It took a while, mind.

"They offered me something to eat. Sandwiches. I couldn't remember the last time I had eaten bread, let alone sandwiches. They said they were there at the request of my daughter and that she had instructed them to pick me up and look after me. I collapsed right there and then at the news. Until that point, I had no idea whether my daughter was alive, let alone where she was or what she was doing.

"They took their time to wait until I had recovered from the shock a little before asking me if I wouldn't mind getting into the back of the armoured personnel carrier. I asked where they would take me and they just said we were going somewhere safe. It was a while since I had known anywhere safe and the thought appealed to me. I climbed into the back of the vehicle with a little help, and about four other men got in with me. They looked like soldiers while at the same time looking like they might not be. I didn't question them. The prospect of somewhere safe was too enticing to risk losing over idle chatter. I struggled to hold on as the APC descended the track. I hadn't remembered how potholed the track had become. It seemed a while since I had dragged the trolley up the hill, even though it wasn't that long ago.

"There were no windows in the back of that truck, but I had a rough idea of where we were by the twists and the turns. I knew that road very well, and I wondered whether this would be the last time I travelled this road, I looked at the faces of the soldiers who sat in the back with me, I say soldiers, but even then there was something strange about them, something that was not quite 'soldier' about them, I didn't trust the situation but what was I to do? I couldn't fool myself about the state of my smallholding, I was starving and, although this could be the frying pan into the fire, anything must be better than starving to death. Right?"

Jack nodded agreement but said nothing.

"The sandwich had been chicken. It was so long since I had eaten a chicken sandwich. It was so good. I could still feel it going down. We kept driving over bumps, and although it was never the best road in the world, I knew that some of those bumps were bodies. I was both relieved that they had liberated me from this nightmare and anxious about what would happen next.

"As we progressed, the road became smoother, and then we slowed down for what I guessed was the junction. It was then that the fighting began. Someone was firing shots. I heard bullets bouncing off the APC. They returned the shots. Unintelligible shouting. The APC accelerated, more shots, from both sides. More shouts. The APC picked up speed and then, after that, I lost track of where I might be. We sped along what must have been still a reasonable quality road, not common these days. I imagined what the countryside might look like as it passed.

"The countryside I pictured in my mind was the countryside of my youth, not the countryside as it is now, dysfunctional and messy, but the neat farms that I knew when I grew up. I know that all of that is gone, but it does no harm to imagine. The more we drove, the wearier I became. Perhaps it was the movement of the APC, rocking me to sleep. Before I realised what was happening, I was nodding off. I kept trying to wake myself up, but the need to rest was overwhelming, I succumbed to the urge, and when I awoke, the APC had stopped.

"I was told to wait while two of my fellow passengers got out. The wait was painful and seemed to go on forever, to my dismay, after the wait, my fellow passengers got back in, and we moved off again. I watched their faces for clues, but none of them was giving anything away. I wondered where we could be heading."

Jack wondered whether any of this was true or whether he was doing the old man a disservice by mistrusting him. If he was genuine, then he had been through a terrible ordeal, but if he was making it all up, then he was very good at lying.

"I had lost track of time," the old man continued, "because of nodding off all the time. I was just so tired, I couldn't keep my eyes open. When I next awoke, we had stopped again, and this time they asked me to get out of the APC. I was glad. They're not the most comfortable of vehicles, as you know. I stepped out into what looked like a courtyard and stretched. I don't know how long I had been in the APC for, but my body ached, it must have been quite some time. Brick buildings surrounded the courtyard, and it was into one of these that they led me.

"Two soldiers stayed with the APC, but the rest of them followed us inside. The interior was as drab as the exterior with yellowing cream paint and worn linoleum floors. The soldiers stopped, so I stopped. They were waiting for someone or something. We stood there for what was only a minute but which seemed much longer. I'd now had enough of stretching my legs, and all I wanted to do was sit down again, but this time on something more comfortable. Since those bastards burnt my house down, the softest thing I'd sat on was grass.

"A man, not much younger than myself, came through a door and the soldiers stiffened. He was also wearing military-looking clothes but with no insignia which might give me a clue as to his rank or status. 'Follow me, please,' he said to me and 'thank you, men,' to my escorts, who left through the door opposite to the one which I now followed the man. It led to a small interview room, and he gestured for me to sit at the single table in the centre of the room. I did so, and he joined me, sitting in a chair on the opposite side of the table. 'You'll be wondering why we brought you here,' he began. I nodded. 'First, would you mind telling me who you are?' 'You don't know?' I asked. 'I'd just like to hear it confirmed by you.' I told him who I was, and he told me he worked for my daughter and that she had sent for me. 'Where is she?' I asked. 'Not here, I'm afraid,' he replied. 'But we can take you to her, in good time.' I was keen to see her even though I hadn't been sure that she wanted to see me again."

"What happened between you two?" asked Jack, and then felt he had overstepped the mark. "Sorry, I didn't mean…"

"It's okay," said the old man. "It's not a state secret. We disagreed. She wanted to marry a man of whom I didn't approve. He was my age. Our views differed on many subjects. I never trusted him."

"What happened?"

"She married him. We stopped speaking, and I never saw her again."

"So, why did she send for you?"

"Good question. That's what I wanted to know, although the desire to know the reason was insignificant compared to my desire to see my daughter again. The officer of uncertain rank (I assumed he was an officer), told me she was now chair of the guild at Freetown and that they had been asked to arrange transport there for me, but that the route was very hazardous and I would need to accept those risks before undertaking the journey.

"I told them that the risks were of small concern to me and that if they could spare the men, I would go. 'Therein lies the problem,' explained the officer. 'We don't have men to spare. Overland routes are too dangerous to travel without a sizeable escort, and I can't spare that kind of workforce at the moment. We've been experiencing raids all over the region, and I need to keep the small number of personnel I have to police the region, however impossible a task that might seem. If I gave you a narrowboat, do you think you could navigate it down the Aire? The Aire Calder navigation is still open, and it's much safer than the overland route. There are checkpoints at all the locks, but you'll find our men at all of them, and I'll give you a pass which will guarantee safe passage all the way into the Humber and through the gates of Freetown.' 'A narrowboat on the Humber?' I asked, surprised. 'They travel back and forth. Just make sure you steer clear of the sandbanks, on the Ouse near Goole.' 'OK, I think I can do that,' I said. 'We'll give you charts and information about the tides. The boat we give you will have spare fuel filters. Just keep the engine cool in case you need to run it at full speed. You'll be fine on the Humber unless it is rough, but I advise you to wait for the falling tide before making the run from Goole to Freetown, the narrowboat will never make the run against the tide. Don't travel at night. We will provide a list of suitable moorings. The forecast for winds is favourable, both direction and speed, so you should be okay. The boat we will give you is reconditioned, so it should be more than capable of making the run.' 'You want me to do this alone?' 'I can give you a pilot, they have made this run before.'

"I can't tell you how relieved this made me feel, the thought of taking a narrowboat down the Aire wasn't a problem, but taking it out onto the estuary was something I knew I was not qualified to do, I would need someone who knew what they were doing, and I hoped this person did, I agreed to his plan. He asked me to wait and said he would be back soon. I hadn't waited very long when the door opened again, and a woman entered. She was no older than you."

The old man eyed Jack for a moment as if trying to confirm his estimate to himself.

"I stood up, and she introduced herself. 'Hello,' she said. 'My name is Sandra Williams.' 'Pleased to meet you, Ms Williams,' I said. 'Are you the one who will get us to Freetown?' 'I'm the one who will try.' 'I heard you've made this run before.' 'Sometimes.' 'How long will it take?' 'Three days. You'll spend the night here. I'll take you to your room in a moment. We'll leave first thing in the morning. I've already prepared the boat near the Royal Armoury. Tomorrow we'll go as far as Gaggs Bridge. The days after we'll go to the junction of the Ouse. We'll wait there for the tide to be right and then we'll head straight for Freetown.' 'Three days?' 'Yes, I know. In your day, I expect you would make the journey from Leeds to Freetown in, what, an hour? Back in the day when there were motorways and security and...' 'I wasn't complaining.' 'I never said you were. Follow me please, sir.'

"I followed her out of the room and along the corridor to the end, then through another door. She opened the first door on the right and showed me into what looked like a cell. There was a bed, a washbasin and a small window high on the wall. The only thing that stopped it looking like a real prison cell was a shower box in the corner. 'There are clean clothes on the bed,' she said. 'I'll be back later to take you to get something to eat.' I thanked her and watched her close the door behind her. This was the first shower I had had in a very long time, and I was very glad to discard my clothes and stand under a warm shower, yes warm, for a very long time. There was even a bar of ambiguous looking soap there..."

"Where was this?" asked Jack.

"Leeds, somewhere. In some barracks, I guess."

"But you said that Dr Jones controlled this place."

"That's right."

"Are you trying to take the piss?"

"What do you mean?"

"Well, I just describe a barracks to you and then when you tell me your story, you describe the self-same barracks."

The old man looked puzzled.

"What do you mean?" he said.

"You are sitting there describing the place where I told you they took me, prisoner," said Jack.

"I'm sorry," said the old man. "I must not have been paying attention. I was describing the place they took me."

"But if the place they took you is the same as the place where they took me if what you say is true, then that means your daughter is complicit in slavery."

The old man sighed.

"Look," he said. "I don't know whether the place they took me is the same as the place you were taken or not. But I very much doubt whether my daughter would be involved in slavery."

"Then what's your explanation?" said Jack.

"My explanation? I don't know enough about it," said the old man. "All I know was that I was taken to somewhere in Leeds. I know that because I got on a boat by the Old Royal Armoury but the idea that my daughter is running a network of slavery...no, I don't believe that."

"Have you asked her?"

"Have I asked her? No. The first I heard about slavery was from you."

"Are you going to ask her?"

The old man thought about it for a moment.

"Yes I am," he said at last.

"When?"

"When we meet her. Why don't you ask her yourself?"

"I will."

The old man looked at Jack. Jack looked at the old man.

"Can I continue?" asked the old man.

"Yes, sorry," said Jack.

"Well, I don't have to describe the canteen if you've been there. I'll skip to the next morning when Williams and I were driven down to the river in an APC. I don't know whether you saw much of Leeds when you were there..."

Jack shook his head.

"It looks terrible now," said the old man. "It didn't look that great in the first place, but now it looks bloody awful. There's not much of it left. Not by the river. There were plenty of guards by the dock. I guess there're a lot of goods that come in by the river. Once we were alone in the boat, I asked Williams why the raiders don't attack the boats. 'They do,' she said, showing me a gun in a chest next to the tiller. This didn't fill me with confidence. We set off and at… Have you been in a narrow boat?"

Jack shook his head again.

"Well, they go slow. Very slow. I guess that's why they get attacked less. The raiders assume they would send nothing valuable by such a slow means of transport. I felt very vulnerable on that deck with the fields passing by at a snail's pace."

"Are all the farms fenced?" asked Jack.

"Some are, but not all," said the old man. "I didn't see anyone pointing guns at farm labourers if that's what you're asking. In fact, we didn't see many people at all, and those we saw gave us a wide berth. I'm not sure whether it's just this close to the border which makes people nervous. Or because they had painted the boat in Guild colours and they know better than to mess with the Guild."

"How did the Guild become so powerful?" Jack asked.

"Did your mum not teach you your history?"

Jack shook his head once more. The old man sighed.

"Who controls the food, controls the power," he said. "After separation, when things were even more chaotic than they are now if you can believe it, the State was crumbling, and the Guild stepped in to protect its supply routes, and before long the Guild was the only real source of security, and so they started calling the shots. They became the de facto government, and no-one minded because the Guild provided a level of security that no-one had experienced for a long time."

"So what went wrong?"

"Nothing. There have always been raids. Ever since the collapse. Some periods are worse than others. This is a busy period."

"But you had no problems?"

"I didn't say that. The first night we stayed at Gaggs Bridge. There are guards stationed on the bridge, so we thought it would be a safe place to overnight."

"But..."

"At about midnight, I awoke to gunshots and shouting. Williams was already awake and was gesturing for me to be quiet and stay where I was. She was holding the gun which she had taken from the chest. I froze, listening for sounds from outside, trying to work out what was happening and how worried we should be.

"After a few moments, the gunshots and shouting ended. Williams and I strained our ears to hear what was going on, and then we heard footsteps on the towpath coming closer. Just one person by the sound of it. As the footsteps drew closer, I felt my body tense. Williams aimed the rifle at the door. The footsteps drew alongside the boat and stopped, then began again but the sound had changed. They had stepped onto the boat. Williams braced herself.

"There was a knock at the door. We said nothing. The handle began to turn, and the door swung open. It was a guard from the bridge. 'I just wanted to check everything was OK,' he said. 'There was a raiding party, but I think we scared them off.' 'We heard,' said Williams. 'We thought you might be one of them.' The guard laughed. 'I doubt we'll see them again tonight,' he said. 'Get some rest.' 'Thanks,' said Williams, watching him close the door. She got up and bolted it.

"The guard was right though, there were no more disturbances that night, and the next morning we left the mooring and continued downstream. Williams told me to steer, I'm not sure what the nautical terminology is, while she made us some breakfast. She had bread and eggs. The smell alone almost did me in. We moored while we ate, although Williams warned that we shouldn't stop for long, we'd left the locks behind, and therefore the guards, meaning that this stretch of the waterway was less safe. 'We need to get to Ouse Junction before nightfall,' said Williams. 'Is it far?' I asked. 'Not really, but at this pace, it will take us about six hours.'

"I imagine it can be very relaxing travelling on a narrow boat, but I didn't feel relaxed that day. I felt very tense, and the pace was so slow it was almost intolerable. The winding of the river made progress even more tortuous. 'Make yourself useful,' said Williams. 'Make a cup of tea.' I didn't complain, I went below, filled the kettle and put it on the small wood stove, which seemed like a bit too much of a fire hazard, but it had kept us warm the previous night.

"I stood there waiting for the kettle to boil, a task which surprised me as being even more tedious than standing on the deck watching the fields go by. It boiled, and I made the tea and took it up onto the deck. Do narrowboats have decks? Williams thanked me for the tea, and I went back to watching the farms trickle by. Some fences, some not. But I didn't see any labourers. No evidence of slavery."

Jack raised his eyebrows in an open expression of his cynicism.

"I know you don't believe me," said the old man. "But your story is the first I've heard of it. Anyway, the rest of the day continued in very much the same way. We reached Ouse Junction before nightfall, though the sun was very low in the sky. There were a few buildings near the mooring and plenty of guards around, which was reassuring in the sense that we would be well defended but also unnerving because the requirement for so many guards suggests a requirement for such a defence. But against what? 'Are we likely to receive any visitors tonight?' I asked Williams. 'It's likely,' she said. 'That's why they have so many guards stationed here.' That didn't fill me with confidence.

"It was getting dark, and Williams had cooked more eggs and bread. 'We have to leave very early tomorrow," she said. We have to catch the tide just as it is turning to stand a chance of getting all the way to Freetown before it turns again. If we don't make it, we will have to moor somewhere and wait for it to turn back. But that will mean travelling the last leg at night, which we want to avoid.' 'What sort of time are you thinking of leaving?' I asked. 'About five am,' she said. 'It'll still be dark but dawn won't be far away.' 'We must get an early night tonight then,' I said. 'Exactly.' She handed me a plate. 'You like eggs, don't you?' I said. 'Not really," she admitted. 'But they are easy to get hold of, to transport, and don't go off that fast.' I didn't care.

"Everything I'd tasted in the last couple of days tasted great after living on whatever I could find in that garden. I had no trouble falling asleep, but I'm not sure whether Williams slept at all. She was sitting up with the gun on her lap when I fell asleep, and she was still there when I awoke. She gestured for me to be quiet. I was. I sat up and watched the door like she was, listening to the noises outside, trying to work out how many people there were, where they were and what they were doing. I'm sure that Williams had a better idea than me, but I guessed that there were maybe half a dozen men, talking in low tones and moving along the towpath. Where were the guards? Where were the bloody guards?

"We waited until the men were alongside our boat and then, suddenly we heard shouting and rapid movement. It was the guards. They were ambushing the interlopers. That was when the shooting began. Shooting and shouting. It was difficult for me to tell whose shots were whose or who had the upper hand. The gunfire seemed to get more intense, and that was when a bullet entered the boat. It came through the wood panel beside my head and buried itself in Williams' bed in front of me.

"After a frozen moment, I leapt off the bed and onto the floor. Williams had quite a different reaction. 'Stay here,' she ordered before opening the door and going outside with her gun, closing the door behind her. I heard her footsteps on the deck above me. She ran to the bow and then back to the stern. A moment later I heard the engine start, and then the boat began to move. The gunfire intensified, and I could have sworn that Williams was firing too. Another bullet entered the side of the boat, flew over my head and then exited the boat through the panel on the other side.

"The shouts and shots grew louder and then began to recede. I heard another motor start. In the direction of where we had just come. Williams had our motor at full throttle, and I wanted to get out of this cabin into the air, but I was too scared, even though the gunshots seemed a long way away now. There was a thud, and the boat jolted. 'Smith! Get up here!' Williams shouted. I picked myself up, opened the door and crept up onto the deck. 'Grab that pole up there!' Williams shouted. 'We've hit a sandbank.'

"As I emerged onto the deck, I could see that it was close to dawn and that we were already on the Ouse. I took the pole Williams was pointing at, hung it over the side of the boat and tried to push but it just sunk into the sand. 'It's sinking into the sand,' I said to Williams. 'Try again. Hurry,' she shouted. 'We have to get out of here before they arrivboat which was coming up the Aire Calder Navigation towards us. I could see a man crouched on the bow holding a rifle. I pushed the pole back into the sand again. It sank, as before, but this time I put all of my weight into the end. At first, it continued to sink but then it stopped, and I pushed against it letting the force run through my body and my feet, into the boat. Nothing.

"I tried to pull the pole out, but it was stuck, I used all my strength to wiggle it backwards and forwards, and it moved. I tried again and pulled it out, I lifted it up and pushed it in at another spot. Williams cut the engine and came round to join me, grabbing a second pole which she inserted near to mine. Together, we pushed down into the sand. 'It's moving,' said Williams after an almost imperceptible shift in the boat's position. 'Again,' she said pulling the pole out of the mud to reposition it. I did the same, and we both pushed all our weight into the pole and our feet into the boat. It moved.

"We repeated the procedure, and two pushes later, we were free of the sandbank. Williams rushed back to the rudder and restarted the engine. It didn't catch the first time, and my heart almost stopped as I saw that the other narrowboat had almost reached the Ouse and the man crouched on the front was raising his rifle and aiming to shoot. The engine kicked into life. Williams pointed the narrowboat downstream and set the engine to full throttle.

"The boat surged forward with surprising speed just as a shot crossed the bow. I heard Williams shout out in pain and then curse and take her hand off the tiller to clutch her other hand, which I saw was bleeding. 'Smith! Grab the tiller!' she ordered, waiting for me to take control of the boat so she could dress the wound which, as I drew closer, looked nasty. 'Just steer clear of the sandbank,' she said. We seemed to pull away from the other boat, and I said as much to Williams. 'The engine in this boat is bigger than your average narrowboat,' she explained. 'We need a big engine to get down the Humber in time.'

"Having dressed her hand, she took the rudder from me and steered her way down the river with far more confidence. I was relieved. I kept expecting to steer into a sandbank. I looked back and saw we were leaving the other boat behind. The sun was just beginning to rise, casting an orange glow of what was left of the Goole skyline and the rows and rows of broken wind machines in the surrounding fields. Williams was staring straight ahead. I looked too and saw the expanse of the estuary opening out in front of us. The bare trees on the riverbank looked like skeletons and made me feel colder than I was.

"The water was so still it looked like a mirror and Williams said this was a good thing because if it was rough, there was a risk that the narrowboat could capsize. This made me feel even more nervous, and I consoled myself with the sunlight reflecting on the water. 'How long is it going to take us to get to Freetown?' I asked. Williams sighed. 'We have to make it in less than six hours,' she said. 'After that, the tide will turn, and we must find a mooring. 'And wait?' I asked. 'And wait,' she confirmed. I didn't fancy that very much. Unsavoury people had a habit of turning up every time we stopped. Williams must have been thinking similar thoughts because she cranked the throttle up to what I assumed was full.

"Even though we still seemed to travel at a snail's pace, the scenery moving past so slow. I sometimes wondered whether we were moving at all and had to look over the side of the boat at the wake to reassure myself that we were making any progress at all."

The old man paused.

"Do you know why it's called Freetown?" he asked Jack.

"Because the people there are free?" Jack shrugged.

The old man laughed.

"No, the Guild controls everything. It goes back to the days of monarchy, to the very end of the Monarchy, when everything associated with the Monarchy was being vandalised or destroyed. The Guild was still very new then. They hadn't been in control long, and the wall was still going up. The city had, many years before, a twin town with the capital of a country in Africa called Freetown, so they renamed the city, seal it off and run it as a little republic. No-one complained. They hadn't paid too much attention to it anyway, and everyone was too busy attempting to suppress their masses they didn't worry too much about a city on the border. In fact, the Guild did the surrounding countries a favour by policing this part of their land."

The sound of trumpets and drums suddenly filled the air.

"What the hell is that?" asked Jack, still recovering from the shock.

"Sounds like Chet Baker," said the old man. "The landlord is a big Chet Baker fan, but he says he only has enough energy to play it for an hour a day, so he plays it an hour before closing. He says it helps get rid of the customers."

Piano and guitar have joined the trumpet and drums, along with a bass guitar, and Jack taps his foot.

"You don't like it?" the old man observed.

"It's terrible," said Jack. "Not bad enough to make me want to leave the pub. But only just. So, did you make it in six hours?"

The old man grimaced.

"We were doing great for a while. Then the engine started making different sounds. 'Have you ever made this journey in six hours?' I asked. 'Six and a quarter is my fastest,' she said. 'High tide was at eight, if we make it by three we'll be fine.' 'The engine seems different,' I said. 'Look at the river,' she told me. I did and then offered her a quizzical look. 'What colour is it?' she asked. 'Well, I guess it's a kind of brown,' I said. 'Kind of brown?' She laughed. 'I don't think I've seen a browner river in my life. Why do you think it's brown?' 'Mud?' I surmised. 'Mud.,' she said. 'We changed all the filters before we started the journey, but there is so much mud in this river from all the soil erosion that, running the engine at full throttle for so long sucks in all the mud and blocks the filters.' She eased off the throttle. 'I have spare filters,' she says 'but having to stop and change them would waste valuable time. We should take it steady for a while. I don't want to risk anything.'

"Take it steady? Full throttle was steady enough. This was worse. We went past a white post sticking up out of the water. She told me that this was Trent falls. 'What's that?' I asked. 'It's where the Ouse and the Trent meet,' she said. 'This is where the Humber begins.' I thought I was already on the Humber and when I said this, she laughed. We must have been travelling for two hours. 'How far have we gone?' I asked. She thought for a moment. 'About seven miles.' I could walk faster than that, I thought. 'And how far do we have to go?' 'About another 18 miles,' she said. 'It should take us about another four hours, as long as the filters hold out.' That didn't seem so bad."

"But..." Jack anticipated.

"That's right," said the old man. "The filters didn't hold out. The engine started overheating. Williams thought it was that she was running it too hard at first and so just eased off the throttle for a while, but the temperature shot up, and so she turned it off altogether, and we just began drifting downstream with the tide. She told me to take the rudder and opened the engine cover. 'The drive belt is OK,' she said, feeling it with her hand, satisfied with the tension. 'That means it's the seawater filter. 'Yep, look at this,' she said, tipping muddy debris over the side of the boat.

"She put the pump back together and restarted the engine. We continued for a little while but the engine overheated and she shut it off again. 'Damn,' she said. 'What is it?' I asked. She looked worried. 'It's burnt the paint off the powerhead,' she said staring at the engine. 'Can you fix it?' I asked. She laughed.

"This filled me with foreboding. 'Best-case scenario,' she said with a sigh. 'Is that we only need to replace the impeller on the water pump. I might need to replace the pump itself, but if it's got hot enough to burn off the paint, then the chances are that it'll have scuffed a piston or even burned it.' 'Is that bad?' I showed my ignorance. 'Even to check the impeller, I have to get the water pump off, and that means dropping the gear case. If it's burned a piston, well...' she trailed off, and I became more conscious that we were drifting in the middle of an estuary. 'What are we going to do?' I asked, but I could tell she could do without my blathering. 'I've got a spare pump,' she mumbled as if talking to herself. 'The trouble is, I can't fix it here. We will need to steer her into the bank and try to get someone to tow us to Freetown.'

"I looked up and down the river. 'How likely is that?' I asked. 'Very unlikely,' she said. 'I will guard the boat until you can get a message to someone.' 'Me?' I was astonished. How was I supposed to get a message to anyone? 'Give me the tiller,' she said and started steering the boat towards the north bank. 'Where are we going?' I asked. 'Brough,' she said. 'It's only about six miles to Boothferry Gate, you can make it in two hours and ask them to send someone for me.' 'I thought it wasn't safe going overland,' I said.

"She raised her eyebrows. 'Well,' she said. 'It should be safer during the day.' 'Oh, great, thanks.' I said. 'We don't have any choice,' she said. 'It's better than just sitting here and waiting for them to come for us.' I sighed. I knew she was right, but all I could think about was what I might find in those six miles. 'And how am I going to convince them to let me in at Boothferry Gate?' I said. 'You'll manage,' she said with confidence, concentrating on getting us to the north bank. 'I'll try to moor at Brough Haven. Have you got any silver?' I nodded. 'Let's hope we find some friendly faces,' she said. 'I will not get into the Haven without a motor, we must beach ourselves on the foreshore as near as we can.' As the north bank drew closer, I could see the mouth of a small river, in which were moored a variety of yachts and barges, some in good condition but most rotting away.

"This must have been the Haven. With the tide going out, the water would flow downstream, and there would be no way we could navigate our way to moorings without a motor. Alongside the mouth of the river was a grassy bank. This must have been where Williams was planning to stop. As we drew near to the bank, I could see that a group of people had gathered and stood on what looked like a harbour wall. I wondered what their intentions were. I hoped they were not hostile, but our experience so far pointed to the opposite.

"As we reached the bank, two of them ran down through the grass and helped us to secure the boat. This was a good sign. Williams jumped out of the boat and climbed through the grass to speak to the group standing on the wall. I saw her chatting with an old man and then shaking hands before she came back to the boat. 'We are in luck,' she said. 'I just spoke to a man willing to tow us the rest of the way to Freetown.' I breathed a huge sigh of relief. 'I told him you would pay him in silver,' she said. 'That's OK,' I said. I was happy to part with a fair amount of silver not to have to walk the six miles to Boothferry Gate with all the risks that would entail. But I was also surprised that someone had agreed to help us, even for silver. I said as much to Williams, but she just shrugged and said that silver buys a lot these days."

The old man got out of his chair.

"Another?"

"Are you trying to get me drunk?" asked Jack.

"On this stuff," laughed the old man. "It's not very strong."

"OK," Jack agreed, thinking his definition of strong and the old man's must be very different.

The old man returned with two more drinks and a four-litre bottle.

"This'll have to be the last," he said. "They're closing soon. The batteries have almost run out of power."

"Thank goodness for that," said Jack. "This jazz music is driving me mad."

Jack thought to himself that it was also just as well because he was feeling the effects of the ale.

"So, was the man good as his word?" asked Jack.

The old man smiled.

"Around the corner, we saw this yacht emerge from the mouth of the river. Williams and I both raised our eyebrows, wondering whether it would be capable of towing us all the way. They must have access to fuel because they were using the motor, they tied two ropes to our bow, one on either side, fastened to the opposite sides of their stern so they crossed over, they said it makes it easier to steer. Once they had pulled us out into the estuary, the skipper of the yacht hoisted the sails to assist the motor. The wind was northwesterly, so there was no need for him to tack. Before long, we were in the middle of the estuary, and I could see the ruins of the old bridge getting closer. Did you know it was the longest bridge in the world when they first built it?"

Jack nodded his head.

"Just a pile of ruins now, a real shame." The old man took another sip of ale.

"What happened to it?" asked Jack.

"It was a victim of the separation," the old man explained. "Not long after the collapse, when the Union broke apart. There was a lot of friction between Northumberland and Mercia. The Mercians blew it up to stop incursions from the north."

"Such a shame," said Jack.

"You can say that again," said the old man.

"Such a shame," Jack repeated.

The old man stared at him for a moment and then laughed.

"Anyway," he said. "The man was as good as his word. He towed us all the way to Myton Gate, and I had to part with a fair bit of silver. At Myton Gate, they knew Williams. They arranged for another narrow boat to come and tow us to a mooring up the river where Williams said they would have to pull her boat out of the water to fix it. She wasn't happy, but since she was working for the Guild, at least they were looking after her. I was met at the dock and showed apartments in the Guildhall where they told me I could stay. The rooms are much nicer than anything I've had in a very long time. They told me that my daughter, Dr Jones, is travelling."

"When will she be back?"

"Tomorrow."

"Tomorrow?" Jack said with surprise.

"Yes, I know," said the old man. "Very disappointing, don't worry. The apartments where they are accommodating me are very spacious. There'll be room for you, and I'm sure I'll have no problem convincing my friends, the guards, to let you in."

Jack felt very nervous. He wished he hadn't let the old man ply him with so much alcohol, he was feeling a little drunk and realised that he had nowhere to stay. He was sure that even the streets of Freetown were not an advisable place to spend the night, but he was even less sure he should trust this man who, despite the sharing of their stories, was still a stranger.

The old man seemed to sense Jack's discomfort and sought to re-assure him.

"I know what you're thinking," he began. "You don't know me from Adam, and here I am, taking you to a pub, plying you with drinks, and then inviting you to spend the night. I appreciate that might look odd but, please, believe me, my motives are honourable, and the apartments are all separate, so you'll have your bedroom and bathroom. You won't be sharing with me, so don't worry."

Jack was not convinced, but he also realised he didn't have an-other option.

"What do you say?" asked the old man.

"Well, if I'm honest," said Jack. "I don't have anywhere else to stay."

"Great," said the old man. "Drink up, let's go."

Jack looked at his pint. There was still three-quarters of it left. He took a large gulp and was dismayed to see more than half a pint in the bottom. The old man only had a quarter of his pint left.

"Tomorrow, we'll take the diary to Dr Jones," the old man promised.

Jack smiled and patted his bag, checking that the diary was still inside.

"Come on then," said the old man as he downed the rest of his pint.

Jack took another large swig and then looked with disappointment at the amount of beer left in his glass.

"Take your time," said the old man.

"Thanks," said Jack, but with another couple of swigs, he finished his beer and the old man stood up, picking up the four-litre bottle from the table.

Jack rose, too, and followed him to the door just as the lights and the music died.

"Thank goodness for that," said Jack. "Peace and quiet at last."

"Perfect timing," laughed the old man, as he sat in the flickering light from the candles the landlord had placed around the bar in anticipation of the solar charged batteries running dry.

Jack followed him through a narrow passage, which led onto a cobbled street.

"They re-cobbled many streets for the horses," the old man observed. "But this one never had the cobbles removed."

They turned right and at the end of the street turned left, past a church and into the square in which Jack recognised he had met the old man earlier. The streets looked deserted, but Jack couldn't help but feel that people were lurking in the shadows. They walked to the front of the Guildhall where the same guards were still on duty. The old man handed the four-litre bottle to one of them. They exchanged nods, and as the old man led Jack away, a guard followed.

"Where are we going?" Jack asked.

"The entrance is around the back," said the old man.

Jack followed him into a dark side street in between the Guildhall and what looked like an allotment. Ten yards into the street, the old man turned to face him. Jack was conscious of the guard behind him.

"Give me the bag," said the old man.

Jack did not respond until he felt the barrel of a rifle press into the back of his neck. He handed the bag to the old man.

The old man took the bag and walked passed Jack and the guard towards the front of the Guildhall.

"Get rid of him," he told the guard, without stopping or looking around.

Part Four

Ryan Jones smiled at the guards as he walked past them through the door of the Guildhall they were holding open for him. He took the diary out of the bag and eyed the pale blue cover as he ascended the stairs on his way to the private chambers of the Alder. The Alder was the leader of the city. The term derived from Alderman, but Alder had evolved as a gender-neutral title, which was just as well given that the current Alder was a woman.

Entering the chambers, he found the Alder, Dr Jones still sat at her writing desk where he had left her earlier in the evening. He had received two calls, the first from Myton Gate, the second from North Bridge, both confirming the same thing, he asked her if she wanted to go out for a drink, knowing she would refuse, made his excuses and left just in time to meet the young man in front of the Guildhall. He did not know how much of the young man's story was true, he didn't trust anyone who seemed so ignorant of the Alder and her father. It had been truer than the pack of lies he had woven for the young man. Ryan congratulated himself on how well he had fooled the boy and weighed his prize, the battered pale blue diary, in his hand. He watched his wife work for a moment before sitting in a chair opposite.

"I have some news," he said at last.

The doctor looked up from her work and at her husband, waiting to see what he had to say.

Ryan contemplated how much weight his wife had put on since becoming the Alder. Sitting at this desk all day wasn't helping her figure. Ryan was one of those annoying people who could eat as much as they wanted and remain as thin as a beanpole. He handed her the tattered diary.

"Not good news," he said.

"What is it?" she asked, running her hand over the pale blue cover and then flicking through the pages.

"It's your father's diary."

She observed the diary with much more interest, having learnt its author's identity.

"Where did you get it?" she asked.

"They picked up an insurgent trying to sneak it into the city."

"I want to speak to him," she said.

"They have already dealt with him."

"What?"

"I know. I have made sure that I have also dealt with the guard responsible, but, they had the presence of mind to question the individual a little before they disposed of him."

"And?"

Ryan sighed.

"Bandits killed your father out west. They found the diary with his body. I'm sorry, Olivia."

She placed the diary on the desk and stared at the pale blue cover.

"Are you sure?" she asked.

"There's no doubt," Ryan said, trying to look as if he sympathised with her grief.

"Well that's that then, I suppose." She turned back to her papers. "Was there anything else?"

"No," said Ryan, wondering what other news there could be besides the death of her father and the last remaining hope for the reunification of the nation.

"Will you be coming to bed soon?" he asked, knowing what the answer would be.

"I've got some things to finish first," she said.

Ryan pulled himself out of his seat and shuffled off into the other room. He had a warm feeling inside. His plans could bear fruit. Once he had destroyed her hopes of a settlement, she would have no choice but to implement his plan. As long as her father didn't turn up and spoil everything. That was unlikely. Even though he had no proof, Ryan was sure the old man was dead. Old men didn't last very long outside of the free cities.

Olivia had abandoned her papers. She was now poring over the last writings of her father. Could it be true? Could he be dead? She had pinned all her hopes on finding him. One of her teams had sent promising reports of someone spotted living in his home, then they had gone missing, and no-one had heard from them since. How did Ryan know he was dead? Who was this insurgent they had interrogated and then disposed of, and how did he come to possess her father's diary? Was there even an insurgent? If Olivia had learnt anything over the years, it was not to trust anyone. Even her husband. Especially her husband.

Her father had warned her about Ryan, but she hadn't listened. Ryan had her under his spell and was the reason she hadn't spoken to her father for so long. How she wished she could be with him right now and tell him how sorry she was for not listening.

Perhaps it was too late for that. She'd never get the opportunity now if what Ryan had told her was true, she pushed the diary aside and looked towards the bedroom where Ryan had already retired. She was sleepy, she couldn't do any more work tonight, but she also had no desire to share her husband's bed, she was even too tired to read her father's diary.

She opened a desk drawer and pulled out a glass and a bottle. One advantage of being the Alder is a supply of single malt, which arrives under armed convoy from the very far north. She poured it into the glass and then added a similar amount of water from a glass jug on her desk. She savoured the taste, rolling the whiskey around her mouth before swallowing.

Olivia had been drinking more of late. She felt fat and unhealthy. She was feeling the pressure more than usual. Keeping the peace and the food flowing in a city which had more or less separated itself from the neighbouring states, was no small task, and many would like to depose her and take control themselves. Although Olivia had no desire to run a free city, the thought of what might happen to the people if she ceded control to one of the power-hungry pretenders kept her going, trying to find fair solutions for all. She understood that this sometimes required an iron fist, and she controlled her force of vigilantes, which kept peace in the streets by engendering fear among the populace. This, she knew, was not ideal, but the alternative was worse. For the moment at least.

She was used to fighting fires. Tackling each crisis as it emerged. The insurgency was under control but only that. She had hoped that the return of her father might help unite the disparate groups and create a sense of unity that she could build upon. He had done it before when the collapse was already underway, and the regions were first threatening to separate. He had got all the leaders into the same room and hammered out an accord. As the collapse progressed, the accord fell through, but that had been because corrupt officials betrayed him. Maybe he could do it again. However, if he was dead, then that hope had gone, and she would have to continue fighting fires for the foreseeable future.

Not asking too many questions was the secret to her sanity. The arrival and distribution of food happened. She tried to ask as little as possible about how it was produced and what had to happen to ensure it arrived. The city was experiencing a rare moment of peace caused by the disarray of the surrounding states, but it was a situation that would not last forever. Olivia feared that, once they became organised, the states would once again look to Freetown to plunder its fortune.

Olivia stood up and wandered around the room. Although she was tired, exhausted, she did not want to sleep, not yet anyway. She didn't want to be in the same space as Ryan, she thought about playing some music but feared that would bring Ryan back into the room, she decided she would go for a walk. The guards were always warning her not to go out alone at night and would want to accompany her. She always refused and went by herself. She liked the streets at night. They were always so quiet compared to the bustle of the day. People wouldn't go out at night. They were afraid. Afraid of the guards maybe. They could be brutal. As a result, there was no crime at night. There seemed to be a price to pay for everything. The people of Freetown didn't complain about the draconian guards. They wouldn't, would they? Olivia convinced herself this was not due to fear. She believed that the people of Freetown were content that justice was swift and brutal. That it offered them a sense of security. That they just wanted to get on with their lives without the criminal fraternity bothering them. There were occasions when innocent citizens were wrongly accused, but these incidents almost never resulted in summary execution and on the rare occasions they did, the family of the innocent was always well compensated.

Olivia drank the rest of her whiskey in one gulp, set the glass down on the table and headed out of the door for the front entrance. She needed to get some exercise. The guards looked guilty when they snapped to attention. They hadn't expected to see her, they were drinking again, they offered to accompany her, but she refused. It occurred to Olivia that the greatest danger to her on the streets at night was from the guards themselves. If someone deposed her and won the favour of the guards, she would be helpless. They could strike anytime, anywhere, and Olivia would be helpless to prevent it. She just had to hope that none of her citizens ever became so dissatisfied that they would organise such a coup.

She turned right out of the door and then right again to walk alongside the Guildhall, she could hear the guards laughing behind her. They were relieved she hadn't reprimanded them for drinking.

Olivia walked all the way to the entrance of the gardens, which provided most of the fresh vegetables she found on her dinner plate. She contemplated the fact that despite the impressive yields the city's gardeners could deliver from this garden and many others like it, Olivia still had the task of sourcing half of their food needs from outside the city's walls. She already felt out of breath.

From Citizens Gardens, it was only a short walk to Prince's Dock, which the town still could not use because of the scrap metal that still filled the water after the old shopping centre collapsed. Olivia had remembered going to the shopping centre as a little girl. It was one of her priorities to get the metal removed. Not only would the metal and rubble be useful for other projects, but it would also make the dock usable again and expand the city's harbour capacity. It was an easy decision, and yet she was being frustrated at every turn. The workforce was not available, or they had to wait for the correct machinery, or the funds to pay the workforce were engaged elsewhere. She felt very frustrated as she looked out over the mess, which sat in the centre of the dock. She walked alongside its edge, past the warehouses, which could store goods from Europe or further afield, ready to be distributed to the neighbouring states who might pay well if only there could be a prolonged period of stability. At the other end of the dock, she crossed the road to the marina where there was much more activity. Olivia could see lights in the boats, smoke rising from stovepipes and the sound of chatting, laughing and even singing. It always amazed Olivia how many boats they could cram into this tiny space, and it gave her courage to redouble her efforts to get Prince's Dock cleared. As she reached the waterfront, she could hear the voices of late night drinkers still revelling in the candlelit darkness within the Minerva.

She could not see the estuary because of the wall, so she climbed the steps to one of the guard posts, where the guard snapped to attention on seeing her.

"Beautiful night," she commented to the guard, observing how still the estuary appeared. The guard grunted his agreement, no doubt too scared to engage the Alder in conversation.

Olivia smiled at him and descended the stairs again, much to the guard's relief. She continued, following the wall around to Myron Gate, where there was always activity, day or night. There were some guards. Some on duty, some playing cards and drinking. They all stood upon seeing her.

"At ease, boys," she said, waving them to sit. "I don't know how you can see to play cards in this light, anyway."

The guards acknowledged her good-natured comment but were not comfortable returning to their games until she had walked out of sight towards the old town.

Olivia left the river and cut through the warehouses towards the marketplace. Even at this late hour, there were porters busy re-arranging boxes of produce ready for sale the next day. She enjoyed seeing the city when it was busy. It meant that the system was working. She wandered through the frames of the empty stalls. When she had first become Alder, she used to walk past rows of bodies of the homeless trying to rest. She prided herself that it was no longer the case. They took anyone caught sleeping rough straight to one of the rehabilitation centres. There was no space in the city for anyone who wasn't functioning as a positive citizen, contributing to the wellbeing of the whole community.

She left the market square and walked through the quiet back streets until she reached the side of the Guildhall once more. She took a deep breath. There was nothing for it, she would have to get some sleep which meant returning to her chambers, even if Ryan was there.

The guards at the front of the Guildhall stood to attention once more as she approached. She couldn't be sure, but there was something about these guards which suggested to her they respected her less than the other guards she had met during the evening.

She walked past them and up the stairs to her chambers. As she entered her office, she could already hear Ryan snoring from the room beyond. He'd drunk a fair bit this evening. He always snored like this when he was drunk. Olivia entered the bedroom, she could see him, lying on his back, mouth open. She changed her clothes, not wanting to wake him, she paused for a moment to examine her naked body in the mirror, and she did not like what she saw. Getting into bed, tried to ease him over to his side, he rolled over, grunting as he did so and, as Olivia had hoped, he stopped snoring but continued breathing heavily. She could smell the alcohol on him. She turned her back to him, plumped up the pillow and lay down her head, closing her eyes and trying to suppress the building anxiety around the knowledge that when she would next wake up there would be another day of challenges she would need to tackle.

When she awoke, Ryan was already gone, and she could hear the hubbub coming from the banqueting hall downstairs. She washed, dressed, and hurried downstairs to eat breakfast with all the guards and staff who worked for the Guild and were, therefore, eligible to eat in the banqueting hall. Olivia's breakfast comprised porridge with honey and a mug of mint tea. She had given the kitchen strict instructions regarding the diet she was following to lose weight. She collected her breakfast from the buffet table and sat at a spare table by herself, as far from the crowds of workers as she could. This suited everyone, as the workers were keen to keep their distance from her. She finished her breakfast as quickly as she could and left her bowl and mug on the trolley where the kitchen staff would come and take them.

When she returned to her office, Ryan was there, waiting for her. She raised her eyebrows at him, which was her way of asking him what he wanted.

"Why do you always assume I want something," he asked.

"Because you always do."

"You are so cynical."

Olivia ignored him and sat at her desk, her father's diary where she had left it. She put it in the drawer with her bottle of single malt, making a mental note to get a clean glass from the banquet hall.

"We need to clear Prince's Dock," she said.

"I know," said Ryan. It was a familiar subject.

"So why aren't we?"

"We've been through this," he reasoned. "We don't have the funds available to hire the workforce required for such a task."

"But we could use all that material. There's valuable metal, just lying there."

Ryan nodded to show he understood.

Olivia sighed. She'd had this conversation often enough to know that nothing would change soon.

"Another thing," she said, just as Ryan was leaving. "I'm not happy about the guards you've assigned to the front of the Guildhall at night."

"Oh," he said, taking more interest. "Why is that?"

"I have a bad feeling about them. I'd feel more comfortable if you replaced them with another group. The group at Myton Gate look conscientious."

"OK," said Ryan. "I'll see what I can do."

He turned to leave and then stopped.

"Did you go for a walk last night?" he asked.

"Yes, why?"

"You saw nothing unusual?"

"No, why?"

"Last night one of the Guildhall guards was killed."

"Killed? How?"

"Garrotted. They found the body in the gardens."

"Right in front of the guards' barracks?"

"Are you sure you saw nothing strange last night?"

"The Guildhall guards were behaving a little odd, but I just assumed it was because they were trying to hide the fact they were drinking. They don't seem as respectful as the other guards. Do you know who gives them the ale?"

Ryan shook his head.

"Any idea who did it?" she asked.

"Who gave them the ale?"

"No, who killed the guard?"

"Not a clue," Ryan admitted.

"OK, keep me updated."

"I will," he said, turning to go. Then he stopped again and turned back to her. "Listen, with this killer on the loose maybe you should stop going on your midnight walks for a while. Just until we find him or her. For your safety, eh? I'm only concerned for your wellbeing."

"Thanks." She did not watch Ryan leave. She was concentrating on the papers in front of her. The papers she knew she should have dealt with last night.

Ryan strides out of the room and down the stairs. He marches straight up to a guard who has been waiting for him outside on the street.

"Find him, as quick as you can, before anyone else...." the sight of a tall, thin man entering the Guildhall distracts him. Ryan turns back to the guard. "Wait for me here. There might be another way."

Olivia barely had time to focus on the first sheet when there was a knock at the door. She sighed. "Yes?"

"Sorry to disturb you, ma'am," the tall, thin man said.

"I am not the Queen," Olivia complained.

"You are to me," said the man.

"Whatever is it, Harry?" she was losing her patience. "Can't you see that I'm busy?"

"Begging your pardon, ma'am," he said. "It's just. There's something you need to see, or rather someone you need to meet."

"Show them in," she said.

"They're not here," said Harry. "You must come and see them."

"Harry, I'm very busy."

"This is important, ma'am."

She stopped what she was doing. For Harry to speak to her that way, she knew that this was important.

"Let's go," she said, heading for the door, but Harry did not move.

"The back way, ma'am," he said, and she followed him through the bedroom, through a partition door into a storeroom, out into a corridor which Harry checked was clear before they hurried to the end, to a set of stairs. At the bottom of the stairs, Harry led Olivia through another small corridor and through a door which led to the street. Harry popped his head out the door first.

"Come on," he said, leading her out into the street and straight into a covered carriage. They had barely closed the door by the time the coachman had taken the reins, and the carriage was speeding along, watched from the front corner of the Guildhall by Ryan Jones.

Olivia tried not to look out of the window until she was clear of the centre but she knew the streets well enough to know that she was heading west. After a few minutes, she peeked through the curtain. It wasn't every day that she could get out of the Guildhall, much less out of the centre and seeing the world of her citizens, so she wanted to make the most of this journey by seeing what was happening in the suburbs. She was impressed by how many neatly pruned fruit trees lined the road. There was no waste of space, every spare piece of land had been dug up for cultivation. Not just gardens, but spaces between buildings, at the sides of the roads, even rooftops had all manner of vegetation sprouting. This was even more impressive because spring had not sprung yet and this was the leanest period of the year.

Yet, despite all of this cultivation, it still only supplied half of what the city needed to feed itself.

The coach negotiated the ruins of the old flyover, across what used to be the railway lines, now occupied by rows and rows of allotments. On the other side, Olivia could see the ruin of the old football stadium, also surrounded by allotments, too numerous to mention. Olivia remembered that when she was a child, this was a park filled with trees, which, to her, seemed huge. The trees had gone, long ago felled for timber, but were now replaced by many more fruit trees, all pruned and waiting for their spring buds.

Olivia tried to look at the tree-lined street itself, but before she could view more, the carriage made a sharp right turn into the courtyard of what Olivia recognised as the old Anlaby Road barracks. Harry helped her from the carriage and led her inside and straight down to the detention cells. He stopped in front of a cell and opened the small observation window to show Olivia the occupant. Olivia glanced in and then looked at Harry.

"Who is he?" she asked.

"Who he is and who he claims to be are two different things," Harry replied.

"So who is he?"

"I know," said Harry. "That he is one of the Mercian insurgents that we have been looking for."

"And who does he say he is?"

"Come with me," Harry said, leading Olivia to an interrogation room and offering her a seat.

"Why do I need to sit down?"

"Because," Harry continued. "I saw him talking to your husband in the Stag last night."

"Okay."

"So I followed them when they left, and your husband was going to have him killed."

"And?"

"And I intervened and brought him here."

"Harry, did you kill that Guildhall guard last night?"

Harry looked guilty.

"Why? You said yourself he is an insurgent."

"He had your father's diary."

"I see." Olivia looked at Harry for a moment, waiting for him to continue but he stared back. She sighed. "And what have you found out?"

"Not a lot. He wanted to see you. I think he might know where your father is."

"OK, bring him in."

Olivia sat back in her chair and waited while Harry got the man from his cell and brought him into the interrogation room. Harry told the man to sit opposite Olivia, closed the door and stood behind him.

"So, Mr..." Olivia began.

"You can call me George," he said.

"Is that your name?"

"Does it matter?"

"Well, that depends on whether you want me to believe you."

"I do."

"So, is it?"

"Let's say yes."

"Harry tells me my husband entertained you last night."

George laughs.

"You could say that," he says.

"What would you say?"

"I would say that your husband listened to my lies, and then I listened to his lies, before he asked someone to kill me. If it weren't for your friend Harry here, I would be feeding the vegetables instead of that guard."

"It's not true what they say about our plant food."

"I'm sure it's not."

"So how did you end up spending an evening in the pub with my husband?"

"I was trying to reach you, ma'am."

"Did he tell you to call me that?" she said, looking at Harry.

"I was on my way to see you when he cut me off. I had no opportunity but to go along with him hoping he would lead me to you."

"And what did you tell him?"

"I made up a story which would give my presence in Freetown plausibility."

"And what did he say to you?"

"He told me he was your father."

Olivia laughed.

"And you didn't believe him?" she asked.

"No."

"Why not?"

"Because I've met your father."

"When?"

"I last saw him only two days ago."

"He's alive?"

"He was when I last saw him."

Olivia tried to suppress her emotions.

"How do I know what you are telling me is true?"

"You don't."

"So why should I believe you?"

George paused for a moment and then looked at Olivia.

"I know this might be difficult to believe, but I work for the Mercian government."

"The Mercians?"

George nods.

"The Mercians who have been raiding our land? The Mercians who destroyed our bridge."

"We've always disputed the ownership of the bridge," said George.

"Whatever." Olivia felt she had every right to be cynical. "So you've come here to tell me you have kidnapped my father, and you have come to deliver your demands."

"He hasn't been kidnapped. He's just being kept safe."

"Ha! That's one way of putting it," Olivia laughed.

"It's the truth."

"I'm sure you can understand my cynicism... George."

"I can."

"So, what do you want?"

"We want to deliver your father to you."

"And...?"

"That's it."

"That's it?"

"Yes."

"Why?"

"We believe that your father could play a crucial role in repairing the divisions. Between Freetown and its neighbouring states."

"Why didn't you bring him then?"

"It's not safe. Some people do not want to see him here. People who are not interested in seeing the divisions repaired and who may be interested in seeing the divisions widen. We believe these people would rather kill your father than see him in Freetown."

"Where is he now?"

"He was being held as a slave on a farm. I lost some very good men breaking him out of that farm, and even more good men are now guarding him in a secure location."

"How is he?"

"He's fine now. He was not in a very good condition when we found him, but they are looking after him, and he is fine now."

"What do you need from me?"

"I need a team of good men, some arms, and a good boat."

"Harry? Can you organise that?"

"If you are sure, ma'am."

Olivia cringes at being called ma'am.

"I don't see what we have to lose. If he is telling the truth, he will bring us my father. If he is lying, then I can't see what he hopes to achieve. Loyal Freetown men will surround him. There's very little damage he can do."

"If you say so, ma'am."

"And stop calling me ma'am."

"Yes, ma'am."

Olivia sighed.

"Take me back to the Guildhall, then assemble your team and take whichever vessel you need."

"Yes, ma'am."

Harry led George back to his cell, apologised for his temporary continued detention, and then drove Olivia back to the Guildhall. He dropped her off at the back entrance once more.

"Take care, Harry," she said as she left the carriage and scurried through the rear entrance of the Guildhall.

"Let's go," Harry told the driver who turned the carriage and sped towards the barracks.

Not far past the old railway line, Harry noticed smoke rising from the direction of the barracks. He reached under his coat and pulled out his revolver. The coachman pulled a rifle from a holster by his side.

The carriage was less than twenty yards from the barracks when Harry saw a gang drag a man-shaped bundle from the courtyard and throw him on the back of a cart. Harry fired a round from his revolver and hit one of the gang. The coachman raised his rifle and fired a shot, which knocked the driver from the cart, the carthorse was startled and bolted. The coachman made chase while Harry shot at the remaining two members of the gang. He picked off one as they passed but the other was soon out of range and fled.

Before the coachman could draw alongside the cart, the man's bound body, which had been bouncing around in the back of the cart, fell out onto the road and the coachman brought his horses to a stop so that Harry could jump off and run to the man's aid.

They had tied him up in a blanket which also covered his head. Harry untied the ropes and pulled the blanket away from George's head. He was unconscious.

"Give me a hand," Harry shouted up to the coachman. "We need to get him to the infirmary."

The coachman helped Harry lift George's body into the coach and then turned around and headed back towards the city centre and the infirmary.

The main infirmary building was no longer in use as they considered it unsafe, and so they had transferred all the functions of the infirmary to many buildings, which littered its grounds. Gardens used to grow many of the therapeutic plants and herbs that they used inside surrounded every building.

The coachman drew up in front of the entrance to the accident and emergency department and, having secured the horses, helped Harry to carry George inside. The staff, on seeing that Harry and the coachman wore the insignia of the Guild, could not be more helpful, finding George a stretcher and wheeling him straight into a treatment room past the frustrated hoards who had probably been waiting for hours.

The coachman asked whether he could take his leave and Harry said he could go. He could offer no further help now, and Harry could call the Guild if he needed him. Harry asked the coachman to go straight to the Alder to report what had happened.

Harry watched as the doctor examined George.

"What happened?" she asked.

"I'm not sure," said Harry. "He was set upon by a gang. When we found him, they tied him up. He fell off the back of a cart."

"Hmm," the doctor examined George. "Looks like they beat him up pretty well."

"Will he be OK?"

"Well, we've no x-ray so we can't tell for sure whether he has a skull fracture. We'll just have to wrap him up, give him plenty of Arnica, and hope for the best."

When Olivia returned to her office, her husband, Ryan was hanging around.

"Where were you?" he asked. "I was looking for you."

"Why?"

"I was just worried when I couldn't find you."

"When have you been worried about me?"

"Come on, Olivia. Don't be like that."

"Why did you tell me my father is dead?"

"Because that's the information I had."

"From whom?"

"From the insurgent, I told you about him."

"The insurgent to whom you gave the death sentence?"

"It's too dangerous to have people like that hanging around."

"Only he's not dead, is he?"

Ryan did not answer.

"He's the one who killed your guard, isn't he?"

"I've got my best men on it," Ryan said at last.

"I just spoke to him. He told me my father is alive."

"He would. I'd tell you your father was alive if I thought it would stop you from killing me."

Olivia slumped into her seat.

"From what he told me, he does not understand who your father is," said Ryan. "He just happened upon his diary and was trying to use it to get close to you. He can't be trusted."

There was a knock at the door. It was the coachman.

"Yes, what is it?" Olivia asked.

"I need a word with you, ma'am."

"Why does everyone insist on calling me that?" Olivia sighed. "Go on then. What is it?"

The coachman glanced at Ryan.

"In private," he said.

"Give us a minute, Ryan," said Olivia.

"What?" Ryan began to protest.

"Step outside please, Ryan."

Ryan did as she told him, staring at the coachman as he closed the door.

"Now, what is it?" Olivia asked.

The coachman looked at the closed door and then approached Olivia's desk.

"When we got back to the barracks," he said. "They had George tied up and were putting him in the back of a cart."

"Who's they?"

"Don't know, ma'am. Harry shot one of them. I shot another. One more got away. George fell out of the cart. Harry is with him at the infirmary."

"How is he?"

"I don't know, ma'am."

"OK, thank you..." Olivia struggled to remember the coachman's name.

"Brown. Ma'am."

"Thank you, Brown. Go back to the infirmary and help Harry monitor George."

"Yes, ma'am."

Brown turns to leave.

"Brown," Olivia calls after him.

"Yes, ma'am?"

"What do you think of this George fellow?"

"I don't know, ma'am. The first I saw of him was when they bundled him into the cart."

"OK, thanks, Brown. Let me know if there are any developments."

"Will do, ma'am."

Brown opened the door to leave. Ryan was on the other side talking to a guard; he seemed surprised to see the door open and told the guard to go away. He watched Brown leave and then walked into Olivia's office.

"What are you doing with this guy, Olivia? He might be dangerous," he said.

Olivia was tired of having to justify herself to Ryan.

"I have men watching him," she said.

Ryan was seething, but he knew he couldn't give away how much he knew.

"Where is he now?" he asked.

"Never mind where he is now. You had your chance to deal with him, and you blew it. Now it's my turn to deal with him as I see fit." She watched Ryan fill with rage, turn and leave before she picked up the phone.

"Connect me to the infirmary, please."

*

When Brown arrived at the infirmary, Harry was waiting for him.

"Give me a hand with George," he said. "We need to leave."

"Where are we going?" Brown asked as he helped carry George to the carriage.

"Somewhere safe," said Harry.

He directed Brown through the back streets on a route that Brown felt was tortuous but which Harry told him was just to make sure that no-one was following them.

They arrived at an anonymous-looking semi-detached house, surrounded by gardens containing many herbs and plants. Harry banged on the door, and a moment later, a thin old woman with short grey hair opened it.

Brown helped Harry to carry George into the house. The old woman instructed them to set him down on the large table in the kitchen. The kitchen itself was lined wall to wall with shelves containing jars of all manner of shapes and sizes, each containing mixtures, powders, liquids or dried plants in a range of hues, which spanned the spectrum.

"They beat him up," said Harry. "He might have a fractured skull."

"Are you bringing trouble to my home?" the old woman asked.

"I hope not," said Harry. "But if anyone comes asking, you haven't seen us."

"Get out then," the old woman said. "Before anyone sees that coach of yours, leave him with me. I assume it's my niece I need to keep informed."

Harry nods and the two men return to the coach.

"Who's her niece?" Brown asked once they had begun another circuitous route back to the Guildhall.

"The Alder," Harry replied.

"That was the Alder's aunt?" said Brown. "Dr Smith's sister?"

"That's right," said Harry.

"I didn't even know she had an aunt," said Brown.

"Few people do," said Harry. "But she's the best herbalist in Freetown."

"Do you think she can heal that boy?"

"If she can't, then no-one can."

While Harry navigates, Brown becomes frustrated at the round-about route they are taking to return to the Guildhall.

"Don't look now, but I think someone is following us," said Brown when they were near Cottingham Gate.

"I think you're right," said Harry. "We may as well go straight back to the Guildhall."

"Good," said Brown. "I think the horses have had enough."

At the Guildhall, Harry reported to Olivia before going to the banquet hall for something to eat. After a while, Brown joined him.

"They are still watching us," said Brown as he sat down next to Harry. "Table of guards over there."

Harry pretended to stretch so he could glance across the room at the table of guards who were watching them.

"Better take care," said Harry.

"They might be chums of the couple we finished off at the barracks," said Brown.

"Maybe," said Harry.

*

Olivia had summoned Ryan back into the office.

"Your guards are meant to be keeping the peace in the city," she complained.

"They are."

"So how come three men could walk into the old Anlaby Road barracks, set fire to it, and then walk out with a prisoner."

"Where is he now?"

"Never mind where he is. He's somewhere safe."

"I sent some men to the infirmary to guard him, but..."

"You did. Don't worry, Ryan. Someone is looking after him."

"You will regret taking care of this man," said Ryan.

"Well, that's a risk I'll take," she said. "Make sure your guards are keeping the peace, not breaching it."

"You can't think my men were involved."

"I hope not, Ryan. That'll be all."

Disgruntled, Ryan left and descended the stairs to the front of the building where he met another one of his guards.

"We picked them up near Cottingham Gate, they were coming from the west," said the guard.

"The west?" Ryan paused for thought. "OK. Concentrate the search in the west. Let me know what you find."

The guard nodded and walked away.

*

Brown and Harry had long finished their meals, and the guards were still waiting at the other table.

"Do you think they're waiting for us?" said Brown.

"Possibly," said Harry.

"What do we do?"

"Wait."

Another guard came into the otherwise empty hall and marched straight over to his colleagues, imparting hurried instructions and gesticulating towards the door before leaving in the direction he had pointed. They didn't want to, but the other guards followed him, glancing across at Brown and Harry's table, content that this fight would have to wait for another day.

Brown and Harry breathed a sigh of relief in unison, got up, dumped their trays on the serving hatch and then left through the back door.

"What are we going to do?" said Brown when they got out into the street.

"Run," said Harry starting to sprint. "Follow me."

Harry shot across the street and down a lane. Brown followed him. He kept running until he was in the market square. Hidden amongst the bustle of traders. Brown catches him.

"What if they've put out the word?" asked Brown.

"It's a possibility," said Harry. "Do you know a safe house? Somewhere we can go until we figure out what to do?"

Brown thought for a moment.

"Not really," he said. "I always thought the Guild was the safest place."

"Hmm, we have to think of something," said Harry. "We can't lead them back to George. It has to be somewhere they won't think of looking until we can get word to the Alder."

"Can't we go straight to the Alder?"

"No, we can't put her at risk."

"What if she's already at risk?"

Harry thought about it.

"Good point," he said. "Let's tell her."

They filed their way out of the market crowds and started to run back to the Guildhall, but their path was blocked by half a dozen guards, all carrying weapons.

"Harry Davies, Jacob Brown," said one guard. "You are under arrest for the murder of Charlie Evans."

"Charlie Evans?" asked Harry.

"The guard you murdered last night. Now come quietly, or something might happen if you resist arrest."

Harry guessed what that 'something' might be and suspected that it involved the weapons the guards were carrying. It wouldn't be the first time they had beaten someone to death in the streets in broad daylight.

Harry and Brown went quietly, allowing the guards to lead them towards the Citizens' Gardens barracks. Harry contemplated running, but he knew the guards outnumbered them and there were plenty of other guards on the streets taking an interest.

The guards led them into the barracks and down the stairs to the cells. Harry's mind raced, the further they went, the slimmer their chances of escape.

It was on the stairs that Harry took his chance. He grabbed the rifle from one guard behind, pulling it forward, sending the guard off balance and tumbling forward into the guards in front. Harry tried the same with the second guard who didn't go over as easily. Brown took this opportunity to kick two floored guards in the teeth before they got up while Harry got the better of his guard and send him tumbling down the stairs on top of the others sprawled in the stairwell. Harry and Brown leapt up the stairs two at a time until they were back on the street, running away from the confused guards outside the barracks, not sure whether they should shoot.

By the time the fallen guards had reached the street and alerted their colleagues, the fugitives were too far away.

Harry and Brown knew they had to get out of the centre, to somewhere they could lie low for a while.

"So where are we going to go?" Harry asked Brown as the two hurried away from the centre. "I don't know any safe houses either."

"Only the Alder's aunt."

"Yes, but we can't go there in case they follow us. We'd lead them straight to George."

"So what do you suggest?"

Harry sighed, at a loss of what to do.

"I know one place," Brown said at last. "It's not a house, but we might hide out there for a while."

"Let's go," said Harry. "But don't take us straight there. Let's make sure they are not following us first."

"OK," said Brown. "This way."

He turned left down the next street they came to. Then crossed the next road and led them down a small road, which ran alongside the shell of what used to be a shopping centre.

Brown was trying to stick to the back streets as much as possible where it would be more difficult for Ryan Jones's guards to spot them.

They took a path through the garden, which ran along what used to be the old railway line. On the other side of the garden, they crossed a busy road and over a small wall which surrounded a ruinous housing estate. The homes were in a terrible state of repair, but the gardens looked very well maintained. Brown and Harry weaved in and out of the gardens until they reached the far side of the estate where they had to cross another busy road, before ducking into another side street on the corner of which stood three prostitutes who all propositioned the two of them.

"You take me to the nicest of places," Harry joked.

"It's on the next corner," said Brown.

"What? I thought we were meant to take a roundabout route?"

"There's no point being on the streets longer than we need to."

Brown turned the next corner and walked straight through the open doors of what looked to Harry like coachworks.

"Noah fixes my carriage for me," Brown explained as he approached a man whom Harry assumed must be Noah.

"Jake!" said the man, catching sight of Brown. "Your wreck playing up again?"

"'Fraid not Noah, I need a big favour. This is Harry."

"Pleased to meet you, Harry," said Noah extended his hand for Harry to shake.

"We need to hide in your loft for a while," said Brown.

"Oh yes, anything I need to be worried about?" asked Noah.

"Not if no-one finds us," said Brown. "I also need you to get a message to someone. Can we talk about it upstairs?"

"Of course," said Noah. "You head up there while I lock up. Tea?"

"You read my mind," said Brown as he led Harry up a set of old rickety wooden stairs to a mezzanine floor also constructed of wood. Shelves filled with all manner of parts covered most of the floor. In the centre was an old carpet, on top of which stood an old sofa, a coffee table and a lamp. Around the carpet were two old armchairs and some piles of books. Harry and Brown made themselves comfortable in the armchairs. They could hear Noah downstairs bolting the doors and then making tea.

"Are you sure we can trust this guy?" Harry asked.

"Noah? Noah and I go way back. I'd trust him with my life."

"I think you are, and with mine. Can he get a message to the Alder? He can't go himself. That would lead them back here."

"I'll have to ask," said Brown. "I'm sure he knows someone he can trust. That we can trust."

"I haven't got any milk," Noah shouted from downstairs. "Or sugar."

"No problem," Brown shouted back.

The old wooden staircase creaked as Noah ascended with the tray of drinks.

"I'd offer you a beer," he said as he emerged at the top of the stairs. "But I don't have any of those either."

Noah offered the tray to them to take their teas and then took his own and slumped on the sofa.

"So what is it this time, Jake?" he asked in expectation of an amusing story.

"There are people after us," explained Brown. "We need somewhere to hide for a while."

"I see," Noah scratched his head. "You're welcome to crash here as long as you need."

"I need another favour," said Brown.

"Does it never end?" Noah addresses Harry.

"We need you to get a message to the Alder," said Harry. "But you must not deliver the message yourself, and you must not meet the messenger here. We can't risk them following you back here. That would have serious repercussions, not only for us but for yourself as well."

Noah leant forward. He was intrigued.

"What's the message?" he asked.

"Do you know someone you can trust?" asked Harry.

Noah leant back and thought for a moment.

"Yeah. I know someone," he said.

"Good," said Harry. "Tell them they need to deliver the message to the Alder, and in private. Not even the Alder's husband must hear the message."

"Most of all, the Alder's husband," said Brown.

"Tell the Alder that Ryan Jones's men are after us. Which means any of the Guild's guards."

"Ryan Jones, the Alder's husband?"

"Tell her we are hiding in a safe place and that she can get messages to us through your friend."

"OK," said Noah. "Well, Jake, it looks like you have got yourself in hot water this time."

"Can you trust your man?" asked Harry.

"No," said Noah. "But you can trust my woman."

He laughed, and Harry and Brown couldn't help but smile at his good humour. It was a relief from the tension they had been feeling.

"No problem," said Noah. "I know the girl."

*

Amelia Wilson walked into the Alder's office and closed the door behind her.

"Are you alone?" she asked as she approached Olivia's desk.

"How did you get in here?" Olivia said, staring at the strange woman.

"That's not important," she said. "I have a message from Harry."

She now had Olivia's attention.

"He and Brown are in hiding. The guards are after them."

"Why?"

"Because Harry killed a guard, and they both killed friends of the guards yesterday."

"Hmm."

"Did they tell you anything else?"

"No, ma'am. They are waiting for instructions."

"Did they tell you to call me 'ma'am'? And how am I going to get instructions to them?"

"Through me, ma'am."

"And how do I contact you?"

"I'll come here every day, ma'am."

"I see."

"Any message?"

"Tell them to hold tight. I'll think of something."

"Anything else, ma'am?"

"Yes. Stop calling me ma'am."

"Yes, ma'am. I'll come back tomorrow then."

Amelia turned to go, opening the door to the office and shutting it behind her, leaving Olivia deep in thought.

Ryan and the guards observed Amelia leaving the office, descending the steps and leaving the Guildhall.

"Follow her," Ryan said to one guard.

Amelia walked through the old town until she reached the marina then she turned right and walked through the estate of old factory outlet stores now converted into warehouses, then into a road of old warehouses. About halfway along this road she entered a doorway and ascended a set of stairs. The guard waited across the road some distance away, waiting for her to emerge. The guard stayed out of sight watching the doorway. Five minutes later the guard observed Noah walk up the street, enter the doorway and ascend the stairs. The guard waited until Amelia emerged again and then followed her back towards the centre and across the other side of town until she arrived at a private house and went inside. The guard stayed until nightfall before returning to the Guildhall to report to Ryan Jones. He told him everything he had seen, and Ryan told him to take two men the next day.

The next day when Amelia walked into the Alder's office, Olivia was not surprised.

"Let them know that George is doing well and that in a few days he will be able to travel. When that is the case, I will ask them to escort him on his mission. They are to remain in hiding until further notice."

Amelia left the Guildhall, followed at a distance by two guards. They followed her as far as the door in the warehouse, watched her ascend the stairs and waited. A few minutes later, they saw Noah approach the door then ascend the stairs. They waited until Amelia emerged once more and then one guard followed her back to the same private house. The second waited for Noah to leave and then followed him only a short distance to some kind of workshop. He waited there until dusk when Noah locked up for the evening. He then followed him to a nearby private house. Satisfied that Noah would spend the night there, the guard returned to the Guildhall to report.

"They're at the workshop, I am sure of it," said Ryan. "Or in one of the private houses. Arrange for all three properties to be searched at dawn and have any survivors taken to the cells at Citizens' Gardens."

*

The noise of the wicket door being broken down woke Harry and Brown. They grabbed two heavy looking pipes from the shelves and waited for the intruders to ascend the stairs.

Harry and Brown stood with their backs to a shelf, which stood against the bannister so they would not be seen until the intruders emerged from the top of the stairs. They could hear the intruders' footsteps on the old wooden boards getting closer to the top.

Harry, closest to the stairs, saw the barrel of the rifle first. He waited until the intruder was on the top step, the intruder saw them and spun around firing a shot before Harry could bring the pipe crashing down on the intruder's skull. As the intruder fell to the floor, Harry swung around the edge of the shelves and thrust the pipe into the face of the second intruder who also fired a shot before falling back down the stairs, knocking over the third intruder who toppled backwards, breaking his neck. Harry grabbed the rifle off the first intruder and then turned to see why Brown was not backing him up.

Brown was lying on his back nursing his arm, a victim of the shot the first intruder could fire. He nodded to Harry to show he was OK. Harry looked at the first intruder, lying at the top of the stairs, his skull caved in. He eased himself around the shelves and saw the second and third intruders lying at the foot of the stairs in unnatural positions. The face of one was a bloody mess, and the second was staring wide-eyed at the wall, his head at a right angle to his body. Harry descended, pointing the rifle towards the workshop in case a fourth intruder was lurking within.

There was a metallic crash, and the fourth guard made a run for the door but Harry fired, and the man fell. Harry rushed to the door, checking the fourth guard was dead before opening the door and checking there were no more outside. Satisfied, Harry shut the door, collected the rifles, searched the bodies for additional ammunition, which he pocketed, and then climbed the stairs to check on Brown who was busy wrapping a cloth around his arm.

"It's only a flesh wound," he said. "I'll be fine."

"Let's go," Harry said, handing Brown two of the rifles and then sharing out the ammunition. "Are you going to be OK?"

"I'll have to be," says Brown. "What about Noah?"

"He'll have to take his chances. If they knew we were here, then they must have got to Noah, anyway."

Harry poked his head out of the door, looked up and down the street before he nodded to Brown that all was clear, and stepped out into the deserted road, across which the dawn light was only just beginning to creep.

When Amelia did not arrive at the Guildhall, Olivia became concerned. She avoided the gaze of Ryan and his guards, worried that she might expose her true feelings, she realised it was possible that Amelia's role had been compromised and that Harry and Brown's hiding place might have been compromised. She knew that she now had no coachman she could trust, but she also knew that she had to get away from the Guildhall unnoticed. Her information about George had come from coded telephone conversations with her aunt. She knew they would have listened these conversations, but she was confident that they were cryptic enough to not have given anything away.

Olivia went into her bedroom and changed into a pair of jeans and a hoodie top then left through the connecting door to the corridor. She went down the stairs, out the back door and into the street where she hurried along as quickly as she could, ducking into the first back street to get away from the prying eyes of any guards who might be lingering around. She hurried around the gardens, in between the houses, crossing main roads as fast as she could and sticking to the back streets wherever possible. She also avoided any of the collective transport buses in case they recognised her. This meant a six or seven-mile walk, but she knew it was the only sure way she could avoid being spotted.

It was cold, but Olivia was walking at a brisk pace, and the exercise kept her warm although she soon became out of breath. It was already getting dark, and the risk of being spotted on the streets by guards was much greater after dark as people still observed the curfew, even though it had been rescinded months ago.

Olivia kept her head down and kept walking, staying off the main streets as much as she could. By the time she reached Hessle, she was exhausted and was very relieved to arrive at the street on which her aunt lived. She approached the door and knocked, keeping an eye on whether there was anyone else on the street watching her. She couldn't see anyone. Her aunt opened the door and appeared shocked.

"Olivia? What are you doing here?" she asked. "Come in."

Olivia stepped into the house and breathed a sigh of relief when her aunt closed the door behind her.

"Aunt Lisa," Olivia gave her aunt a big hug.

George came out of the lounge to see who was at the door.

"You look fine," said Olivia.

"Thank you," said George. "Your aunt has looked after me very well."

He moved out of the doorway of the lounge to make room for Harry and Brown to come into the hall.

"Goodness," said Olivia. "This is a right reunion."

"Yes," said Aunt Lisa. "I'm surprised a platoon of guards hasn't followed you all here."

"We were careful," said Harry.

"Me too," said Olivia. "Well now we are all here, I guess there is no reason you shouldn't get started on your mission. It will be no more dangerous than staying here."

"We could do with one more man," said Harry.

"We could all do with a lot of things," said Olivia. "But it's been a long time since we could get everything that we could do with."

"Let's take the weight off our feet while we talk about this," Aunt Lisa said, gesturing towards the lounge.

They all followed Olivia into the lounge and sat down. Olivia noticed the rifles propped up against the wall.

"I see you've armed yourself," she said, nodding towards the weapons.

"We have four rifles," said Harry. "Enough for one more man."

"Any idea?" Olivia asked.

"I had someone in mind," said Harry. "But I'm afraid they might have already got to him."

"Who was it?" asked Olivia.

"Noah Thomas," said Harry. "The blacksmith. He hid us above his workshop."

"I'll try to find out," she said.

There was a knock on the door.

"You've led them here," said Aunt Lisa, getting out of her chair.

Harry distributed the rifles.

As the aunt left the room, she closed the lounge door behind her. She opened the front door and breathed a sigh of relief when she saw young Charlie Roberts stood on her doorstep.

"The Alder's missing. Everyone thinks she's dead," he said, out of breath.

"No, she's not," said Aunt Lisa. "Come in, close the door."

"She is," Charlie insisted. "I've just come from town. Ryan Jones is the Alder now."

"Come into the lounge," said Aunt Lisa, leading Charlie through the hall. "There's someone you need to meet."

Charlie jumped back when Aunt Lisa opened the door, not just because he saw the Alder sitting there, but also because he saw four rifles pointing at him.

"Everyone thinks you're dead," he said, emboldened by the removal of the rifles which were being handed back to Harry, who was propping them back up against the wall.

"I'm not," Olivia said.

"Ryan Jones said you were missing. He's sworn himself in as Alder."

"Has he now?" said Olivia. "Well, that's an interesting development. I leave my office for five minutes and look what happens."

"We have to get you back there," said Harry. "Show everyone you are still alive."

"I think if I go back there then I might not be alive for very long."

"What are you going to do?" asked Brown.

"I may as well come with you, and then if we return with my father, we will have the people on our side when we confront Ryan."

"Isn't it dangerous?" asked Brown.

"Not as dangerous as it would be to stay here," she answered.

"What's going on?" asked Charlie.

"Nothing for you to worry about," said the aunt.

"If you will get the Alder's father... *the* Dr Smith... then I want to help," said Charlie.

"Thanks, but I think we've got all the help we need," said Olivia.

"I don't know," said Harry. "An extra pair of eyes wouldn't hurt."

"But you don't know this man," Olivia protested.

"I know him," said the aunt. "I can trust him."

"But will he be of any use?"

"I've always found him very useful," Aunt Lisa assured Olivia.

Olivia sighed.

"OK. That makes five of us then," she conceded.

Charlie could not disguise his excitement, which only filled Olivia with more foreboding.

"So when shall we leave?" asked Harry.

"That all depends on George," said Olivia.

"I'm ready now," said George.

"First thing in the morning?" suggested Olivia.

"Only one problem," said Harry. "Guards on every gate will be looking out for all of us except Charlie. The wall is good at keeping people out, but it's also good at keeping people in."

"I know people at the shipbuilders on the foreshore," Aunt Lisa said. "We can load you all on the back of Charlie's cart."

"Charlie has a cart?" said Brown.

"We'll drive you down to the boatyard and get you a boat," Aunt Lisa said, ignoring Brown. "You'll do better in a boat. It's much safer than travelling by land. And quicker."

"You think you can get us a boat?" asked Harry.

"Like I said, I have friends." Aunt Lisa smiled. "Come on, let's eat. Who knows where your next decent meal is coming from."

The five sat around the aunt's large kitchen table while she served them a variety of dishes.

"You'd be forgiven for thinking there was no food shortage," said Olivia gesticulating at all the plates.

"I have a well-stocked garden," she replied. "And I use permaculture, so my yield is high."

"It's delicious," said Olivia.

"Thank you."

"Yes, it's superb," agreed Harry.

"I have plenty of dried food for you to pack as provisions."

"How can we repay you?" asked Olivia.

"You've paid me enough over the years," said the aunt.

"I only did what any niece would do for her family. The collapse was a difficult time for everyone, and I'm glad we could find you a home here," Olivia gave her aunt a big smile and then turned her attention to George. "How long is it going to take to reach my father?"

"Well that all depends whether he is still in the same place," said George. "But if he is, it should only take about a day to get there."

"Wait a minute," said Harry. "You mean to say you're not even sure where he is?"

"I know where I left him," said George.

"This could be a wild goose chase," said Harry.

George shrugged. Harry looked at Olivia.

"I can't guarantee he hasn't moved," said George. "But even if he has moved, we should be able to find him."

"We have little choice," said Olivia. "Our best hope of ousting Ryan is bringing my father to Freetown."

"Absolutely!" said Charlie with a little too much enthusiasm, which earned a frown from almost everyone around the table.

"You can have the guest bedroom," Aunt Lisa said to Olivia. "The rest of you will have to sleep on the lounge floor. I can give you blankets."

"No problem," said Harry. "Thanks."

Charlie cleared away the dishes and Brown helped him do the washing up, while the aunt went to get the blankets she promised. Blankets allocated and dishes done, she set about gathering a collection of dried food that the group could take with them as provisions.

Charlie said goodnight to everyone and promised to return in the morning with a horse and cart. Olivia went upstairs to the guest room and left the others to get an early night in the lounge.

It was just before dawn when Charlie returned with the horse and cart. Everyone was already up when Olivia went downstairs, and she had thought she was getting up early.

Part Five

When she got downstairs, Olivia found the others in the kitchen, already having breakfast. She had had nagging doubts about the mission. She now felt that she was the weak link in the group and that the others were concerned about having to carry her. She knew that she would be the person most capable of persuading her father to return to Freetown, even though they hadn't spoken for so long and also taking into account the circumstances of their separation. She was convinced that if she admitted he had been right all along that he would see the benefits of returning, not just for herself or Freetown, but also for the whole region. If nothing else, she knew that his hatred of Ryan would be sufficient reason alone.

Charlie was clearing the breakfast things away when Olivia's Aunt Lisa said: "Come on, leave these, time to get going. I'll sort these out later."

They gathered the provisions that Aunt Lisa had prepared and Harry handed out the rifles.

"Don't I get a gun?" Olivia asked.

"I only have four," Harry explained.

"Have mine," offered Charlie.

"No wait," said Aunt Lisa, moving to a kitchen drawer, which she opened, pulling out a pistol and a box of ammunition.

"Take this."

"Thanks," said Olivia, taking the weapon and placing it, with the bullets, in the outside pockets on either side of her Barbour jacket. She picked up her duffle bag. "Is that it then? Shall we go?"

The rest of the group seemed to agree, and Aunt Lisa opened the back door so they could climb into the back of the cart which Charlie had pulled alongside the house so they wouldn't be seen from the street.

Once the group was in position in the back of the cart, Charlie and Aunt Lisa covered them with old blankets and then climbed up on the front. Charlie drove the horse and cart into the street and towards the foreshore and the shipbuilder's yard.

The roads were potholed, and the cart bumped around. Olivia was forever having to rearrange the blanket to remain covered, and the others were often being tossed onto her. After what seemed like a very long time, the cart halted, and Olivia could hear her aunt speaking to someone.

The conversation was short and soon followed by the sounds of metal gates opening. Then the cart moved again, over what must have been a very uneven surface because the passengers in the back were thrown around with a force they had not yet experienced.

The cart stopped, and Aunt Lisa told the passengers it was safe to disembark, which they did with great relief. The cart had stopped next to a large shed, and two strangers whom Olivia assumed must be men who work in the boatyard ushered them all inside.

"They have a boat you can use," Aunt Lisa said. "They're going to get it now."

"Thank you," said Olivia

The group waited in the shed until the men returned, then the men led them a short distance to the water, where a barge with a mast was waiting.

"She's full of fuel," said one of the men.

"Thank you," said Olivia. "We didn't expect this."

"It was my father's boat," said the man. "He would have wanted you to use it. Bring your father back, and we will help you reunite both the city and the region."

Olivia gave her aunt a look that suggested she felt her aunt may have gone into too much detail with the boatmen.

"Muhammad and Ethan are two of my most trusted associates," said Aunt Lisa. "You can trust them not only to keep our secrets but to be of the utmost help on your return."

"Thank you," said Olivia. "We need all the help we can get."

"Muhammad will go with you to skipper the boat," said Ethan.

"Are you sure?" asked Aunt Lisa.

"You don't think I'm going to let you damage my dad's boat do you?"

"It might be dangerous," said Olivia.

"No more dangerous than staying here with that nutter Ryan in charge," said Muhammad. "Begging your pardon, ma'am."

"No offence taken, unless you don't stop calling me ma'am," said Olivia.

They boarded the barge, going below deck and out of the way. Once everyone was on board, Ethan untied the ropes, tossed them to Muhammad and then went to the end of the dock and turned a large iron wheel. A section of the corrugated iron wall, which surrounded the city even on the riverside, began to move. Ethan kept turning the wheel until a large enough gap had opened for the barge to pass through. He waved Muhammad off, and he and Aunt Lisa watched until the barge cleared the opening, and then turned the large wheel back in the opposite direction until the gap closed once more.

"Keep out of sight until we are clear of the city walls," Muhammad whispered through the port to his passengers. "South Ferriby right?"

"Exactly," came George's hushed voice from inside.

The sky was grey, and there was a strong breeze. Muhammad left the motor running but unfurled the mainsail to assist. The wind was creating some waves, and the boat bobbed through the choppy water.

"Are you okay?" Harry asked Brown with a laugh, as he observed his colleague's uncomfortable countenance.

"I prefer to be on land," admitted Brown.

"The toilet is in there if you need it," laughed Charlie, pointing towards the head of the boat.

Before long, the north bank became more distant, the south bank grew closer, and they were out of view of the city walls. George poked his head through the port.

"Safe to come out now?" he asked.

"For the moment," Muhammad confirmed.

The passengers made their way on deck.

"Come on," Harry took Brown by the arm. "The fresh air on deck will be good for you."

He led his ill-looking colleague up on deck, but Brown did not look any happier.

"You can take her straight up the river," George told Muhammad. "You'll be OK as long as you are with me."

"Are you sure about that?" asked Muhammad.

"As sure as I can be about anything these days," said George.

"Hmm," Muhammad frowned.

Muhammad followed the south bank until the village of South Ferriby came into view. An important trading post 2,000 years ago, the village had found itself important again because it was strategically on the frontier between Mercia and Northumberland, and because of its proximity to Freetown. He stowed the mainsail, and the others helped him to lower the mast, which hinged on a plinth. He steered the barge into the mouth of the River Ancholme and brought the boat to a standstill within the South Ferriby lock.

"Have your guns ready," said George, as he climbed up onto the lockside where an old man soon met him. The others watched the two converse for a while before the old man nodded and went to open the lock gate while George returned to the barge.

"So far, so good," said George, as Muhammad steered the barge through the lock, scanning the riverbank as he went. "It looks quiet, but you never know."

Harry sat at the bow, rifle at the ready. On the starboard side, Charlie crouched. George was on the port with Brown who still looked ill. Olivia crouched at the stern next to Muhammad.

"We're going all the way to Brigg," Muhammad told Olivia.

"It's quiet, isn't it?" she replied. She had got used to the city.

"Let's hope it stays that way," said Muhammad.

"Ahead," said Harry. "On the bridge."

Olivia looked forward just in time to see three figures disappear from a suspension bridge. She checked her gun was ready, and then continued her vigil towards the rear of the boat, watching the banks of the river above where their wake was lapping the banks.

"Well, they know we're here," said Harry, scanning the land to see where the figures went.

"In five minutes, everyone will know we are here," said George. "That'll mean we won't see anyone else. But if we do, we'd better be ready."

Charlie tapped his pocket. His spare ammunition was still there. He could feel his heart racing. He scanned the riverbank, glancing behind from time to time to see whether any of the others had spotted anyone. Not only could he see no people, but he could also see no buildings, farmland seemed to surround the river on all sides.

The situation remained unchanged until they began to approach another bridge.

"Look," shouted Harry, pointing to an iron bridge in the distance on which a group had gathered, some of which appeared to be pointing rifles.

George went to the bow while Muhammad slowed the boat to a crawl.

"Bring her into the bank," said George. "I think I've got some talking to do."

"Do you know them?" asked Harry.

"Yes," said George.

Muhammad brought the boat into the bank, and George jumped off, climbing the grass bank and walking along the towpath down which the group was coming to meet him.

"George," the leader of the group greeted him.

"Saxby," said George, holding out his hand for his acquaintance to shake.

Saxby observed the hand with suspicion but decided at last to shake it.

"I didn't expect a welcoming committee," said George.

"We welcome all strangers who cross our land without asking," said Saxby.

"I'm not a stranger."

Saxby nodded to the barge.

"Aye, but they are," he said.

"Just friends I'm taking to Brigg."

"Why?"

"Official business."

"Official business, eh?"

George nodded.

"Well, any business is my business in Saxby country."

George sighed.

"Not when it's Dr Smith's business," he said.

Saxby laughed.

"Dr Smith's dead."

"You have proof of that?"

"Well..." Saxby scratched his grey stubble.

"What if I told you I saw him only last week?"

"Serious?" Saxby scratched his bald head.

"Not only that," said George. "My friends and I are going to get him now."

"He's in Brigg?"

"Near Brigg."

"And what are you going to do when you get him?"

"I can't tell you that right now."

"You can't, eh?"

"What if I were to tell you it involved sorting out Ryan Jones once and for all?"

"Then you could count on Saxby's help," said Saxby.

"Thought so," said George. "I hope to be back through this way as early as tomorrow. See who and what you can muster."

"I will," Saxby smiled. "Give the old man my regards."

"I will," said George, scrambling back down the grass bank to the boat.

"Come on," said Saxby, turning to the crowd and gesticulating for them to return to the village.

"You seem to have the gift of the gab," said Harry, as George climbed back on the barge.

"It helps that I know these people," said George. "We'll need a bit of support if we're going to pull this thing off. But don't get too relaxed. There are plenty of people out there who are not on our side. Be on your guard. Let's go."

George looked to Muhammad, who restarted the engine and steered the barge away from the bank. The group resumed their positions, observing the fields either side of the river which stretched out over the flat land as far as the eye could see.

"Hold on," Olivia addressed George. "That all seemed a little too easy."

"Saxby and I go way back," said George.

"Far back enough for him to let a bunch of strangers from Freetown wander through Mercia."

"Yes, but not just that. It's a convenient fact that Saxby hates your husband and loves your father."

"But there must be more in it for him than that."

"Don't worry. I owe Saxby, and he will get paid back in full, don't you worry. I will make sure he gets what he's got coming to him."

Olivia raised her eyebrows.

When another bridge came into view, the group sat up, expecting another band of rifle-wielding locals.

"Under the bridge," yelled Harry, pointing towards what looked like a shadow emerging.

"It's another barge," shouted Muhammad, slowing down and steering closer to the side.

As the barge approached, it became clear that there was a similar group of rifle-brandishing individuals guarding cargo.

"Hello, friends," George shouted from the bow. "We're heading for Brigg. You?"

They greeted him with silence. They were aiming every rifle towards George and, as the boats passed each other, the guards adjusted their aim, fingers poised over triggers, even after the boats were moving away.

"That was tense," Olivia commented, watching the other barge recede into the distance.

"Not very chatty, were they?" said Muhammad, as the shadow of the old railway bridge passed over them.

"Lots of barges get robbed," George explained. "Hence the armed guards. That could have gone very wrong if any of them had a nervous trigger finger."

Soon, another bridge came into view, and the tension on the boat increased. It was an iron arch in the style of the Sydney Harbour Bridge. Everyone on the boat except Muhammad held their weapons tightly until it became clear that the bridge was a pipe bridge and not for pedestrians or vehicles.

Everyone relaxed, but the feeling was short-lived because it soon became clear that their time alone was about to end.

George could see at least six shadows on the bridge, and Harry confirmed this.

"Go below, ma'am," George said.

"What? No, I..." Olivia began to protest.

"Go below, ma'am!" Harry interrupted her with a force in his voice she had never experienced. She was so surprised that she obeyed without further protest.

Once inside, George closed the port and Olivia could no longer see what was going on above, she could only hear.

Muhammad opened the throttle, and the barge started to pick up speed. She heard him take a rifle from the case near the tiller.

"Fire as soon as you have a clear shot," George said.

There was a terrible silence filled only by the sound of the barge's straining motor.

She flinched when the first shot rang out. It sounded like it was fired from the barge. Then, a moment later there was a cacophony of gunfire from all around the boat. Olivia could hear the returning fire and the sound of bullets as they ricocheted off the deck.

Brown was the first she heard call out. He must have taken a bullet. The noise of the returned fire was getting louder, and she could hear bullets hitting the metal bridge. Another shout, Charlie this time but moans of pain followed his shout, which concerned her even more. Olivia felt the shadow of the bridge passing overhead, accompanied by a brief cessation of fire, which resumed as soon as the barge was clear of the other side of the bridge. Muhammad called out, and the barge veered to starboard. Its course was corrected moments later, but Olivia could sense it scraping against the bank. There was lots of shouting now, and she could not make out the shouting amongst the gunfire.

The shots became less frequent, and then died away, and the throttle was eased back.

"You can come out now," said Harry, opening the port. "See if you can find a first aid kit. Muhammad said there's one in one of the cupboards."

Olivia searched through the cupboards until she found an old biscuit tin, on each side of which was a red cross. She took it up on deck.

When she got there, she saw Muhammad first. George had taken the wheel. Brown was not far away. Both were clutching wounds, which were bleeding. She knelt by Muhammad and then saw Charlie whose cries of pain were drowning out all other noise.

"Give me a bandage and go to him," said Muhammad.

Olivia prised the lid off the tin and handed Muhammad a bandage. She passed another to Brown then took the tin over to where Charlie lay on the starboard side. Harry was applying pressure to a wound on Charlie's abdomen.

Harry and Olivia exchanged glances both well aware that a bandage would be insufficient in this case.

"Is there anywhere we can take him?" Olivia asked George.

"Only in Brigg," said George.

"How far is that?" Olivia asked.

"Only two miles," said George.

"Forty-five minutes," said Muhammad, as he wrapped the bandage around his wound.

Olivia thought for a moment.

"We have to stop the bleeding," she thought aloud. If only her aunt were here, she would know what to do.

Harry looked at her for an answer. She looked through the tin and found some absorbent gauze, some dressings, a large roll of bandage and a small bottle of surgical alcohol. She placed the gauze and the lint together and doused them with alcohol, and then she nodded at Harry. He removed his hands, and she lifted Charlie's shirt, pouring some alcohol on the wound before pressing down with the lint. Charlie writhed in pain. Olivia held the pad in place, applying pressure to the wound while Harry unfurled the bandage, trying to pass it under Charlie. Every movement caused the boy more pain.

"Pull it tight," said Olivia, worried that their efforts would not be enough to stem the bleeding.

Harry pulled the bandage as tight as he could while being careful not to restrict Charlie's ability to breathe. Olivia kept pressing until Harry had tied the final knot. She released the pressure, watching to see what would happen and, as she feared, a small red dot appeared then grew little by little. She grabbed another lint from the tin and applied more pressure.

"I don't know what more we can do," she admitted to Harry.

Harry just stared back, alternating glances between Olivia and her hands pressing on the wound. He did not know either. They both looked at George, who pulled back on the throttle but then offered an apologetic look as the barge picked up speed as if to say he was going as fast as he could.

Having bandaged himself, Muhammad got up and went to the tiller to relieve George.

"Are you sure?" asked George.

"Yes, I'll be fine," said Muhammad. "I'll tell you one thing, though. Ethan will not be happy about his paintwork."

He pointed to a dent in the handrail caused by one of the stray bullets.

"I'll paint it myself," said George going over to check on Brown. "How are you?"

"I've had worse," said Brown.

Olivia stared ahead and kept the lint pressed onto the wound for what felt like a very long time. Charlie's screams turned to moans and then from moans to grunts. The barge, despite travelling at full speed, seemed very slow. The fields passing by looked identical. They went under another bridge, which George told them was the old motorway, and then the river forked, and George told Muhammad to take the left fork, down what he said was the old river. They had created the new river, or canal, as recently as the seventeenth century.

"Not long now," George told her, looking past the bow for the place he wanted Muhammad to moor the boat.

"Is there a hospital?" Olivia asked.

"No," said George. "It wouldn't be safe there if there was. I know a man. Like your aunt."

Olivia wasn't sure whether this made her feel better.

"Easy," said George to Muhammad. "That mooring over there. See it?"

Muhammad nodded, shutting off the throttle and allowing the barge to drift alongside the mooring, putting the engine in reverse to bring the barge to a halt while Harry and George fastened the ropes to the mooring.

"How are we going to move him?" asked Olivia.

"Can he walk?" asked George.

Olivia looked at Charlie, who was slipping in and out of consciousness.

"I doubt it," she said.

George looked at Muhammad, who shrugged.

"I think there might be some old sheets below. You could try wrapping him in those and then carry him like a hammock?" he said.

George thought about this for a moment.

"It's OK. You all wait here," he said. "I'll get the doctor and bring him here. Don't talk to strangers."

Harry and Muhammad smiled. Olivia was beyond humour.

"Hurry," she said.

With that, George headed off down the towpath.

Olivia looked around. She could see a bridge in the distance. Trees bordered the river, but she could see some buildings in the distance. She looked over at Brown, who looked very pale. It was difficult to tell how much resulted from his wound and how much was because of seasickness.

"How are you feeling?" she asked him.

Brown raised his head. Even this seemed an effort.

"I've felt better," he said.

"How about you, Muhammad?" she turned and looked at the skipper who had sat on the deck.

"What he said." Muhammad smiled, but his smile masked a grimace which betrayed his pain.

Olivia turned back to Charlie, keeping the pressure on the wound.

"It's OK, Charlie," she said. "George has gone to get help. He'll be back soon."

Charlie did not seem to hear.

Time dragged. Olivia looked up the towpath towards the bridge, looking for signs of George returning with the doctor. It started to spot with rain.

"We have to get him below deck," she said.

Harry took Charlie's head, and Muhammad the legs and they carried him down inside the boat where they laid him on the floor. Brown followed them inside and sat on a bench at the side.

"Stay here, I'll keep a lookout," said Harry.

Muhammad pointed to a cupboard.

"You'll find a waterproof in there," he said.

"Thanks," Harry opened the cupboard, found the waterproof and took it outside.

"Where's George with that doctor?" Olivia thought aloud.

"Do you think something has happened?" asked Brown.

"No," said Olivia. "But I wish he would hurry."

"What if he's gone?" Brown was looking at her with concern.

"What do you mean?" she was confused.

"What if this was his plan all the time?" said Brown. "To get here and then disappear."

Olivia examined Brown's face looking for signs he was joking. He wasn't. He was serious.

"No, I don't believe it," she said.

"He's coming," Harry shouted down from the deck.

"See," Olivia said to Brown, who just looked away.

"Let's hope he's coming with a doctor," said Muhammad.

"My God, you two are a right pair of optimists aren't you?" said Olivia.

They heard footsteps on the deck and then George came below, followed by a man carrying a large leather bag.

"There he is," George said to the man, who then knelt beside Charlie.

"Are you trying to waste my time?" the man said after a few seconds.

"What do you mean?" said George.

"He's already dead," said the man.

Olivia looked at Charlie's lifeless face. She'd been so worried about whether George was coming back that she hadn't checked to see whether he was breathing. Then she realised that Charlie was lying in a pool of blood. They had failed to stop the bleeding. She released the pressure from his wound and sat on the floor. All eyes were on Charlie, except the man who got up and turned to George.

"Anything else?" he asked.

"What?..Er... yes," George returned from his thoughts. "These two were hit."

He pointed to Brown and Muhammad, who both proffered their respective limbs.

The man went to Brown first, removing his bandage.

"I need the toilet," said Olivia.

"Go ahead," said Muhammad. "It's in there."

He pointed towards the bow of the barge where it narrowed, in the centre of which was a door.

"Thank you," she said, as she went through the door.

The little room with a toilet smelled terrible. Olivia sat on top of the seat and began to cry. She removed a handkerchief from her pocket and began to mop her tears. After she had regained her composure, she returned to the main room to find Harry wrapping Charlie in a sheet and the man dressing Muhammad's wound.

"Everything OK?" she asked Brown, who nodded.

"It's not serious," he said.

"Why don't we all eat something?" suggested Olivia. "We have had nothing since breakfast."

"Good idea," said Brown.

"Care to join us?" she asked the man who was still tending to Muhammad's dressing.

"Don't mind if I do," the man said.

"Let's go up on deck," she said, looking at the sheets wrapped around Charlie's body.

Olivia grabbed her bag and went up on deck. She sat down and opened it up, taking out some of the contents. Harry and Brown soon joined her followed by George, Muhammad and the man, once he had finished with Muhammad's dressing.

Olivia offered some dry meat, some cheese, some bread and an apple.

"Thank you," the man said, taking the small parcel of food.

The group ate in silence.

"I'm sorry I can't offer you anything other than water to drink," Olivia told him.

"That's OK," he replied. "We have to be grateful for anything these days."

"Actually," said Brown, reaching into his pocket and retrieving a flask. "This might help a little."

He passed the flask to Muhammad, who unscrewed the cap which hung from a chain, then took a swig, grimacing at the strength of the liquor.

"My goodness. What is that stuff?" Muhammad asked, passing the flask to the man, who took a hearty swig.

"Thank you," he said, once his power of speech returned. Then he passed the flask to Harry, who took a similar draught.

"That's strong stuff," he said, passing the flask to George.

George sniffed the contents first before raising the flask to his lips.

"Phew," he shook his head, trying to shake off the effects of the swig.

He offered it to Olivia, who extended her hand to receive the flask.

"Are you sure?" George asked.

"Why wouldn't I be?" she said and took the flask.

It tasted as strong as she had expected and she fought back the urge to cough. She could feel the liquid burning her insides as it trickled down her oesophagus.

"My God, what is that?" she asked, as she handed the flask back to Brown.

Brown almost managed a laugh.

"It's alcohol," he said.

"Of that, I have no doubt," said Olivia.

Brown took a swig for himself. He was more accustomed to the taste than the others.

"It's warmed us up, anyway," said Muhammad.

"I thought you didn't drink," said Brown.

"Why?" asked Muhammad.

"Aren't you Muslim?"

"Why did you think that?" asked Muhammad.

"Your name?"

"So why did you offer me the flask?"

"Well, I wasn't sure."

Muhammad smiled.

Olivia avoided his stare. She was trying to put on a brave face despite the death of Charlie, she wanted everyone else to feel she was strong but inside she was a mess. She knew that if she dwelled on Charlie's fate too long, it would be the end of her, so she shook herself and tried to focus on what needed to happen next.

"Where do we go from here?" Olivia asked George.

"It's not far," he said.

"Aren't you going to tell me?" Brown asked Muhammad.

"No," said Muhammad.

"By boat?" Olivia asked.

"On foot," said George.

"Why not?" asked Brown.

"I don't ask you about your religion," said Muhammad.

"You can."

"I don't want to."

"No, but you could if you wanted to."

"OK, what religion are you?"

"I don't have a religion," said Brown. "Now you."

"Now me what?" said Muhammad.

"What religion are you?"

"I don't have a religion."

"Then why are you called Muhammad?"

"Because my father was religious. Just because my father was Muslim doesn't make me a Muslim."

"Doesn't it?" asked Brown.

"No, it doesn't," said Muhammad.

"When you two have finished discussing religion," said Olivia. "We should get a move on. How long will it take to get to my father?"

"Not long," said George.

"Good. Shall we leave Brown and Muhammad here to look after the barge? You, Harry and I can fetch my father."

George thought about it for a moment.

"Seems like a good plan," he said.

Muhammad grimaced.

"You're going to leave me with him?" he said. "He'll have me practising Islam by the time you get back."

"Might do you some good," said Olivia. "Come on then. No time like the present."

They packed their provisions away in their bags and Harry, Olivia, George and the man, stepped off the barge onto the towpath.

Muhammad and Brown watched them walk to the bridge, cross it and then disappear behind trees towards what looked like the town.

Olivia had short legs, and she had to work hard to keep pace with the men with their long legs. Only the man, whom she assumed was a doctor, was anywhere near as short as her but even he, overweight though he looked, seemed to outpace her. By the time they crossed the bridge, she was out of breath. It was only then that George realised she was struggling to keep up and signalled to Harry to slow down. Olivia noticed that the man was relieved at the slackening of pace and appeared to be just as out of breath as her.

"Is it far?" she asked, not wanting to sound tired but creating that impression.

"Not far," said George. "Do you need to rest?"

"Not at all," she said, failing to disguise her laboured breathing. "We've only just started."

"Let me know if you do," said George.

Olivia kept her mouth shut from now on to save her breath, but couldn't help wondering why the man was still with them. If George had just popped out to get him, then the man should have been home by now. If not, then where had he found him and why was he going with them now?

"You're coming with us?" she asked him.

"Yes," he said breathlessly that proved he was as unfit as she was. "George thought I might help."

Olivia nodded, but it was the first she had heard of it. She watched George as he glanced back at them from time to time. Was he checking that they were not lagging or on how much they were talking? Olivia probed more.

"How do you know George?" she asked.

"Through a friend," he said,

"I'm sorry," said Olivia. "I'm afraid I don't know your name."

"My name is Christopher," he said. "Or Chris, but most just call me Doc."

"Because you're a doctor?"

"I'm not a doctor," said Chris.

"I see," said Olivia.

"I work as a doctor," said Chris. "We passed my surgery back there. However, I never qualified. Everyone knows that, but they come to me, anyway."

"Why?"

"Because I make them better."

Olivia was almost at the end of her tether. The death of Charlie had hit her hard. She hadn't even been sure he should have been with them at all, and now she felt responsible for his death. She had to dig deep. She couldn't show her true feelings to those around her, she must remain strong, she would have time to grieve later. She had to behave like a leader, she had to be strong.

The road they were walking along was large, and the houses all had gardens in front, most of which were budding into life with a variety of seedlings. Some gardens had people tending them, and they raised their heads at the rifle-wielding group as it passed. None of them seemed to be surprised at the sight of armed individuals passing their houses, and they remained focused on their gardening.

On the corner of a crossroads stood a derelict church, which looked as if a fire had damaged it.

"What happened there?" asked Olivia.

"The riots," said Chris.

A few yards further on there was another derelict building.

"The riots as well?"

"Yup."

"What was that?"

"The police station."

At the next junction, they turned left into another large road. Olivia wished they had taken back streets. They continued in this direction until they reached a pub set back from the road. George led them inside. It was a grotty looking place with wooden floorboards and yellowing wallpaper. Somewhere in another room, someone was playing Depeche Mode.

"Things will change," she heard someone singing from a back room. Otherwise, the pub seemed deserted.

"Liam," George shouted, loud enough to be heard over the music. It was turned off and replaced by Benny Goodman's *Behave Yourself*. Then a middle-aged man emerged from the back room to stand behind the bar.

"Oh Christ, it's only you," said Liam to George. "I thought it was the boss. He hates me playing anything electronic. Prefers me to play this jazz shit. It's like living in the 20th century around here."

"Aren't Depeche Mode 20th century?" asked Olivia.

Liam stared at her.

"Did he tell you I was bringing guests?" asked George.

"He did," said Liam, and smiled a sickly smile which made Olivia feel a little uncomfortable.

"Well here they are," said George.

"OK. Bring them back here," Liam said, lifting a hinged section of the bar and beckoning them to come behind.

He opened a trapdoor which revealed a set of stairs leading down into a basement.

"After you," he said to Olivia.

"Wait," said Harry. "Let me go first."

"What's down there?" Olivia asked.

"Your husband, I mean, your father," said George.

"Wait," said Olivia to Harry. Then to George: "You go first."

"OK," said George.

Olivia and Harry stepped aside for George to pass. He descended the stairs. Harry and Olivia followed him. The basement was very large and comprised more than one room. As soon as he reached the bottom of the stairs, George headed for one of the other rooms. By the time Olivia and Harry reached the door of this room, George was coming out and heading for the entrance of the other room with some haste.

"What is it?" asked Harry.

"Just a minute," said George, disappearing into the other room.

Olivia and Harry followed, and George emerged as they reached the door. He looked very pensive.

"What is it?" asked Harry, becoming impatient.

"See for yourself," said George.

Olivia followed Harry into the room. It was empty. By the time they returned, George was halfway up the stairs.

"They have tricked us," shouted George.

Harry and Olivia reached the bottom of the stairs in time to witness a commotion at the top. The trap door slammed shut, and shots fired. Then everything went quiet.

Harry rushed up the staircase and pushed at the trapdoor, but the iron door would not budge. He descended the stairs again and stood next to Olivia, looking up at the door.

"Shit," said Olivia. "What just happened?"

Harry looked around the basement. It was empty apart from some metal shelves with some old barrels and a few cardboard boxes. There was electric light, but Harry realised this was unlikely to be illuminated for long, so he began to explore the rooms, searching the shelves and boxes for anything useful, but most of them just contained ancient copies of the Financial Times.

Then the lights went off, and they found themselves in complete darkness.

"Are you OK?" Harry asked.

"Yes, shhh, listen," she said.

They listened. They could hear voices above, but the sound was too indistinct to make out any words. The tone of the voices was jovial, and Harry felt his way up the stairs to see whether he could hear any better. But he couldn't.

"What now?" Olivia asked.

"We have to hope they come back for us," said Harry. "I can't see any other exits."

"What happened to George, do you think?"

Harry thought about the question for a moment.

"I don't know. I don't trust him."

"Me neither," she said. "He said 'they have tricked us', but I think it was him who was doing the tricking."

She sighed.

"I've been such a fool, trusting him. Coming all this way. Getting Charlie killed. If I hadn't left the Guildhall, Ryan wouldn't have taken over, and none of this would have happened."

"I wouldn't be so sure of that," said Harry. "If you had stayed, then you would just be imprisoned there instead of here. Maybe worse."

"What now?" she felt for a wall and slid down it until she was sitting on the floor. She felt very guilty. She never should have come. Now Charlie was dead, and their enemies had trapped in a basement. Perhaps they would be dead soon.

"Well, we have guns. We have ammunition. All is not lost. We even have some food from your aunt," said Harry. "We can sit it out for a while if we have to."

They sat in silence for a while.

"Hold on a second," said Harry. "It's not completely dark."

"Seems dark to me," Olivia said.

"Yes but it's not completely dark."

"Well, there's light coming in around the trap door."

"Yes, that's true," said Harry. "But look in that room over there. There's light coming in from there, too."

Olivia couldn't see Harry or where he was pointing, but she looked towards the rooms and realised that one was lighter than the other. Not much light but light all the same.

Harry went into the room, and Olivia got up and followed him.

"There must be a hatch up there," he said, looking at the ceiling. "It's where they used to bring the beer barrels down off the street."

"I don't think they've served beer in this place for a long time," she said.

"Maybe not," said Harry. "But that trap door leads to the street, and we need to find a way of opening it."

Olivia helped Harry to empty everything off one of the metal shelves and then drag it under the trap door. Then, he climbed up the shelves while Olivia tried to hold them steady.

"I think only a padlock secures it and the padlock is on the inside. I could try shooting it off, but you had better go into the other room. I'm not sure where the bullet will go."

"OK," said Olivia from the other room, once she was clear of the doorway.

"Here we go," said Harry, bracing himself for the loud crack of the rifle and the inevitable ricochet.

Click.

The rifle was empty. He reached into his pocket for the box of bullets. It was empty too.

"That's strange," he said. "I have no more bullets. I don't remember using them all."

"Here, take the revolver," said Olivia coming back into the room and offering the gun up to Harry.

"Thanks," he said, taking the weapon.

Olivia scuttled outside again as Harry pressed the barrel of the revolver against the padlock and pulled the trigger.

Click.

Click. Click. Click. Click. Click.

Harry opened the cylinder and felt for bullets. There were none.

"Have you got ammunition?" he shouted to Olivia.

She felt for the box in her jacket pocket and took it out. As soon as she felt how light it was, she knew it was empty. How did she not notice this before? She put her hand back in her pocket and pulled out a stone.

"Bastard," she muttered to herself, then remembered Harry. "No. It's gone."

Harry climbed down off the shelves.

"When did that happen?" he wondered aloud.

"On the boat at some point I suppose," she said. "George?"

"Who else would it be? The doctor guy?"

Olivia shrugged and then remembered that Harry couldn't see her.

"I don't know," she said.

"What now?" he asked.

"I suppose we could find something with which we can prise open the lock. How about the barrel of the rifle or the revolver?"

"Too thick."

They began searching the basement for something with which they could prise the lock.

Part Six

"It's starting to get dark," said Muhammad.

Brown looked to the west, where the sun had already dipped below the horizon, and a pink hue was spreading across the darkening clouds.

"I didn't realise they would be this long," he said.

"How long did you think it would take?" asked Muhammad.

"I don't know, I hadn't thought about it, I mean, we don't know where he is being kept or anything, right?"

"Right. George said nothing about how long it would take."

"It looks like we might have to spend the night here."

"We can take it in shifts. One of us keeping watch while the other sleeps."

"I don't think we will have to," said Brown, pointing up the towpath at the dishevelled figure of George making his way toward them.

"They tricked us," George said as he drew closer.

He looked as if he had been in a fight. His face was bruised and bloody and his jacket torn.

"What happened?" asked Brown.

"When we got to the rendezvous, everything was gone. They tried to shut us in the basement. They trapped the Alder and Harry in there. I escaped."

"Where's your rifle?" asked Muhammad.

"They took it," said George. "Can you give me yours so that Brown and I can get Harry and the Alder?"

"How will defend myself if anyone comes for the boat?"

"Lock yourself inside."

"How many of them are there?" asked Brown. "How are we supposed to just walk in there?"

"There's only two of them."

"But they disarmed you," said Muhammad.

"They took me by surprise. If two of us go with rifles, we should have no problem."

Muhammad looked dissatisfied. Brown shrugged.

"What else can we do?" he said. "We can't resolve anything just sitting here."

Muhammad had to concede the point. He might not like the plan, but he didn't have a better one.

"OK," he said, handing over the rifle. "I'll lock myself in the bloody barge. Don't lose this one."

George smiled as he took the rifle.

"Thanks," he said. "Sometimes we have to make small sacrifices for the common good."

Muhammad wasn't sure about whose common good he was speaking.

"Let's go?" George asked Brown, who gathered his bag and rifle and followed George off the boat and up the towpath.

Muhammad watched them go until he lost sight of them, then he went below and locked the port behind him. He felt exhausted, but he dare not sleep. He made himself a coffee from his secret stash. But even with the help of caffeine, he was struggling to keep his eyes open. He must have nodded off because around midnight he was awoken with a start by a noise on the deck, then a knocking on the port.

"Who is it?" Muhammad called out.

"It's George," came the reply.

Muhammad opened the port and let him in.

"Where's Brown?" he asked.

"With the others," said George. "I need your help to get them back. Brown, Harry and The Alder are all injured. They can walk, but only with support. I need your help to get them back here."

"And Dr Smith?"

George shrugged.

"Let's get everyone back here then we can decide what to do," he said.

Muhammad still felt very dissatisfied, but he was still devoid of any alternative plan and so felt he had no choice but to go ahead with George's scheme. He followed George up onto the deck and locked the port.

George led him up the towpath to the bridge and then crossed it, leading Muhammad the same way he had led Olivia and Harry. Muhammad followed him all the way to the disused pub and led him round to the car park at the back.

"Where are they?" Muhammad asked.

"This is the end of the road," said George, pointing his rifle at the skipper.

"I knew there was something dodgy about you," Muhammad was both proud and disgusted that his fears about George were correct.

As George raised his rifle, a metallic crashing sound came from the opposite side of the building. George became distracted by the commotion, but when Muhammad tried to make a move, George shouted for him to get back. He raised his rifle again, but then a shout made him turn around. He saw Harry standing at the corner of the building and fired, dislodging a section of brickwork. Before he could fire again, Muhammad had jumped on him from behind. As George struggled on the floor with Muhammad, Harry and Olivia came to Muhammad's assistance and separated George from the rifle.

Harry stood up, pointing the rifle at George so that Muhammad and Olivia could release him without fear he would escape or attack.

George stood, facing the others.

"Where is Brown?" asked Harry.

George did not answer but just smirked.

Harry slammed the butt of his rifle into George's jaw, and he fell to the ground.

"So you don't know where Dr Smith is," Harry spat out the words. "You're not interested in getting rid of Ryan Jones."

"Ryan Jones isn't the slaver, she is," said George, pointing to Olivia with one hand while nursing his jaw with the other. "Dr Smith would want Ryan Jones to be in charge. He will set the people free she has imprisoned."

Harry and Muhammad glanced at Olivia who stood, devoid of emotion.

At that moment, Christopher and Liam rounded the corner, brandishing rifles and stopped with surprise to see Olivia, Harry and Muhammad pointing a rifle at George.

Muhammad fired the first shot. It tore into Christopher's chest at the same moment that Liam's shot left the barrel of his rifle. This bullet buried itself in the chest of Harry, who fell to the floor. Before Muhammad could fire again, Liam had let off a second shot, which entered Muhammad's forehead just as Muhammad's shot left his rifle. This bullet entered Liam's throat and exited through the back of his neck.

Without thinking very much about it, Olivia picked up Muhammad's rifle and pointed it at George, who surveyed the bodies which surrounded him.

"Do you know where my father is?" Olivia asked in the tone of someone who has run out of patience.

"Even if I did, I wouldn't lead you to him," said George. "He is the one to bring freedom to our people. You just want to kill him."

"Kill my father? Don't be ridiculous."

"You would," said George. "He would dismantle all the evil you have constructed to protect your power."

"So do you know where he is or not?"

"I do not."

Olivia pulled the trigger, but again a click was the only sound to leave the rifle.

By the time she realised what had happened, George had grabbed Christopher's rifle, and Olivia found she was the one staring down the end of a barrel.

"You need to reload," said George. "But then you don't have any ammo, do you?"

"You're deluded," said Olivia. "It's Ryan who wants to use forced labour, not me. He's the one who terrorises the city with his private army."

"He just does what you tell him."

"Is that what he told you? He does nothing he doesn't want to."

"No, that's what your father told me."

"What? When?"

"When I spoke to him."

"But I thought you said you didn't know where my father is."

"I don't. But I didn't say I'd never seen him."

George used the end of the barrel of the rifle to gesture to Olivia that she should move.

Olivia did as she was told and moved in the direction George was pointing, walking around the bodies lying on the floor.

"Now what?" she asked.

"You're coming with me," said George, leading her around to the front of the pub.

"Where are we going?" she asked.

"Never you mind. Somewhere safe."

"For you or for me?" she asked.

George didn't answer, he just forced Olivia to keep walking by keeping the rifle pointed at her back. Her mind raced as she walked. Now it wasn't only Charlie who had died. Now Harry and Muhammad were both dead as well as Liam and Christopher. Olivia didn't know what to think. She just knew that she had to hold it together for as long as possible. As long as there was a possibility that her father was alive, she knew there was a possibility to salvage something from this mess.

They retraced their steps back towards the river, but before they got to the river, George made her turn right onto a smaller road. The streets looked deserted. Olivia assumed that, like Freetown, the residents were too scared to venture out after dark. The gunfight at the disused pub had drawn no observers. The nearby residents were sensible enough not to explore the sounds of gunfire.

Not far up the side street, George directed Olivia to a house. George did not knock on the door, he opened it and told her to step inside the sparsely decorated hallway. He showed her into the living room.

"Where are we?" Olivia asked.

"Welcome to my house," said George.

"You leave your door unlocked?"

"Oh yes, no-one would be stupid enough to steal anything from me."

"You wield a bit of power in these parts then?"

"Let's just say I am known."

Olivia almost laughed at the arrogant self-confidence of George. That he had dared to enter Freetown, survived a beating, convinced her to leave, had murdered all her colleagues, and all the time he had left the front door of his house unlocked. Olivia heard footsteps in a room upstairs.

"Plus, I'm not the only one living here," George said.

Olivia heard the footsteps of someone coming down the stairs.

She looked at the door, waiting for who was about to enter and when they did, she staggered a little and almost lost her footing altogether. There in the doorway, stood her father.

Dr Smith entered the room and hugged Olivia, before offering her a place on the sofa into which she slumped. Her father sat on the edge of the sofa next to her. Olivia was speechless.

"It's good to see you again," her father told her.

"But you... he... I don't understand," she said.

"I know this must seem all very confusing for you," he said.

Olivia gathered herself.

"He just murdered all my colleagues," she said.

"What you have to understand," Dr Smith said, "Is that while they seemed to be your friends, they have been deceiving you for longer than you realise."

"What?"

"Yes, when they realised that they could get to me, they helped to engineer this whole situation. George had to lure them to the pub to dispose of them. Otherwise, had they been led to me they would have disposed of us both."

"I don't believe it," said Olivia. "Brown and Harry wanted to kill you? What about Muhammad?"

"He was a bit too eager to come with us on a dangerous mission, don't you think?" said George.

"Your sister recommended Muhammad," Olivia told her father.

"You must excuse George," her father said. "He tends to get carried away with his conspiracy theories."

"He thinks I want to kill you."

"You see what I mean," Dr Smith laughed.

"And what about Charlie?"

"No, Charlie was innocent. That was most regrettable," George sighed. He too sat down. "We lost Liam and Chris."

"What?" said Dr Smith.

"There was an exchange of gunfire at the pub, and both Liam and Chris got shot."

"Where are they now?" the doctor asked.

"They're still in the car park. I had to bring your daughter here at gunpoint. Otherwise, she would have shot me."

Dr Smith smiled.

"That's my girl," he said. "Well, we can't just leave them there."

"Of course not," said George. "But I had to get her back here to see you first. Otherwise, she would have been unmanageable."

"I am here," said Olivia. "I can hear you."

"I'm sorry you had to go through all this," Dr Smith said to her. "But you will come to realise, I hope, that it was all necessary. For us to achieve our goals."

"But he said he didn't know where you were," Olivia told her father, pointing to George. "He said I had constructed evil."

George shrugged. Dr Smith sighed.

"They have done lots of terrible things in your name," Dr Smith said.

"He said Ryan was trying to dismantle the damage I had done."

"Sometimes, the truth is difficult to hear."

"I don't believe it."

"What are we going to do with the bodies?" Dr Smith asked George.

"I'll deal with them," George said, getting up and heading for the door, taking the rifle with him.

"Do you need a hand?" Dr Smith asked.

"No, I'll be fine. You look after her." George nodded towards Olivia, before turning and leaving her and her father alone.

"You must excuse George. To be honest, he's a little mad, and I'm not sure he realises what is going on. He might even be a pathological liar. But he is the best mercenary that money can buy. He feels passionate about forced labour camps. I think he has personal history. A lot is going on in Freetown that has been hidden from you, Olivia. Insurgents have been pulling the wool over your eyes, and over the eyes of Ryan as well."

"I don't understand," she said. "I thought you had retired from politics?"

"I had, I was trying to live a sustainable life and making quite a good go of it for a while. But the situation has got so bad that it's not possible for people to exist without being hounded out of their homes by criminals."

"So you thought you would come out of retirement and clean everything up."

"It wasn't a choice. I had no alternative. They had taken everything else from me. Olivia, you do not understand what they have done in your name."

"Are you talking about these so-called forced labour camps?"

"Nothing so-called about them, I was in one Olivia. They are very real."

"But they are nothing to do with me."

"They supply Freetown from places like these."

"What am I supposed to do?" she said, her voice cracking. "Let my people starve?"

"So you knew."

Olivia was silent.

"Olivia," her father's tone was soft and understanding. "Knowing and doing nothing about it is as bad as being the instigator."

"I had no proof. They were only rumours," she looked at her father who was staring back at her, but he didn't look like he was judging her. "Do you think Ryan knew?"

"I don't know. That's what I hope to find out."

"So what do you plan to do?"

"We return to Freetown, where I'm led to believe my popularity is undiminished?"

Olivia acknowledged this more or less true.

"Many of your permaculture theories are still practised there. The people remember your achievements during the collapse to bring the regions together. It may not have worked in the long term, but the people know that was not your fault. You are a bit of a hero, a legend of sorts. Even your name in the back of a diary turns it into a passport which seems to admit free entry into Freetown. I suppose that does your ego no end of good."

Dr Smith laughed.

"I'll try to leave my ego out of this for now. We need to go to Freetown. There, we will find out what Ryan did or didn't know but, either way, we will support Ryan to make the changes required to devolve Freetown from forced labour."

"So why not just come to Freetown and tell me this? Why all this cloak and dagger stuff?"

"Olivia. There are some things that I can't tell you right now. For your own safety. But, don't you see how you have been surrounded by people who want to keep the situation as it is? Ryan could not guarantee my safety, but perhaps if we enter Freetown together..." he trailed off, knowing nothing was certain. "We'll go back on the barge. George thinks he has found us some help, but there is always the risk of bandits."

"Yes, we ran into some of those on the way here,"

"It's good to see you again," he smiled.

"I wish it had been under better circumstances," she forced a smile.

"Look," he leant forward. "I know we had our differences in the past, and we didn't part under the best of circumstances, but..."

"Don't worry," she interrupted. "That's all in the past now. I understand you had your reasons."

"But all the same, I would like to think next time we could find a way of resolving our differences."

"Yes," she contemplated his words. "It would be nice to think."

"Are you tired? Your journey must have tired you. Would you like to rest for a bit?" he got up. "I can prepare a bed for you."

"No, that's fine. I'd rather wait until George comes back."

"We won't be going anywhere until the morning. It would be better to get some sleep. Tomorrow will be a long day. I'll make your bed. Would you like a drink while you wait?"

"What have you got?"

"George has got some scotch."

"You haven't forgotten," she said.

"I'll get some," he left her alone in the lounge.

She looked around the room. Everything looked old and tatty. A faded throw covered the sofa, the carpet was worn in patches, the wallpaper was peeling or missing in various places. There was a record player in one corner, under which rows of vinyl records were stacked.

Dr Smith returned with a glass filled a third of the way with a dark golden liquid.

"Water?" the doctor asked.

"No thank you," she said. "I can't trust the water, but I'm sure I can trust the scotch."

Her father sat down next to her on the sofa, pulling the throw straight.

"Olivia," he said. "I know we've had our differences over the years. And I know I might not have been the best father I could have been."

Olivia protests, but her father puts his hand up to stop her.

"No, it's OK," he said. "I know that a career in public life did not give me the opportunity to give you as much attention as I might have liked. And I know that we haven't seen eye to eye on a lot of things. Especially where Ryan was concerned."

"Actually," said Olivia. "I've been coming round to your way of thinking where Ryan is concerned."

"And," said her father. "I've been coming round to your way of thinking. I may have been hasty in my judgment of Ryan."

"You may not have been."

"It's difficult running a city," said Dr Smith. "Especially when that city is surrounded by regions that have been fighting with each other. It's easy to lose sight of the big picture, and sometimes we make decisions based on our need to survive rather than what is the right thing to do."

"What are you trying to say?"

"Olivia, you've tasked yourself with feeding a city. Feeding a city when food and resources are scarce, you've listened to people who have convinced you that feeding the city is more important than anything else, and you've accepted suppliers without questioning where the produce is coming from."

"You seem convinced that I've been accepting supplies from producers that used forced labour?"

"The evidence seems to point in that direction. People who benefit from your use of these suppliers have surrounded you. People who will stop at nothing to keep those supply links open. We need to find out how deep Ryan has got into this. Maybe he needs our help, Olivia. Many people will do anything to maintain the status quo. You need to return to Freetown and show your support for any efforts to rid the town of these suppliers and stand up against those who are trying to maintain the status quo. Freetown is riddled with insurgents, Olivia. If they succeed, then it is not only the indentured labourers whose future is in jeopardy but also the people of Freetown might be at risk from these tyrants. It's not just the insurgents within Freetown you need to worry about, there are those outside the city ready to make a move."

"You think anyone can remove the liberty of the people of Freetown?"

"Is that a risk you will take?" he asked. "The people will get behind you, even behind you and Ryan together. If we don't go back, there is a very great risk that the insurgents will take over the city. They were already there in the Guildhall at your very side."

"I still find it very hard to believe that Harry was an insurgent. He was the one who believed George."

"He did. George would lead him to me."

"But if George is on the same side as Ryan, then why did his Ryan's men attack him at the barracks?"

"They weren't Ryan's men. They were rival insurgents trying to kidnap George. That's why Harry and Brown killed them. They were trying to get George for themselves. I told you it was complicated."

"And the men who Harry and Brown killed in that man's workshop?"

"No, they were Ryan's men. He was trying to protect you from them."

"Why didn't he stop me from getting on a boat with them?"

"How could he? He didn't know where you were."

"George could have told him."

"Ryan didn't trust George. And George's head is so full of conspiracy theories he didn't trust Ryan either. I don't blame him. He fed Ryan a false story because he did not want to risk giving away where his own allegiances lay. It was too risky. But Ryan didn't believe him."

"Riskier than bringing me here?"

"Fair point, we needed to get you away from the city for your own safety. We didn't think you would believe him unless you met me first."

"And they thought I would believe you?"

"Don't you?"

"Do I have much choice?"

"Look, Olivia. I am sorry about what happened between us."

"It's not just about Ryan. Who told me you were dead and that your diary had been found with your body. Why would he do that?"

"I don't know," said Dr Smith. "If it's not just about Ryan then what else?"

She downed the rest of the whisky in one go.

"It's also about mum."

"Oh."

He downed the rest of his whisky.

"More?" he asked.

She handed him her glass, and he went out into the kitchen to refill them. She got up and followed him. The kitchen was in a terrible state. It looked like it hadn't been cleaned for years.

"Looks like you need a cleaner," she said.

"Don't blame me, blame George, it's his place." He finished pouring the glasses and handed her one. "Shall we?"

They both returned to the living room.

"What were we talking about?" he asked.

"Mum."

"Ah, yes." He took another large gulp of whisky. "I have something to show you."

Dr Smith left the room, and Olivia heard him walk through the kitchen and into another room at the back of the house. He returned with a cardboard box and a cat chasing at his heels, meowing. Dr Smith set the box down next to the dwindling fire, and the cat brushed against it.

Olivia leant forward and peered inside. She saw two small bundles of fur and in the middle of each a pair of round black eyes staring up at her. They both squeaked every time that they opened their mouths. The sound was too weak for a meow.

"There were three, but one of them died," explained the doctor.

"They are very cute," said Olivia, as the cat joined her in observing its offspring. "Molly?"

The doctor nodded.

"Hello girl," Olivia said to the cat. "Aren't you proud of your little ones?"

She stroked Molly, who made the most of it.

"To be honest, I'm struggling to feed her. She needs meat, you see."

"Wait," said Olivia, reaching into her bag. "See if she likes this."

She pulled out a strip of the dried mutton her aunt had given her and offered it to Molly. The cat sniffed at it and then gave it an experimental lick. Olivia dropped the meat on the floor in front of the cat. Molly sniffed it once more and then looked up at Olivia.

"What?" Olivia asked. "Eat it!"

Molly just stared at her, glancing at the meat from time to time.

"Stupid cat," Olivia grumbled.

The doctor laughed.

"You always had a way with her," he said.

"She's always been stupid," Olivia complained.

"She was hunting for herself for quite a while. I think she met their father down in the village," he said, nodding towards the kittens. "Do you ever wish you had children?"

"You are great at changing the subject, aren't you?"

"From what?"

"From mum."

"Oh," he said and took another swig.

"Why did you leave her?" she asked.

"I didn't leave her. She left me."

"She didn't follow you. There's a difference."

"Semantics."

"It's not semantics. She didn't want to follow you, so you went anyway."

"Well, if you know the story, why do you want to talk about it?"

"I just wanted to know why."

"They needed me. Just like you are needed by Freetown now."

"But I don't have a family I'm leaving behind."

"Why not?"

"Because I didn't want there to come a day when I had to make a decision about leaving them behind."

The doctor sighed.

"Look," he said. "You should get some rest. We can continue this conversation tomorrow. We'll have plenty of time on the boat to talk about everything we want."

He rose and started to leave.

"I'll make your bed," he said, and he left the room and went upstairs.

He left Olivia alone once more, feeling the familiar dissatisfaction of a conversation with her father. She could hear him upstairs, moving about the bedroom above her. She drank her whisky.

Although it felt like she would never get to sleep, she must have, because George, returning, awakened her. She could hear the mumbles of the conversation taking place between George and her father in the room below her. Then footsteps coming up the stairs, the door of one of the other bedrooms shutting, and then silence. In what seemed like moments later, there was a knock on her door.

"Olivia," she heard her father's voice through the door. "It's time to get up."

"OK," she said through her fatigue.

Olivia slipped out of the duvet and brought her feet down onto the old carpet, which she felt needed a good shampoo, she found her boots, pulled them on and looked around the room. The dim light of dawn was seeping through the curtains. This was a man's room, she thought. There were no mirrors. She got to her feet and found the door. Stepping out into the landing, she saw George coming out of the bathroom.

"All yours," he said and headed downstairs.

She went to the bathroom. George had left the toilet seat up. She put it down and then found some paper to give the seat a precautionary wipe, before sitting down and emptying her bladder with a satisfying rush of urine into the bowl.

She sat for a moment, then worrying she might fall asleep again, she wiped herself, stood up, rearranged her underwear and trousers, and flushed.

Here was a mirror. She looked in it and then wished she hadn't. She rummaged in her bag for a hairbrush and did the best that she could with her unmanageable locks. After a while, she gave up and went downstairs.

"Eggs?" her father asked her as she entered the kitchen.

At first, she wasn't sure given the state of the kitchen, but the smell of the frying eggs combined with her hunger outweighed any considerations of hygiene.

"Yes, please," she said, after a pause which betrayed her doubts.

"I washed the pan and the plates," her father said.

"Thank you." She sat down at the kitchen table and tried to clear a space in front of her while touching the least number of items possible.

"I've put the kettle on. Would you like tea?" asked George.

The stove they were using seemed to be some kind of wood burning range, and George was checking the progress of an enamel pot.

"We have no more coffee," he said.

"That's okay," said Olivia. "Tea's fine."

"It's green tea," George apologised.

"No problem," she said.

Her father set a plate down in front of her with two fried eggs and an oddly cut slice of bread.

"There you go," he said.

"Thanks," she looked at the plate of food. "Where do you get all of this stuff from?"

"We're connected," said her father. "Or rather George is connected."

George was wearing a smug smile. She didn't trust George anymore, even though her father vouched for him. Perhaps because her father vouched for him, but then, it was because of her father she had come on this expedition.

The egg and bread tasted delicious.

"Let me do the washing up," she offered when she had finished.

"It's okay," George said, taking her plate and placing it in the sink on top of a substantial pile of dirty plates. "I'll do them later."

Olivia could see why the kitchen was in the state it was.

"We need to get going," said George to Dr Smith, who nodded and pushed his chair away from the table.

"Right ho," he said getting to his feet. "No peace for the wicked."

"What about Molly and the kittens?" Olivia asked.

"I've asked a friend to look after them," said George.

Olivia couldn't imagine George having any friends. She followed the two men out of the house and noticed that George did not lock the door, she followed them out into the main road and back to the canal, she could see the barge from the bridge, and it reminded her that the wrapped body of Charlie was still on board.

"Do you want to go below?" George asked as they stepped onto the deck.

"No thanks," said Olivia, thinking of the body lying there.

"You sure?" her father asked as he descended the steps.

After a moment, he returned above deck.

"I see," he said taking his place on a bench.

George started the engine.

"Biodiesel?" asked Dr Smith.

George nodded. It was a tight squeeze, but with some effort, he could turn the barge and head back the way Olivia had come with the others only the day before.

"We've got a stop to make but, all being well, we should be back in Freetown this afternoon," George said.

Olivia wasn't sure now whether this was a good or a bad thing. Her father seemed happy about the prospect though.

"We have some people to collect first," said George.

"People?" Olivia asked.

"That's right," said George. "We'll have a bit of help."

"From who?" she asked.

"From some sympathetic parties."

"The people you met on the way here?"

"That's right. Well, not the people who shot at us."

"Thank God for that," she said. "I wouldn't want to bump into them again."

"There's no guarantee we won't," said George.

"But we have no guns," said Olivia.

"They're below," said George. "Plus, I have your revolver here."

He pulled up his jumper to reveal the revolver sticking out of his trousers. He pulled it out and handed it to her.

"I hope you have bullets," she said.

"Oh yes, they're all loaded now."

"You know I'm a terrible shot," said Dr Smith.

"Hopefully we won't need to find out," said George.

Olivia hoped that too. She looked with trepidation as the bridge under which the gunfight had taken place approached. She started breathing again when she realised it was empty. George and the doctor were scanning the fields for signs of any danger but, as the fields were higher than the canal, it was not possible to see anyone until they were on top of them.

The surrounding fields seemed quiet, but Olivia was not sure whether this reassured or frightened her. She put her hand in her pocket and felt the bulk of her revolver. Its weight was reassuring, but her inability to either fire it or defend herself against any shots fired at her outweighed any confidence that having it gave her.

It didn't surprise her that her father was a terrible shot. He'd be fine if they gave him something to smash up. She remembered when she was younger, and he was still living with her and her mother, that he was always breaking things. She was forever coming home from school to discover that something had been replaced because daddy had broken it by accident. He was very clumsy, and the accidents always seemed to follow arguments with her mother. He broke nothing of Olivia's though, not that she could remember. Perhaps he had but had replaced it before she had noticed. Olivia remembered overhearing an argument where her mother compared herself to a favourite mug he had just broken in one of his accidents, saying that he could apologise and glue the mug back together if he wanted and, from a distance, the mug might look as good as new, but look a little closer and the cracks would be visible. They would always be there.

It wasn't surprising, Olivia thought, that her mother hadn't wanted to follow her father. It probably relieved her to see him go, and the fact that he hadn't insisted she follow him spoke volumes about him being fatigued with the constant arguments.

She watched him staring into the distance, towards the next stretch of the canal. He'd always had this sense of being right, of doing the right thing and looking down on those who weren't as righteous as he. Olivia wondered how many of her genes were his and how many were her mother's. Olivia realised she had followed her father into public office and that she too was stubborn when she felt she was right. She had willed herself to be like her mother, but she realised now, looking at her father, that she was, whether she liked it or not, very much like him.

"We will stop here for a bit," said George, bringing the barge into the bank.

Olivia looked around. She recognised this stretch of the canal. It was where they had stopped yesterday for George to speak to the locals. There was no-one to be seen now, and once George and her father had secured the barge, they stepped off onto the bank and climbed up to the edge of the fields.

"You two stay here," said George. "I'll see if I can find anyone."

Dr Smith scrambled back down the bank and jumped back onto the barge.

"Don't take too long," he warned George.

"I'll be as quick as I can," said George, disappearing towards the bridge.

Olivia and her father looked at each other.

"Are you sure about him?" Olivia asked, gesturing towards the direction in which George had just disappeared from view.

"As sure as I'll ever be about anyone," the doctor said.

"I hope you're right," she said.

They sat in silence for a long time. Olivia wondered whether it was strange that she had nothing to say to this man, her father, who she had not seen for so long and who, it seemed, had nothing to say to her.

She watched the water trickle past the boat and then thought maybe she had better look towards the fields in case anyone was coming.

No-one came. That is until George came back alone.

"They're waiting for us in South Ferriby," he said, leaping back onto the deck.

The doctor helped him unfasten the barge and George started the engine, and they set off along the canal once more.

As they drew close to South Ferriby, Olivia could see that the canal ahead was full of boats.

"Oh no, what's happening?" she thought aloud.

"Don't worry," said George. "They're friends."

"Looks like an armada," said the doctor.

"What do we need an armada for?" Olivia asked. "I thought you said that Ryan is on our side."

"He is," said George. "But he might need some help to flush out the insurgents. The wrong kind of insurgents."

Olivia didn't like the sound of this, but she also didn't feel in a very good position to argue about things.

George brought the barge into the bank behind the other boats, and the doctor helped him to secure it once more. By the time they had finished, a crowd of people had walked over to meet them. She recognised one of them as the man George had spoken to the day before.

"Saxby!" George said, holding out his hand for it to be shaken. "You've done very well at very short notice."

George surveyed the boats lined up in the canal.

"Ah it's nothing," said Saxby. "We've been waiting for this moment for a long time."

"Right," said George. "Shall we go then?"

"Right ho," said Saxby. "Come on men, let's go."

This amused Olivia, who noticed that many of the people in the crowd being led to the boats were women.

"Are you not going to introduce me?" Olivia asked George when he got back into the barge.

"Trust me," said George. "You don't want to get to know Saxby very well."

"Don't you think I should be the judge of that?" she asked.

"I think that's a decision you would come to regret."

The doctor untied the boat and then jumped on board.

"Do you know that guy?" Olivia asked him.

"Which guy?" her father said.

"That Saxby guy."

Dr Smith looked in the direction Olivia was pointing and saw Saxby getting on a boat.

"Him?" he asked. "Nope. Never met him before."

"Well, he seems in charge of all these people," she said. "Maybe we should know who he is."

The doctor looked at Saxby, he looked at all the people gathering on the many boats, he looked at George, and then he looked at Olivia.

"I think we'll be ok," he said. "Don't worry."

It worried Olivia. She was still struggling with the idea that George, whom she had thought was on her side and then on the other side was on her side. Not only that but her husband, whom she considered her enemy, was also on her side. And all these people on boats from Mercia, whom she had considered to be on the side of the insurgents and therefore enemies, were insurgents but good insurgents. And they would help her get rid of the bad insurgents, whom she didn't believe she had met.

"Let me get this straight," she asked her father, who nodded in anticipation. "These Mercians are on our side?"

"That's right."

"They want to help us rid Freetown of insurgents? Bad insurgents?"

Her father nodded.

"And these bad insurgents are from where?"

"Northumberland."

"And they want to take over Freetown?"

"That's right."

"But these Mercian insurgents," she said, pointing to the people crowding on the boats. "They don't want to take over Freetown."

"No."

"Why not?"

"Because we are their friends, and we are happy to trade with them, so they need not take over the city."

"Are you sure about that?"

"Yes, I'm sure."

"How can you be?"

"I'm sure."

Olivia watched as, one by one, the boats made their way through the lock gates and into the Humber. Then it was George's turn to steer the barge through the opening and out into the open expanse of the estuary.

She had plenty of time as the boats glided through the water to contemplate her recent experiences. She felt confused by all this talk of good insurgents and bad insurgents and now had no idea who or what to believe.

Olivia watched the ruins of the bridge pass by, a physical reminder of previous conflicts with the Mercians. And as the boats left the ruins behind the wall of the city came into view. Olivia could see the section of wall which only the day before had been slid aside to let her and what she had thought was her team, enter the estuary. So much had happened since then and it had challenged even her idea of reality and truth.

"Don't you think we should return the boat first?" she asked her father.

"No, there'll be plenty of time for that later," Dr Smith said.

Olivia sighed. She had a bad feeling about all of this. She watched the city creep by her on the port side, shielded by that immense wall of corrugated iron, covered in graffiti. The other boats allowed George to pass them so that, by the time they reached the entrance to the marina, their barge was leading the flotilla.

"We'd better go to Minerva Gate," Olivia told George. "This lot won't fit in the river."

George nodded and steered closer to the bank.

"Minerva," the doctor mused. "The Roman goddess of wisdom and strategic warfare. An interesting choice of a name for the entrance to the city."

"It's named after a pub," she said, shattering his illusions.

The guards looked worried as the flotilla approached Minerva Gate.

"They are with me," Olivia reassured them.

"What? All of them?" the guard was taken aback, no-one had told him to expect so many boats this morning. "I must check. Hold on a second, ma'am."

"Why do they all call me that?" she muttered to herself, as she watched the guard pick up a telephone and dial a number. A moment later, the guard replaced the receiver and ordered his colleagues to open the gate.

There wasn't much space in the marina either, but somehow they got all the boats inside.

Part Seven

Ryan hung up the telephone. It relieved him she was safe. What was she doing on a barge at Minerva Gate and with a bloody flotilla as well? He assumed she must have a plan, so he grabbed his coat and headed for the stairs, telling the two guards he passed to follow him.

"Marina," he said to the group of guards stood outside the Guild-hall. "Put the word out."

"Would you like a cab, sir?" one guard asked.

"No, we can walk. Come on," Ryan gestured for the guards to fol-low him.

They hurried, past the ruins of Holy Trinity church and around the edge of the market into the road, which crosses Myton Bridge, from where they could already see the marina.

As they approached, it became clear from the sound of shouting and the sight of people running away from the marina that there was a commotion. Ryan and the guards began to run but then halted when they heard the first shots fired.

The guards held their rifles at the ready and Ryan pulled a pistol from his pocket. They made their way with more caution towards the edge of the marina.

They arrived at the marina to find guards exchanging fire with people on boats moored on the far side.

"What's going on?" Ryan asked one of them.

"The visitors just started shooting at us," a guard told him. "Your wife is with them, sir. That's why they were allowed into the marina."

"Bloody hell," Ryan cursed. "Who have we got?"

"We've called for support from all available."

"Good. Just make sure we have secured everywhere else. Let's get everyone on duty. Volunteers and regulars."

One guard went to a nearby post, opened a box, pulled out a telephone receiver and began relaying the orders to whoever was on the other end of the line.

"Where are we looking?" Ryan asked another guard.

"On boats at the far side of the marina," the guard replied. "They had come out of the boats, but we fought them back."

"OK," said Ryan. "Let's try to get closer."

A small group of guards followed Ryan, crouching behind a small wall until they reached the next corner of the marina where they found another group of guards, sheltering behind the fruit trees on the other side of the wall.

"What can you tell me?" Ryan asked one of these guards.

"Our unit is just holding this corner," said the guard. "Another unit was sent down there behind the trees and forced the hostiles back onto the boats."

The guard pointed to a line of large mature trees, which bordered the marina on the side where the abandoned hotel stood.

"Let's go," said Ryan to his group of guards, who followed him around the trees to the back of a small building which housed the mechanism to raise and lower the small footbridge which, at the moment, was raised to prevent the insurgents crossing. There was a small detachment of guards sheltering there.

From the side of this small building, Ryan could see the insurgents' boats.

"Has anyone seen the Alder?" Ryan asked. "Is she still on a boat?"

"We haven't seen her," said one guard. "A group crossed the bridge before they raised it, but there's no way of crossing now."

"I see," said Ryan, looking towards the boats. He could only see some boats because the mature trees growing alongside the marina were obscuring his view. Ryan could see some guards using the trees for protection. "How do I get there?"

"The only way," said the guard. "Is to go around railway dock."

Ryan looked at the trees where his guards were sheltering and then at the length of railway dock. A shot rang out from the boats.

"Come on," Ryan said to his guards, who followed him at a trot along the side of Railway Dock. Round the far end of the dock and back along the opposite side, past the houses growing vegetables in their front gardens.

By the time the group had returned to the Humber dock marina on the other side of the raised footbridge, Ryan was breathing hard and was glad to slump down behind the first of the giant conifers. A guard ran up to him.

"What are you doing here?" said the guard. "It's not safe here."

"My wife is on one of those boats," said Ryan.

"She was on a boat when they came through the marina gate," said the guard. "But she hasn't been seen since."

"I need to get closer," said Ryan.

"That's not possible," said the guard. "The best thing would be to view from the temporary operations centre we have set up here."

The guard pointed to a building behind them where Ryan could see other guards pointing rifles from upstairs windows. He followed the guard into the building and up the stairs to one of the upper floors, where he could get a commanding view of the marina from a window.

He could hear some gunshots from time to time, and could see some bodies lying motionless on boats or in the water, with a similar number having their wounds treated behind the small wall which surrounded the courtyard of the marine repair company.

They had gathered the boats around a small jetty on a stretch of the marina devoid of trees. Most of the guards sheltered, either behind the low wall of the marine repair company or behind the nearest mature trees, which had outgrown the gravel squares intended to contain them and had cracked the surrounding paving slabs.

The gunfire coming from the boats became fiercer, and Ryan sensed that the mariners outnumbered the guards, but they were somehow managing to contain them. No sooner had this thought crossed his mind, than the insurgents sprang from their boats, firing shots in quick succession. The guards felled many, but many more replaced them, emerging from inside the boats quicker than they were being shot. Moments later, the insurgents had overcome the guards behind the trees and behind the wall, and had gained entry to the building in which Ryan was watching the proceedings, feeling helpless. The guards who had been firing out of the window turned their attention to the stairwell from which they could hear shots below.

Ryan could hear the gunfire getting closer and closer. He saw the guards returning fire with more urgency. Then he watched them as they started to fall. Pools of blood gathering beneath them. Ryan searched for something in the room he could shelter behind. Finding nothing, he turned over the table in the centre of the room and sheltered behind it. The gunfight became more fierce, and Ryan's heart felt like it might leap from his chest. He could hear more guards falling and footsteps on the stairs. Ryan peered around the edge of the table just in time to see an insurgent stepping over the bodies of the guards. He raised his pistol and loosed a shot just as the insurgent turned to see him. The bullet struck the insurgent high in the chest and sent him toppling backwards through the bannister which crumbled under the weight of the insurgent, sending him tumbling down the stairwell. Ryan ducked back behind his makeshift barrier as two more insurgents rounded the corner and let loose a volley of shots into the table. The solid wood absorbed most of the fire, but some bullets passed through, including one, which tore into the flesh of Ryan's right hand. He cried out in pain and dropped the weapon, he tried to reach for the pistol with his left hand, but a boot encountered his face before he could get a grip, he lost consciousness.

When Ryan awoke, he was alone in a cell, he recognised it as a cell in the courthouse which meant that the insurgents must have captured the city at least as far as the Guildhall. He sat on the bench at one end of the cell and read some racist graffiti, which a previous inmate had scratched into the tiles. Ryan felt the pain in his hand and saw that someone had bandaged it.

The door opened, and a guard pushed Olivia inside. Ryan got up and approached her. She stood in front of him for a moment, tears welling up in her eyes, and then rushed to embrace him. Ryan accepted the affection but was surprised. Olivia had not been affectionate towards him for a very long time. Olivia burst into floods of tears, and Ryan helped her to sit down on the bench.

He held his arm around her until she had calmed down enough to talk.

"I've been so stupid," she said at last.

"Why? What happened?" Ryan asked.

She recounted the whole story from George's arrival to the return from the south bank where they used Olivia as a passport into the city.

"We had barely passed through Minerva Gate before they bundled me below deck and tied me up," she said. "And then I started to hear all the gunfire. They left me there for hours. Until now, when they brought me here. What happened to your hand?"

"A bullet. Did you see anything on your journey here?" Ryan asked.

"Nothing," she said. "I was still tied and blindfolded, but I could hear exchanges of gunfire, though they seemed far away. Is your hand OK?"

"I'm sure it will be fine."

They sat in silence for a moment.

"What are we going to do now?" she asked.

"I don't know," said Ryan.

"I can't believe my father was behind this. After everything he wrote in the diary. Was that just a ruse?"

"I don't know. It's possible he made it all up just to fool you. I should have got rid of that George, or Jack, myself when I had a chance, instead of leaving it to that incompetent guard."

"And I should have listened to you," she admitted. "Why did you tell me my father was dead?"

"I told you, I guess my intelligence was wrong. Well it's too late to cry over spilt milk," said Ryan. "Let's concentrate on what we are going to do next. How are we going to get out of here, for example?"

"And what are we going to do if we get out?" she asked.

"No idea," said Ryan. "But the fact that we are both still alive means that we have not yet outlived our usefulness. Maybe even my father-in-law cannot bring himself to dispose of his own daughter and son-in-law. Maybe there's still some humanity left in him."

"Maybe we can appeal to his human side."

"Maybe we can and maybe we can't."

"I love your optimism."

"I'm just realistic." he sighed.

"What do you think he will do?"

"If I'm realistic, then I think before long he'll have turned not only the entire city but the entire region into slaves."

"Now who's being the optimist? You can't believe that my father wants to turn everyone into slaves. He's been living in a house in the woods, and now he's intent on enslaving people? Come on."

"For all we know, the diary could be a complete fabrication. You can lead a popular uprising against your father, but only if we can get out of here."

Ryan stood on the bench and looked at the window, but it was completely sealed. The air was circulating in the room via a vent in the ceiling, which was too high to reach.

"Do you think if I lifted you up, you could open that vent cover in the ceiling?"

"You are too old to lift me. Even if you could lift me," Olivia began. "And even if I could remove the vent, do you think I will squeeze myself in there?"

"Do you have any better ideas?"

Ryan held his hands low to provide a stirrup for Olivia to step onto.

"My god, how much do you weigh?" he said as he attempted to lift her. Pain coursed through his bandaged hand.

"Told you," she said, struggling to reach the vent.

Olivia just got her pudgy fingers around the grill of the vent when Ryan gave way. She held onto the grill and brought it, together with some surrounding roof tiles and part of the vent itself, crashing to the floor.

"Someone is bound to have heard that," Ryan warned. "Quick. Hide these pieces behind the door."

Olivia helped Ryan hide the bits of the broken ceiling just in time before a guard slid open the small slider in the large metal cell door.

"What's happening in there?" asked a voice.

"Nothing," said Ryan, confident that from the small aperture in the door, neither the gaping hole in the roof nor the pile of debris would be visible.

"Keep it down in there," said the voice, and the hatch closed.

Ryan stared up at the hole. He could see that the ventilation ducting, running towards the wall was too small for them to get inside and the supports too flimsy to hold their weight. However, he could see that at one end, the accident had ripped the ducting away from a fan on the wall, which led to the outside. The room seemed to be below ground so that the fan aperture would give them access at street level. The aperture was large enough for him to get through. He wasn't sure about Olivia.

"Do you think you can lift me?" Ryan asked her.

"Not sure," she said. "I can try."

"Wait, I've got a better idea."

Ryan stood on the bench next to the window from where he could reach the ceiling tiles and remove them.

"If you crouch on this bench," he told Olivia. "If I stand on your back I should be able to reach the fan housing and maybe pull myself up."

"OK, let's give it a go," said Olivia, getting into a crouching position on the bench.

"Here goes," said Ryan putting his weight on Olivia's back.

He reached up and grabbed hold of the housing. Grimacing at the pain in his hand, he pulled himself up into the ceiling cavity. The roof tile supports would not hold his weight, but there was a wooden joist, which he could rest on while he examined the fan housing. By pulling himself up and sitting on the joist, Ryan could use his feet to kick the entire fan housing through to the outside of the building leaving a gap he hoped was large enough for him and Olivia to squeeze through.

"You are agile for an old man, aren't you?" she said.

"Stand on the bench," he told her. "I will pull you up."

"You are kidding, right?"

Ryan straddled the joist and held onto it with his good hand while he reached down for Olivia with the other. While he pulled, Olivia used the wall for support until she could reach the empty aperture. Ryan tried not to yelp from the pain in his hand.

"Can you get through?" he asked.

Olivia pulled herself through the aperture. She squeezed her torso through, but when she reached her thighs, she found herself unable to move.

"I'm stuck," she said, her front half dangling outside the building about three foot from the ground. She seemed to be in an alleyway where the rubbish bins were stored. About two metres in front was a large wall obscuring the view from the street. At the other end of the alley was an old car park, now deserted and overgrown.

"Hold on, I'll try to give you a shove," said Ryan, bracing himself against the joist and placing his feet on her buttocks.

"Careful," she warned. "This is not very dignified."

"OK, breathe out," he said and pushed as hard as he could.

"Ow, that hurts," she protested.

"Sorry," said Ryan, releasing the pressure. "Can you come back the other way?"

She tried.

"No, I'm stuck," she complained.

"Okay," said Ryan. "Well, seeing as though we can't get you back in, we may as well try to get you out."

"What if someone comes?"

"Well, we'd better be quick then, hadn't we? Try wriggling about a bit."

Olivia tried wriggling, but it made little difference.

"I'll try pushing you again," suggested Ryan.

"No," she protested.

"Well, we can't leave you there, dangling halfway out of a prison cell. Come on."

He placed his feet on her buttocks once more and pushed while she wriggled. After more effort and complaining she started to move, and before long she had wriggled her way out onto the street. Ryan followed her in what was a much simpler operation given his bony physique.

They stood in the alleyway at the back of the courthouse.

"Now what?" Olivia asked.

"We have to assume that the Mercians have taken the bridge and that they are controlling the old town. We somehow need to get to your aunt without being spotted."

"You know about my aunt?" Olivia was surprised. "Why didn't you come and stop George when you had the chance."

"First, because I don't know where your aunt lives, and because I had no more idea of how this would pan out than you did."

"I'd say you had a better idea."

"Maybe, but not good enough to stop it."

"What did you think would happen?"

"I don't know. I thought maybe if we got your father back here, we could use his influence to our advantage. Why does he have so much respect anyway?"

"Do you not know?"

"No,"

"In the days before the collapse, it was he who stopped the union from disintegrating into the chaos we find ourselves in now."

"Well, yes, I knew that, but do you think he believes he can re-unite the regions again?"

"If anyone can, he can."

"Yes, but at what price?"

"Look, we can have this discussion at my aunt's. The only way to get there without raising suspicion is on foot."

"How far is it?"

"About five miles. Maybe six or seven."

"That's a long way to go without being spotted in broad day-light."

Ryan looked around. The fact there were no Mercians here suggested to him they had to spread their resources.

"Come this way," he said. "We will get over this wall."

Olivia laughed.

"I'm not kidding. We have to get over that wall. Look, I'll give you a lift."

Ryan bent down and held his hands like a stirrup again to give Olivia the boost she needed to get onto the wall. His hand throbbed from all the punishment.

"Can you see anything?" Ryan asked once Olivia had perched herself on top of the wall.

"The lane is clear," said Olivia. "But it looks like there might be some kind of panic on the main streets."

"That might work to our advantage," said Ryan. "Drop down the other side, I'm coming over."

Olivia dropped into the deserted lane, and a moment later, Ryan had taken a running jump at the wall and hauled himself over.

"Damn," he cursed as he landed on the other side, stopping for a moment to examine the grazes he sustained from the coarse brickwork and clutching his bandaged hand. "Never mind, let's go."

"I never knew you were so athletic," Olivia commented.

"I like to keep in shape," he said. "If you paid more attention to me you would know that."

Ryan led Olivia along the lane until they reached the back of the ruined church, St Mary the Virgin. From the back of the church, they could see people running both ways along the street in panic. They picked their moment and then ran across the road and into the next lane, which appeared quiet. The few people they passed in the lane didn't seem bothered about Ryan and Olivia, they seemed too busy with bundles of their own belongings. The far end of the lane ended in a T-junction. Turning right would bring them out next to the Guildhall, which Ryan argued would have guards surrounding it, whereas a left turn would take them towards the market, which should be chaotic enough to hide them. From the next corner, they could see that the marketplace was also full of people and panic seemed to be par for the course. They turned right, struggling to follow behind the people who were going in their direction and avoid those who were coming their way. The end of this street brought them out by the Princes Dock ruins, and they were near the end of the street when Olivia pulled Ryan back by the arm.

"There are armed Mercians by the dock," she said.

"Stay close to me," said Ryan, and they kept their heads down as they tried to disappear with the crowds heading into Victoria Square. They rounded the square towards the old City Hall, which they skirted until they reached Carr Lane. Here, some confused horses and carts added to the confusion of pedestrians and Ryan and Olivia came close to being trampled on two occasions as they tried to cross the road.

In the absence of any Mercians, Ryan and Olivia continued heading west, until they approached the wide junction with Ferensway where some armed Mercians could be seen patrolling the junction. They stood on the side nearest the old railway station, so Ryan nodded for Olivia to head over towards the Old Danish church, long ago ruined with the other churches during the city's spiritual cleansing, well before Olivia was born.

There was enough chaos on the streets for Ryan and Olivia to weave between the people and carts without being noticed, until they found themselves on the street beside the church. This backstreet was a lot quieter, and they could make quicker progress. They passed along the back of gardens, all the way to the road, which led to the infirmary, from which they could hear shooting and see smoke rising above the trees. They followed a path through some allotments.

"This way," said Olivia, leading Ryan a little way along a busy road, before turning into what seemed like another quiet back street full of residential houses and vegetable gardens.

"I need to rest," Olivia panted.

"OK, here," said Ryan, leading her into the shadow of a brick wall. "We'll stop here for a while."

Ryan could see curtains twitching at windows and parents pulling children inside houses.

"We shouldn't stop for long," he said.

"I know," Olivia said. "Just let me get my breath back."

They sat in between the houses, in a clearing filled with allotments and fruit trees.

"What's the plan?" she asked.

"To get to your aunt's house."

"Yes, I know. But what about after that?"

"Survive," Ryan said. "Once we've survived, then we can think about what we will do next."

"So we are just going to let them take over?"

"I don't think we have much of an option. Once the dust settles, then we might come up with a plan, but right now the plan is to not get killed."

Olivia nodded, and Ryan felt he had been successful in articulating his concept of being alive as the first step in his non-existent plan.

He didn't allow Olivia to rest for too long before they continued their journey through the back streets and allotments which formed the west of the city.

"Do you know where we are going?" Ryan asked after a while.

"Once we get to Hessle, I will know the way from there," she said.

"Oh good," said Ryan. "Well, we are heading toward Hessle okay."

"I'm tired again," she complained.

They had reached the western suburbs and hadn't seen a Mercian for well over an hour.

"OK, let's rest in there," said Ryan pointing to a small allotment on one of the street corners.

They crouched behind a makeshift fence and Ryan marvelled at the variety of produce they appeared to be growing in such a small plot of land. He began to wonder whether he should have spent more of his time learning how to grow fruits and vegetables. He didn't know the first thing about how to survive off the land. At least that's one thing Olivia's father had going for him. He could survive off the land if he needed to. All Ryan knew to do was how to administrate. He suspected Olivia was pretty much in the same boat. If they were going to get through this, then they might have to develop some new skills.

"How are you feeling?" he asked her.

"I'm OK," she said. "I'll be ready to go on in a minute."

"Good. The sooner we get off these streets, the better."

"There is one problem I'd overlooked," she said.

"What's that?"

"George knows where my aunt lives. They'll have picked her up by now."

"Shit!"

"What now?"

"No idea."

They sat among the plants wondering what to do next.

"We will have to find some kind of shelter before nightfall," said Ryan. "There's bound to be some kind of curfew tonight."

Olivia nodded.

"How about appealing to the better nature of your father?"

"I'm sure if my father had a better nature, he wouldn't have thrown us both in the cells."

"I wish you'd had this revelation about George and your aunt before we'd walked all this way," said Ryan.

"Yeah. Sorry about that," said Olivia. "But it is safer out here than in the centre."

"Any ideas then?"

They sat in silence for a while.

"Are you sure George will have got to your aunt? She is your father's sister."

"Do you think that'll make much difference?"

"Let's go now. We might get to your aunt before they do."

They rushed now. Olivia showing Ryan the way, but when Olivia arrived in the street where her aunt lived, they found one house in flames. It looked as if the fire had been burning for some time. A neighbour was trying to put out the remaining flames.

"What happened?" Olivia asked.

"They came, and they killed her and then they set fire to the house. We daren't do anything until they left," he said.

"Who are they?" asked Olivia.

"I don't know," said the man. "They weren't from around here."

Olivia thanked the man and then walked away for some distance until she sat down and began to cry.

Ryan knew Olivia's father could be ruthless, but hunting down his own family seemed extreme.

"What about trying to find groups loyal to you?" Olivia suggested after she had regained her composure.

"Loyal to me?" Ryan was surprised. "Don't you mean loyal to you?"

"Whatever. Maybe we can find groups resisting the Mercians."

"Yes, but where?"

"What about the Anlaby Road barracks where George was given his beating?"

"It's a long shot," said Ryan. "But it's better than nothing."

"Which way is it?" she asked.

Ryan looked around for a moment to get his bearings.

"This way," he said, getting up, renewed with vigour.

He led Olivia along a road past a large community food-growing cooperative. They cultivated either side of the road, with the front gardens of every house given over to growing food. Every few metres grew fruit trees, and yet Olivia was very aware of the deals she had to make to import the rest of the fruit needed to satisfy the city's demand. As they approached a large junction at the end of the road, Ryan could see that some Mercians were patrolling. It amazed Ryan that they had secured an area so large already.

"Look, we must make a little diversion," said Ryan, pointing out the Mercians to Olivia. He led her between some very mature trees a little away from the junction, until he reached a point out of sight of the Mercians where he felt it would be safe to cross.

"We will go a long way around," said Ryan. "We can't risk being spotted."

"OK," said Olivia, following Ryan through the trees away from the junction. "How long will it take us to get to the barracks?"

"That depends on how many Mercians we encounter. I'm amazed they are this far into the city already."

"What if it's already too late?"

"Then it's too late. There's nothing we can do about that. We just have to hope that there are still pockets of resistance."

Ryan led Olivia around the edge of a large park, chunks of which residents had sectioned off for allotments. Residents were working on their plots, oblivious to the fact that insurgents had attacked the city.

As they entered the residential area, it struck Ryan how many people appeared to be going along with their everyday business. He wondered how much people knew about what had happened in the city today.

As they turned into the main road, there were none of the signs of panic that was so clear on the streets in the centre.

They were walking now along a boulevard, the centre of which was devoted to food growing.

"All these vegetables growing are making me feel hungry," said Olivia.

"I know," said Ryan. "I have had nothing since breakfast."

"Let's hope we find what we are looking for," said Olivia.

Ryan smiled and just kept walking. He had no idea what he might find at the barracks.

"Can you hear that?" he asked, as they drew closer to their destination.

Olivia listened.

"Gunfire," he said. "I never thought I'd be so relieved to hear gunfire. What I don't understand is how they took Fiveways without Boothferry Road."

"They went down Hessle Road," said Olivia.

"You're not just a pretty face, are you?" said Ryan.

As they drew closer to the gunfire, Ryan and Olivia could see that they had stretched a barricade out across the road, behind which guards were sheltering between shots at another barricade about 100 metres towards the centre.

Ryan approached a guard and introduced himself.

"We thought they had captured you," said the guard. He turned to his colleague. "Put out the word that Dr Jones and the Alder are safe."

"What's the situation here?" asked Ryan.

"We've been holding them here for some time, sir. There is also a barricade at North Road where they have been trying to take us from behind."

Ryan looked back along the road, but he couldn't see the barricade from where they were.

"Do you have any food?" Ryan asked.

"Of course, sir," said the guard, gesturing to another guard. "Take them to the mess."

The guard saluted before leading Ryan and Olivia towards the barracks, into a hall where Guild staff served them bacon and eggs.

"I never imagined bacon and eggs could taste so good," Olivia admitted.

"I know what you mean," said Ryan. "Enjoy it while you can."

A senior looking guard came and hovered over their table.

"Sorry, to disturb you, sir," he apologised.

"That's OK," said Ryan. "What is it?"

"We are fighting them back, sir. I thought you might like to know."

"Yes, thank you," said Ryan. "We'll be there in a moment."

The guard smiled and returned to the action while Ryan and Olivia finished their meals.

"Well, I suppose we had better show our faces," said Ryan, pushing his plate aside.

"I suppose so," said Olivia.

They dragged themselves up and left the mess, heading back outside where the intensity of the gunfire had seemed to increase. They were both handed helmets, which they received with thanks.

When they stepped outside, they realised that the guards had moved on from the first barricade to the second barricade, from which they had already beaten the Mercians back.

Ryan could see the surviving Mercians sheltering in the doorways of shopfronts as they attempted their retreat.

"What's the plan?" Ryan asked the senior guard.

"The plan is to push them back as far as we can," he said. "We have another front at the infirmary. If we can push them as far back as that, then we can combine our efforts."

Ryan nodded. He remembered hearing gunfire at the infirmary earlier.

"That must be one hell of a battle if it's still going on," he said.

"We've had reports of large numbers of casualties," the senior guard confirmed.

Ryan frowned.

"This is, without doubt, the biggest fuck up since I've been here," he said.

"Worse than the war of division?" Olivia asked.

Ryan thought about it for a moment.

"I wasn't responsible for that one," he said.

"You're not responsible for this one," said Olivia.

"I opened the gates for them."

"You weren't to know."

"Beware of Mercians bearing gifts."

"Well they fooled me, and I was the gift."

Olivia put a hand on his shoulder. The whole group was now moving at a walking pace, now that they had dealt with the last of the Mercians. The single obstacle to progress being the caution the group commander insisted on exercising, every time they reached a junction around which more Mercians might be hiding. By the time they reached the old railway line gardens, they could hear gunfire from the infirmary.

On the other side of the gardens, they encountered a group of guards who were very relieved to see them, having been fighting for most of the day without support. The captain of the group told how they had started the day in front of the infirmary but had been pushed back to the old railway line where they had fought on two fronts for a while.

The group commander informed them it was far from over, but he hoped that the tide had turned and it was just a question of flushing them out. He sent out two detachments, the first was to follow the gardens, which ran the length of the old railway line, with instructions to engage with the Mercians from behind the infirmary. The second detachment he sent down the Boulevard, from where he suspected the second front had come. Their instructions were to flush out any insurgents they could find, after which they should loop around and rendezvous at the front of the infirmary where the commander hoped to have reached by then. The re-grouped unit could then consider making an assault on the centre, assuming everything went to plan.

Ryan marvelled at the confidence of the commander and wished he shared the same optimism. He told the commander about the group he had seen at Fiveways, and the commander assured him that the group he had sent to deal with the North Road barricade would deal with them also. It amazed Ryan. Did this man run off arrogance alone or did he have any other energy sources?

Ryan felt his heart race with every gunshot, which flew past. Fortunately for him, the commander seemed to have very low expectations of him and seemed happy for Ryan and Olivia to make up the numbers. At last, Ryan could hold back his desire to know the opinions of the commander no longer.

"We don't seem to be much help," he said to the commander.

"That's okay, sir. The main thing is that we get you both back in the Guildhall in one piece."

Ryan thought it was nice to be wanted and he shared this with Olivia.

"Right now I'd be happy to be a little less wanted," she said.

Ryan knew that none of this could be resolved without a confrontation with his father-in-law. That was something he was not looking forward to, but he resolved to cross that bridge when he came to it. He looked at Olivia, sheltering beneath her oversized helmet and gave a thought to the effect this ultimate confrontation might have on her.

"You know that, at some point, we will have to confront your father," he said.

"I know," she responded.

"How do you feel about that?" he asked.

"How do you think I feel about that?" she snapped.

"I understand how difficult this is for you."

"How can you understand? We're not about to attack your father, are we?"

"I understand."

"You keep saying you understand, but how can you understand. He's not your father."

Ryan wanted to say he understood, but he thought better of it. Instead, he sat in silence.

"I know that he will be dealt with if we will resolve this situation," she said. "But it doesn't make it any easier."

Ryan nodded.

The commander interrupted their contemplation asking them to follow him as the group prepared to advance along the road, which was scattered with rubble and debris.

They were more or less level with the Freetown Omnibus Garage where staff had closed all the doors. Usually, this road would have been a hive of activity, but today the street was deserted except for the commander's group, making their way from the doorway to doorway pursuing the retreating Mercians, the exchanges of fire with whom kept ringing in Ryan's ears.

He couldn't help wondering how this would end. If the rest of the Mercians capitulated in the same way then at some point Olivia's father would have to surrender and then, like it or not, she would have to make an example of him. The citizens of Freetown needed a strong leader, and Olivia would have to prove that she contained the strength required to defend the city against whatever the regions throw at it. Especially given the day's invasion.

Ryan had to shake himself free from his daydreaming. He was counting his chickens before they had hatched, to a certain extent, given that he was crouched on a doorstep with bullets flying past and not in a comfortable chair in the Guildhall.

The commander bid them move forward again, and they had to step over the bodies of two Mercians. Ryan was struck by how young they looked. What a terrible waste of life, it seemed to him. Why did human nature feel the need to control everything?

Ryan knew that the principle was greater than just who ran Freetown. He well knew that allowing the Mercians to take over would return the region to slavery.

"Was there no sign of your father's intention?" Ryan asked Olivia.

"Do you think if I knew what he was up to that I would have gone along with his plans?"

His constant questioning irritated her.

Ryan resolved to keep his mouth shut until he needed to open it again. He couldn't shake the image of the young dead Mercians from his mind. Such a waste.

They were now near to the infirmary itself, and Ryan could sense an increase in the number of combatants from the increase in the intensity of gunfire. They sheltered behind a mature tree, the trunk of which showed scars of gun battle.

The commander asked them to sit tight for a moment while he went forward to assess the situation. Ryan was happy to stay put behind the tree, and Olivia looked like she was happy to stay put, too. He was not surprised she was in no hurry, given the inevitable confrontation that awaited her.

Ryan listened to the shouts and the gunfire. He wondered whether the commander's detachments had found their way back to the infirmary yet. He felt so useless. Like a limp appendage on the body of war. He watched with curiosity a man on the other side of the road, who appeared to be walking home oblivious to all the fighting going on around him. Ryan observed that, as the man walked, he didn't seem to swing his arms. Ryan didn't trust people who didn't swing their arms as they walked. It seemed to Ryan a symptom of mental instability. Of pent-up emotions building up inside, ready to explode in a rash episode of mass murder.

He realised that Olivia was staring at him.

"What?" he asked.

"You looked like you were daydreaming," she said.

"I was just watching that man on the other side of the road," he confessed. "Going about his business as if nothing is different."

"People need a lot to shake them out of their daily routines," Olivia suggested. "Have you ever read War of the Worlds?"

Ryan shook his head.

"The morning after the aliens land on the common, the people go about their business as if nothing has happened. That's how life is. People get on with what they need to do unless someone places an obstacle in their path, and even then, they sometimes carry on as if nothing has happened. Most people in this city don't care whether it is you or I or my father who is in charge, as long as we leave them to get on with their lives."

"But they won't be allowed to get on with their lives if the Mercians take over."

"Yes, but they don't know that. They just see these little battles as an inconvenience they have to deal with."

"So it doesn't matter who's in charge?"

"As long as they have food to eat."

"Then why do you bother?"

"Because I want them to have food to eat. If possible, food that they have grown as free citizens."

"Seems as good a reason as any."

A guard approached and said the Commander had sent him to take them forward. Ryan and Olivia got up, dusted themselves off and followed the guard to what seemed like the next mature tree.

"The Commander doesn't want you to get left too far behind," the guard explained.

Ryan smiled his acknowledgement and joined Olivia, who had already slumped on the ground by the base of the trunk.

"People are dying for these ideals," Ryan reminded them both.

"Let's hope we are on the right side then," Olivia said.

"Well, we don't want to reduce the citizens to slavery," said Ryan. "That's got to be a good start."

"I asked no one to die anyway," said Olivia. "They seem to do it of their own accord."

"Hang on a second," said Ryan. "You heard these guards pledge allegiance to you and to the city. The sacrifices they are making now was implicit in that pledge. "

"Fair point. It's not that I'm not grateful to these men. I am. And I felt guilty for putting them in this situation. The Mercians are pissing me off. What makes someone think they can just walk up to something that people have spent years creating and just take it as theirs? It's fucking ridiculous."

"And their intention wasn't obvious?" Ryan couldn't help asking again.

"No," Olivia was getting irritated. "They strung me a bunch of lies about supporting you to fight the real insurgents. I wouldn't have believed it if it hadn't been because my father was in on it. The bastard."

Ryan let her be. He knew better than to upset her any more than she was already, he just watched her as she sulked, he thought she looked beautiful when she sulked.

The gunfire didn't seem to let up. He wondered from where the Mercians were getting all the ammunition. They must have brought a hell of a lot with them. He hadn't even realised his own guards had stockpiled this much ammo. However, he was glad they had.

The people and the guild would ask serious questions after this about how the city protected itself. He wouldn't be surprised if the city held a vote of no confidence in Olivia and himself. That would be awkward. What would they do then?

The guard received orders to move them again, and Ryan and Olivia got to their feet and followed him further up the road to a point where they were almost at the infirmary.

"What's happening at the infirmary?" Ryan asked when the commander came to update them.

"It's operating as usual," he said. "They are taking some of the wounded. We've more or less secured this area. Once we are confident that this area is secure, then we can advance on the centre."

Ryan thanked him and sat down again with Olivia, who was looking more sullen than ever.

"Is this what it has come down to then?" she asked. "Every day a struggle to survive. Who can go on like this?"

"Don't forget," said Ryan. "That most of the world has always struggled to survive. We have been living for years on the resources we exploited from others, and now that we've used all those resources, we complain when we have to live like those poor bastards we exploited for decades, centuries maybe."

"Well, I don't like it," she said.

Ryan watched her. She looked like a spoilt child now, who had been told she can no longer play with her favourite toys.

"But this isn't news to you," he said. "We've been dealing with this situation for years."

"I know," she said. "But it grinds you down. Always battling to get enough food, source enough produce. And then something like this happens."

"It's the human condition," said Ryan. "The constant struggle against the elements. Trying to survive when everything seems to want to drag you back into the primordial swamp. We just happened to have experienced the tail end of an era in which cheap oil made survival so much easier. But we wasted that oil and now we have to live with the consequences."

Olivia didn't seem convinced.

"We should be proud of what we have achieved here," said Ryan. "We got everyone cooperating together. Working toward a common goal. Feeding each other. It's a real achievement, which is why people like these Mercians want to take it away from us. But they would never succeed because the people will not work together for them the way they have done for you."

Olivia did not look up.

"Look at the surrounding regions," Ryan continued. "They are in chaos. This is why they try to invade us because they haven't been able to achieve what we have achieved here and they are jealous."

"They wouldn't be here if I hadn't let them in," she said.

"Oh stop it, Olivia," Ryan was becoming impatient. "This entire city wouldn't be here if you hadn't galvanised support to make it happen, and people like your father said it couldn't be done. These people are fighting for you, and you have to continue to justify their faith in you."

"I'm sorry I ever doubted you," she told Ryan.

"Doubted me? How?"

"I thought you wanted to usurp my position."

"Usurp you? I've only ever wanted to support you. This is what happens when you listen to the whispering of little birds from Mercia."

"It doesn't help if you don't know the birds are from Mercia. I have to admit that I took notice of Harry more than I should have. Sometimes it's difficult to see the wood for the trees," she said.

The commander returned.

"We've secured the area," he said. "So this is it. The big push on the centre. You can stay here, and we'll send for you once we have secured the centre."

"No, I'll come with you. I want to be there when we defeat them," Olivia said.

"If you are sure," said the commander.

"I'm sure," said Olivia.

"Then I'll be coming too," said Ryan.

Ryan could sense the commander's disappointment that he would have to haul two VIPs through another battle zone. Ryan imagined that even the commander understood the value of having a personality like Olivia in the final moments of a conflict such as this.

They gathered themselves and followed the group along the main road towards the centre. Ryan and Olivia hung around the back of the group with an escort the commander had allocated them, the commander himself had gone back to the front from where Ryan could hear more shouting but not much in the way of gunfire.

The distance from the Infirmary to the Guildhall could not have been more than about a mile, the buildings around the infirmary had been easy to clear of insurgents, but the Guildhall and the law courts would not be so easy, and then there was the question of the marina, which the guards still had to secure. Ryan began to wonder where they might spend the night. He hoped he wouldn't have to get involved in any of the actual gunfighting. The guards had given both he and Olivia pistols, but neither of them intended to use them unless they had to.

Ryan had witnessed some of the fighting and was surprised at how messy and disorganised it seemed.

They walked close to the walls that enclosed the remaining tower blocks with their huge communal gardens. Large fruit trees offered shelter. They were approaching a junction, where earlier Ryan and Olivia had to take a detour to avoid a group of Mercians. Their guard told them to shelter by the corner of a building because at the junction ahead a Mercian had taken up a position as a sniper on a rooftop. A large tree in front of the building offered enough cover for them to cross the road and shelter by the entrance of what used to the railway station.

They rested here until word came that the guards had cleared the sniper. Ryan felt nervous, and he looked up at the rooftops as they followed their escort. On the rooftops, he could see men with guns but the fact he wasn't being shot at reassured him they must be on the same side.

There were many rooftops. And there seemed to be many people on top of the rooftops. Another burst of gunfire halted their progress. The escort told them it was around the telephone exchange. The telephone exchange always reminded Ryan of the days they used to have the cloud. Access to an unlimited source of information. He thought about how much they had taken things for granted.

The gunfire ceased, and a few moments later, their escort beckoned them to follow him again. The next stop was by the ruins of the old shopping centre on the corner of Victoria Square. Ryan watched the escort taking instructions, and then listened as the escort explained that things had become a little complicated and that there were pockets of insurgents fighting all over the place. He explained that they were setting a command post up in the old City Hall and that Ryan and Olivia should accompany him there for the moment. They did as he told them, they were now very close to the marina and Ryan could hear distant gunfire.

Olivia and Ryan followed their escort into the City Hall, where tables had been set up in the main hall, and all manner of activity was going on. Instructions were being given, directions were taken. He noticed that, at the far end of the room, they had set up a makeshift infirmary to treat the wounded.

"Would you like a cup of tea?" the escort asked.

"Would I?" said Ryan. "I'll make you captain of the guard if you bring me a cup of tea."

The escort laughed.

"I should be able to get you both something to eat," he said.

He found them somewhere to sit and told them he would be back soon.

"This conflict is very civilised, isn't?" Ryan commented. "First bacon and eggs, now maybe some sandwiches. We should go to war every day."

"Shut up," she told him.

He shut up. She wasn't in the mood for his poor attempts at jokes right now.

He watched as the people in the hall busied themselves with their various tasks. There was a great sense of cooperation in the room. A sense that everyone was working towards something bigger. He also had to hand it to the Mercians for having the audacity to think they could take over an entire city with just a few thousand men. Ryan understood now that even if they had overwhelmed every guard in Freetown, the people themselves would have stood up against the Mercians and would not have given up until they had overthrown every one of them. It made Ryan feel very proud, but it also gave him a sense of responsibility to these people, that Olivia and he must do their very best to ensure that these people get the very best. He looked at Olivia. She was lost in her thoughts again. The commander approached.

"I apologise for not keeping you more updated," he said.

"That's OK," she said. "This is a military operation. You must do what you think is best. Unless my husband..."

"No, not at all," said Ryan. "You have my utmost confidence, Commander."

"Good. We think we have them contained within three areas. The first is the Guildhall and the law court, the second is the marina, and the third is a small group on Boothferry Road, which is proving tricky to disarm. The best thing is if you stay here until I can bring you more news. You should be able to get something to eat here."

"Thank you," said Ryan.

"Is there anything else you need?" the commander asked.

"We're fine, thank you," said Olivia. "Don't let us distract you from your work."

"Thank you," said the commander, and left them.

"I like him," said Olivia.

"Why?" asked Ryan.

"He doesn't call me ma'am."

"I don't call you ma'am."

"That's true."

"Does that mean you like me too?"

Olivia looked at Ryan for a moment.

"Sometimes you're OK," she said.

The escort returned carrying two plates of sandwiches, which he handed to Ryan and Olivia.

"If you need anything else, I'll be over there," he said pointing to a table busy with people.

They thanked him, and he went over to the table and began discussing matters with the others gathered there.

"Told you it would be sandwiches," said Ryan.

"You should be grateful," Olivia chastised him.

"I am grateful," he said. "Mine's cheese and pickle."

"Do you get the impression that we're surplus to requirements," she said. "It's not as if anyone is asking our opinions on any important decisions."

"Because we've told them to get on with it."

"Only the commander. Are you telling me that no decisions are being made in this room that would have required the approval of the Alder?"

"Maybe they thought you've had a rough time and need a break."

"And look at those guards at that table over there. They look like they're making all kinds of decisions. Yesterday, they wouldn't have dared decide anything without running it past you. They are circumventing you."

Ryan watched the guards.

"I don't mind them circumventing me," he said at last.

"Me neither," she said. "But what do you think will happen to us if we are no longer useful?"

"I'm not sure," said Ryan, still watching the guards and eating his sandwich.

"Is there anything we can help with?" Ryan asked the guard when he came to collect the plates.

"No, I think we're fine," said the guard and took the plates away.

"See," said Olivia. "Circumvented."

The commander returned.

"Would you mind coming with me?" he asked Olivia. "We have someone you might want to talk to."

Ryan followed Olivia and the commander out onto the street where a horse and cart was waiting. In the back of the cart, bound by his hands and feet and bruised from a beating, lay George.

"We picked him up with the group on Boothferry Road," said the commander.

George looked up and saw Olivia.

"I killed your aunt," he said, staring into Olivia's eyes before spitting at her.

"She saved your life, you ungrateful shit," she said.

"What would you like us to do with him?" The commander asked.

"Do you have a cell you can put him in until we can have a public trial?"

"We can improvise something until we regain the courthouse. The cells at Citizens' Gardens are filling up, but I dare say we can find room," the commander said.

"Good," said Olivia. "Thank you for your work, Commander."

"Don't mention it," said the commander. "As soon as I have any news about the Guildhall or the Courts, I'll let you know."

"Is there anything we can help you with?" asked Ryan.

"The best thing you can do for us is to be here when we need you," said the commander.

Ryan nodded and followed Olivia back inside.

"Still feeling circumvented?" he asked her.

"Shut up," she said.

He smiled.

When they entered the main hall, the guard who had acted as their escort approached them.

"We have prepared a room where you can rest for a while if you wish," he said.

"That would be nice, thank you," Olivia said.

He led them both to a room in which they had arranged blankets and sheets on some mattresses.

"That's very kind, thank you," said Olivia.

"I'll wake you if there are any developments you need to know about."

"Thank you," said Ryan as he closed the door behind the guard.

Olivia took her shoes off and lay down on a mattress.

"Mind if I join you?" Ryan asked, taking his shoes off and laying down beside her.

"Suit yourself," she said.

He lay down and closed his eyes. There was knocking on the door, and he realised that he must have fallen asleep and he had no idea how much time must have passed.

"Enter," he said when he had gathered his wits and sat up.

The guard opened the door.

"What time is it?" Ryan asked.

"It's early," said the guard. "The commander asked whether he could speak with you."

"Of course," said Olivia, sitting up.

They followed the guard out of the room and back to to the main hall, where the commander was waiting.

"We've secured both the Guildhall and the courts," he said as they approached.

"Well done, commander," Olivia said. "Your efficiency will not be forgotten."

"Thank you," the commander's demeanour became more sullen. "We took some prisoners. One of them we believe is your father. If you would like, I can take you to him."

"That won't be necessary, thank you, commander," she said. "I'll see him when he stands trial."

Part Eight

Olivia looked up at the ornate dome above, decorated with the white roses of the old county of Yorkshire. Her gaze wandered down to the ornate chandeliers hanging on thick chains. She could hear the clock ticking on the wall behind her as she looked at the paintings adorning the alcoves beneath the dome.

The council chamber was full, but the room was quiet. The clerk whispered in her ear that everything was ready. She banged her gavel to bring the gathering to order, but she already had the attention of the entire room.

"Because of the unusual circumstances that led to today's trial, the Guild has held the trial here in the council chamber to be presided over by all eight sitting judges in the presence of the Guild. Call the accused."

Several guards led a bruised and battered George to a chair beside a table in the centre of the room.

"The accused has only given his name as George," said Olivia. "Would you like to give your real name now?"

"Does it matter?" said George.

Olivia wondered whether George was mad.

"You have been accused of the murders of Harry Davies, Jacob Brown, Charlie Evans, Charlie Roberts, Muhammad Wilson and Lisa Smith. How do you plead?"

"I do not recognise the validity of this court," he said.

There was a titter of amusement from the public gallery.

"You have chosen to defend yourself," said Olivia. "Would you like to make an opening statement to the court."

"I am a Mercian. I will always be a Mercian. Everything I did, I did for Mercia. I regret nothing," he said.

Olivia thought everything George did, he did for money, but she let the Guild get to the truth, as was correct. He never talked about the events that had led him to become a mercenary, but Olivia suspected something terrible must have happened in his path to encourage him to select the route he did.

"Anything else?" asked Olivia.

George sat in silence.

"In that case, I'd like to call the Public Councillor to state the case for the Guild against the defendant."

An old man approached the opposite side of the table to George and opened a file of papers.

"Thank you, ma'am. Learned judges, the man brought before you is only known as George because he refuses to give his real name. That alone should give you some idea of the moral fibre of this individual who hides his identity. This man was smuggled into the city by individuals who the city guards dealt with. However, this man evaded capture and, with the aid of accomplices, kidnapped the Alder, and took her to Mercia where he assembled an attack force and then used the Alder to gain passage into the city with his fellow insurgents. This man is responsible for the deaths of many of our citizens who gave their lives defending our city from the Mercian threat."

Olivia observed the expressions of hate from the members of the public who had queued for hours for an opportunity to observe the proceedings.

The old man turned his papers.

"The Guild would like to call its first witness, Ryan Jones."

Guild staff led Ryan into the room, and they showed him to a seat opposite the row of judges. The clerk brought him a copy of the city constitution and held up a card on which he could read the oath.

"I, Ryan Jones, swear to tell the truth, the whole truth and nothing but the truth, or I will pay the consequences as laid down in the city constitution."

The clerk took the book and card away. The old man approached Ryan.

"Mr Jones, you were in charge of the city guards on the night that this man entered the city, were you not?"

"I was."

"And were you aware that this man had entered the city?"

"I was."

"Can you describe to the court the measures you took on that night?"

"Yes, I interrogated him as to how he came to arrive in the city and what his intentions, were. At the end of the interrogation, I decided that he was a threat to the wellbeing of our community and decided that we should eliminate him."

"So, why wasn't he eliminated?" asked the Councillor.

"He was assisted by an accomplice who facilitated his escape before my guards could deal with him."

"Can you let the court know what happened?"

"I had left him with a guard to be dealt with. The next that I knew was a report that he had escaped and killed the guard and that he was assisted by a group of people who had infiltrated the Guild at the highest level."

"What do you mean by that?" interrupted the Councillor.

"The individuals had gained access to the highest level of city government."

"By that, you mean that they had access to the Alder herself?"

Many of the observers appeared shocked by this revelation.

"That's right," said Ryan. "As far as I could tell, one of his accomplices had got himself into a position of confidence with the Alder and convinced her to see this man where he was held in a safe house."

"Do you know how this man got direct access to the Alder?"

"As far as I understand, they claimed to know the whereabouts of the Alder's father and offered to take her to her father."

"Why did they not just bring her father to the city?"

"They convinced the Alder that there had been a coup and that she had to flee the city and return with her father to overthrow the coup."

"And who did they tell her was responsible for this coup?"

"Me," said Ryan.

"And were you?"

"No, I was not. There was no coup."

"And can you help the court understand how this man entered the city with an armada of boats and close to a thousand men."

"I received a call that the Alder was at Minerva Gate on a boat, so I ordered the guards to let her in. I was not aware at that moment of the number of boats that were being allowed into the marina."

"And what happened to the guards on duty?"

"They were killed in the fighting which ensued once all the Mercian boats had passed through the gate."

"And what did you do when you realised what had happened?"

"I mobilised all of the guards, who were able to overcome the insurgency."

"And the insurgents captured you at one point, did they not?"

"They did."

"Please tell the court how this came about and what happened after your capture?"

"I was in the command centre by the marina when the insurgents overran the building. They held there me for a while, before being transferred to the cells below the courts across the road from here."

Ryan glanced at Olivia who maintained an impassive expression.

"And how long were you kept there?"

"I wasn't there very long before they placed the Alder in the same cell, and together we escaped."

"And what did you do once you escaped?"

"The Alder was concerned that the insurgents would target her aunt in Hessle, so we went straight there to warn her, but we were too late."

"Why did you not attempt to alert the city guards?"

"At that moment, we had no idea whether any city guards were still fighting. As soon as we realised we could not help the Alder's aunt, we headed straight for the barracks on Anlaby Road where we found a group of city guards who had reversed the advance of the insurgents. We stayed with this group until they had liberated all areas of the city."

"And it was during this period they captured this man, was it not?"

"That's correct. They brought him to the Alder, at which point he confessed that he had killed the Alder's aunt. It was the Alder who insisted that they detain him until he could stand trial."

"And you heard him confess yourself that he had killed the Alder's aunt?"

"I did."

"Did you hear him confess to killing anyone else?"

"I did not."

"Is there anything else you can say which would help the court understand the circumstances which led to these events?"

"No, sorry."

"The Guild has no more questions for this witness."

"Would the defence like to question the witness?" asked Olivia.

"I do not recognise the validity of this court," said George.

Another titter from the public gallery. Olivia delivered a stern look, which achieved silence.

"Very well. That is all, Mr Jones. The Guild may proceed," she said.

"If it pleases the court, we would like to call our next witness. The Alder, Dr Jones."

Olivia nodded and descended the platform to take up the chair reserved for witnesses. As she did, Ryan took her place as chair of the proceedings.

The clerk approached her with the constitution and the oath card, and she swore the oath.

"Do you know who killed Charlie Evans?" the Councillor began.

"I don't know for sure," said Olivia. "But I believe it to be Harry Davies."

"Did Mr Davies tell you he killed Mr Evans?"

"He did not. But when I gave him the opportunity to deny it, he did not."

"Why do you think Harry Davies killed Charlie Evans?"

"Because if he hadn't then, we would have lost an opportunity to find out where my father was."

"So you condone his actions then?"

"I didn't say that."

"Do you condone his actions?"

"No, I don't."

"What was Harry Davies' relationship to you?"

"He was an advisor."

"Was he this man's accomplice?" the Councillor asked, pointing to George.

"Not to my knowledge."

"Please tell the court how you came to meet the defendant?"

"I was taken to see him by Harry Davies and Jacob Brown."

"And what was your relationship to Mr Brown?"

"This was the first occasion he had introduced himself. He worked as a coach driver for the Guild so he may have driven me places before without me being aware of his name."

"And where did you meet the defendant?"

"At the barracks on Anlaby Road."

"Citizens' Gardens Barracks?"

"No, the old barracks on Anlaby Road."

"Commander Lewis's unit?"

"Correct."

"So, he was in the custody of the guards?"

"I believe that Harry Davies took him there because he had friends who would monitor him until I could speak to him."

"And is it true that there was an incident in the barracks involving the defendant in which Davies and Brown killed two more guards?"

"I understand that two men died, but whether or not they were guards, I couldn't say."

"And who killed these people?"

"As I understand it, Harry Davies and Jacob Brown killed them because they were trying to kidnap the defendant."

"And then where was the defendant taken?"

"They took him to the infirmary."

"And were you aware that they had taken him there?"

"I was. I arranged for them to then take him to the house of my aunt."

"Why did you do that?"

"So he would be safe."

"From whom?"

"My husband."

"Why was that?"

"I believed that my husband wanted to kill him because he felt he was a threat to the city."

It was Olivia's turn to glance at Ryan and Ryan's turn to maintain an impassive countenance.

"And you didn't agree with your husband?"

"I saw the defendant as a link to my father, and therefore he was a risk worth taking."

"And you joined him at the house of your aunt, is that right?"

"That's right."

"Why was that?"

"My position here at the time seemed in doubt."

"Can you be clearer about that?"

"There were doubts about my safety."

"You didn't feel safe? Who did you feel was threatening you?"

"My husband."

"And do you now feel that your fears were justified?"

Olivia sighed. Ryan was watching her.

"I have no evidence that the threats were justified," she said.

"And yet you felt sufficiently threatened to get on a boat with these individuals and leave the city."

"Apparently."

The Councillor shuffled his papers.

"Would you tell the court from where you procured the boat?"

"It was owned by Muhammad Wilson's father, who had been a friend of my aunt."

"And where did you go on this boat?"

"Brigg."

"In Mercia?"

"That's right."

"And would you tell the court what happened in Brigg."

"They took us to a disused pub where they tried to imprison us."

"Who are 'we' and who are 'they'?"

"We were Harry Davies and I. The 'they' is unclear whether it was the defendant or friends of his."

"Friends?"

"They were called Christopher and Liam. I should clarify that Charlie Roberts died on the way to Brigg when raiders attacked us. When we escaped from the pub, the friends of the defendant confronted us, and they were the ones who killed Harry and Muhammad."

"And who killed Jacob Brown?"

"I don't know. I assume that the defendant killed him, but I have no evidence of that."

"So the only evidence you have is a confession from the defendant that he killed your aunt."

"That is correct."

"And what motive do you think the defendant would have for killing your aunt?"

"He accused me of perpetuating slavery."

"And have you been involved in slavery?"

"Of course not."

"Would it be fair to say that the defendant would never have threatened the life of your aunt if you had not affected his entry into the city?"

"That is speculation."

Olivia was becoming annoyed by the tone of the Councillor.

"This issue of how the insurgents got all of their boats into the marina. Could you enlighten the court as to how this happened?"

"I was told that the Mercians were coming to support my husband against another band of insurgents that had infiltrated the city. They told me that Harry Davies and Jacob Brown had been members of those insurgents."

"So, after believing that your husband was orchestrating a coup which endangered your life, you then believed that a band of Mercians would defend your husband against another group of insurgents."

"That's right."

There was a murmur of confusion among the observers.

"Order," Ryan demanded.

"And this second group of insurgents were meant to be from where?" asked the Councillor.

"From Northumberland."

"I see. Forgive me, ma'am, but all this suggests that you are gullible."

"It would appear that way."

A ripple of laughter crossed the room.

"Order!" shouted Ryan again, and the room fell silent.

"If what you have said is to be believed," continued the Councillor. "Then it was your actions which led to all of the deaths in question today except Charlie Evans, who you think might have been killed by Harry Davies, who himself is now dead."

Olivia sat in silence.

"That concludes our examination of this witness," said the Councillor.

"Would the defendant like to cross-examine the witness?" Ryan asked.

"I do not recognise the validity of this court," said George.

There was a groan from the public gallery.

"I excuse the witness," said Ryan. "Given the nature of the revelations relating to the conduct of the Alder, I suggest to the court that I remain as chair for the rest of the inquiry."

Ryan scanned the faces of the eight judges, who all agreed with his suggestion.

Olivia stepped out of the witness chair and took a seat in the public section of the room.

"Your next witness?" Ryan asked the Councillor.

"Yes, I would like to call Dr James Smith."

A murmur of excitement travelled around the room.

A group of guards led in Dr Smith and asked him to sit in the chair Olivia had just vacated. The clerk swore him in.

"Dr Smith," the Councillor began. "Please tell the court how you persuaded the Alder to return to Freetown with an armada of Mercian insurgents?"

"They were not insurgents," said Dr Smith.

"Then who were they?"

"They were Mercians whom the defendant convinced to help me."

"Help you?"

"That's right. The Mercians came on the understanding that they would help overthrow Ryan Jones."

"But we have just heard testimony from the Alder that the Mercians were there to help Ryan Jones against a group of insurgents from Northumberland."

"The Alder was kept in the dark about many matters. With regards the Mercians, they were led to believe they would overthrow Ryan Jones."

Olivia scowled at her father.

"And why did you want to overthrow Ryan Jones?"

"I never said I wanted to overthrow Ryan Jones. I said that the Mercians came because they understood that they would overthrow Ryan Jones."

The Councillor shook his head as if trying to shake his confusion away and there were chuckles from the confused spectators in the public gallery.

"And were they not going to overthrow Ryan Jones?"

"No."

"But they came very close to doing so, did they not?"

"No, they didn't."

"But they captured Ryan Jones and placed him in a cell with the Alder."

"No, I had them placed in a cell together for their safety. I did not expect them to escape."

The Councillor scratched his head, as did many of the observers. Olivia leaned forward.

"I'm sorry Dr Smith, but I find this all incredible," the Councillor continued. "You say that you placed the Alder and Ryan Jones in the cells."

"That's right. I was in charge of the operation. I led the Mercians here to purge the city of Northumbrians who had infiltrated the city guard."

"Really?" said the Councillor. "I find that difficult to believe."

"Without the knowledge of Ryan Jones, the Northumbrians had infiltrated all but one of the barracks in the city, and had conspired so that the city was buying 50% of its fresh produce from their forced labour camps."

The sense of disbelief in the room was tangible.

"But how could Ryan Jones not know about this and yet you knew about it? Even though you were not in the city."

"I was alerted by one of the city commanders. They came and found me because they knew I might help get support from the Mercians, because of my previous negotiations on reunification. They showed me what was happening on these slave farms and so I sent George to contact my daughter."

"So the defendant's name is George?"

"Yes, George Johnson."

George looked at Dr Smith as if he had just betrayed him.

"And what happened to Mr Johnson when he arrived in the city?"

"Ryan Jones, who pretended to be me intercepted him. George knew that he was not me but could not gain Jones's trust. Fortunately, one of our agents could come to our assistance."

"Harry Davies?"

"That's right. Harry Davies was working for us. He got George to the barracks, where he arranged an interview with the Alder."

"Why did you not just approach Ryan Jones?"

"Ryan Jones was under the influence of the Northumbrians, and couldn't be trusted until we could remove the threat."

"So you took the Alder to Brigg?"

"That is correct. She might not have been in danger from Ryan Jones himself, but she was in danger from the Northumbrian insurgents, so we decided to remove her from the city for her safety until we could resolve the situation."

"Then how do you explain what happened in Brigg?"

"First, let me clarify that it was my sister who arranged for the Alder's safe passage from the city. Without her help, this would not have been possible. Also, it was very unfortunate that the Mercian raiders killed Charlie Roberts. That is just one risk of travelling in hostile territory."

"And Brigg?"

"Yes, so, unbeknownst to us, the Northumbrians had learnt of our plan and had infiltrated our group. Therefore, when George took Harry and the Alder to our original rendezvous, the Northumbrians tricked him. However, luck intervened, and Harry could eliminate the threat, despite losing his own life. George could then bring the Alder to me, and we could prepare for the return journey."

"Which involved the invasion of the city."

"That was what we wanted the Mercians to think. We allowed them to attack all but the Anlaby Road barracks, thus eliminating the Northumbrian threat. Once we had achieved that, the commander of the Anlaby Road barracks could mop up the Mercian attack. When I received word that they had reached the Guildhall, I was able to let them in a rear entrance and take the remaining Mercians by surprise."

"But you say that your sister helped you in this venture. Why then would Mr Johnson want to kill her?"

"He didn't."

"Then why did he?"

"He didn't."

"Then why did he say that he did?"

"It was important to maintain the illusion that we were trying to overthrow Ryan Jones until we could be certain we had eliminated all the Northumbrians and Mercians. It was, therefore, necessary for George to take part in an element of playacting to achieve this. It seems that he is reluctant to give up the play-acting, but I think that is because he feels a little affronted by those who have not understood the real situation."

"Well, you have to admit that the whole story you have presented here seems a little incredible."

"I agree, which is why the Alder agreed to hold this inquiry in front of the whole Guild so that everyone could hear the truth first-hand."

"Well, if you don't mind, I think we have first to corroborate your story. We have no more questions for this witness."

"Do you still not recognise this court, Mr Johnson?" asked Ryan, with a smile.

"I do not," said George.

Olivia raised her eyebrows at George's belligerence. Perhaps her father had been right about George being a pathological liar.

"That will be all for now, thank you, Dr Smith."

Olivia's father stepped down from the witness chair and joined the rest of the observers. The Councillor consulted his notes.

"We would like to call Commander Lucas Lewis," said the Councillor.

The commander entered and sat on the witness chair, as the clerk swore him in.

"Commander Lewis," the Councillor began. "We have just heard testimony from Dr Smith that Northumbrian insurgents had infiltrated the city guard."

"That is correct," said the Commander.

"Would you tell the court how almost the entire city guard could be infiltrated by insurgents?"

"By the time I noticed the situation," said the commander, "It was too late to take any preventative action. It was when attempts were being made to infiltrate my unit that I realised the extent of the situation."

"And what did you do when you realised the extent of the infiltration?"

"I had to go along with it to a certain extent, at first to protect my position. I began to formulate plans to reverse the situation, and it seemed to me that the best way was to get the Mercians and Northumbrians to fight with each other, and the best person to convince a bunch of Mercians to come over and have a fight seemed to be Dr Smith. Therefore, the first thing I had to do was to track down Dr Smith, and with a combination of information from the Alder and some drones, we found him and went to pick him up. He was receptive to the plan, and so we recruited George Johnson, who is a known mercenary who we felt could help in this situation."

"And did you consider the risk to the general population with this approach?"

"Yes, we did. Which is why we set up a command centre in the City Hall to coordinate our efforts with the public. It was the best-kept secret in the city, and it was very important that I kept the Alder and her husband in the dark to a certain extent for our deception to be convincing."

"How many people were involved in this deception?"

"Not very many at all. The more people involved in a secret, the better chance it has of not being a secret for very long. Only my most trusted officers were party to the plan."

"Were you not, in fact, conducting your own insurgency? One could construe this as a coup orchestrated by yourself in which you colluded to keep the community's leaders in the dark."

"You could construe it that way, but I never intended to undertake a coup."

"This was a perilous strategy, was it not? What if the Northumbrians had learned of the plan? You said yourself, Northumbrians infiltrated the city."

"It was perilous, yes. However, it was a risk worth taking. And it paid off."

"And did everything go according to plan?"

"Yes, more or less. We did not expect the Northumbrians infiltrating our plan in Brigg, which led to some regrettable deaths. Johnson encountered some problems when he tried to extract himself from the Mercians, but apart from that, it went according to our original plan. It would have gone wrong if Harry Davies hadn't protected Johnson when he first arrived in the city."

"If it was the Northumbrians who infiltrated your plan, then how was it they did not send word to the Northumbrians in Freetown to warn them you were about to launch an attack using Mercian insurgents."

"That's simple. They infiltrated our cell in Brigg, but they were not party to that aspect of the plan. Even if they had discovered it, they would have needed to get someone to Freetown to raise the alarm. They would never have got past the Mercians by boat and by the time anyone travelling by land reached Freetown it would have been too late."

An assistant whispered in the Councillor's ear.

"I have no more questions for the commander," the Councillor said.

"Unless Mr Johnson has anything to say, you are free to go," Ryan told the commander.

George snarled at him.

"We would now like to call Lisa Smith," said the Councillor.

An audible gasp circled the room.

Olivia's Aunt Lisa walked into the room, took her place in the witness chair, and the clerk swore her in.

"Ms Smith," said the Councillor, "We have heard testimony from your brother, and also from Commander Lewis, that insurgents had infiltrated the city guard and that you were involved in the plan to bring Mercians into the city."

"That is correct," she said.

"How did you first learn about this?"

"Commander Lewis came to me looking for my brother and explained the whole situation. I was more than happy to help."

"Can you confirm that during the conflict with the Mercians, they burned your house to the ground?"

"That is correct."

"How did that happen?"

"Mr Johnson took me to safety, but inadvertently led the Mercians to my door. It was the Mercians who burned the house down, but it was Mr Johnson who saved me from them."

The assistant returned and whispered in the Councillor's ear again.

"Are you sure?" the Councillor asked the assistant, who nodded. The Councillor looked at his papers and then at Ms Smith and then at Ryan. "I don't think we need to ask Ms Smith any more questions."

"Fine, then unless Mr Johnson objects, Ms Smith can step down," said Ryan.

George offered Ryan a forced smile as Ms Smith stepped down from the witness's chair.

"As our final witness, I would like to call Jacob Brown," said the Councillor.

A collective astonished gasp engulfed the room.

"Order!" shouted Ryan.

Brown entered and sat in the witness chair. The clerk handed him the constitution, and he swore the oath.

"Mr. Brown," said the Councillor. "You may have guessed that a lot of people in the room are surprised to see you here. We heard testimony that you were in Brigg the last time anyone saw you. Would you explain to the court what happened in Brigg?"

Jacob took a deep breath.

"We were fulfilling the mission as planned. George had taken the Alder to the rendezvous, but then he discovered that Northumbrians had infiltrated us. So I went with him to the rendezvous, and he told me to hide out of sight in case any more Northumbrian came. There was a gunfight between the infiltrators and our team, and the infiltrators were both shot. They killed Harry and Muhammad. I waited at the pub where this happened, to see whether anyone else would arrive, and it wasn't until George came back to deal with the bodies that a group of them came and we overwhelmed them. I stayed in Brigg, interrogating the prisoners until I had gained all the information I could. Then I made my way back to Freetown."

"And how did you get back to Freetown?"

"I stole a Mercian boat."

"And what information did you get from your prisoners?"

"I don't think I should share that in open court."

"And what happened to the prisoners?"

"Let's just say they will not be a threat to Freetown anymore."

"Are they dead?"

"They are."

"Did you kill them?"

"They died from wounds they sustained when they resisted their detention."

The Councillor consulted his notes.

"Mr Johnson was not involved in the deaths of any of the individuals implicated in this inquiry and that we should drop all charges against him."

"With all due respect, Mr Councillor," Ryan interrupted. "It is up to the judges to decide who if anyone will be sentenced. Are you ready to consider your verdict?"

The judges nodded.

"I will adjourn the court until the judges have reached their verdict," Ryan said and banged the gavel.

The room started to clear amongst excited chatter.

Part Nine

The landlord and his staff had laid out the plotting parlour of Ye Olde White Harte in all its splendour. The best crockery and cutlery on the table and the best wine glasses waiting for vintage from long before the collapse. Only very special occasions received this kind of treatment, but this was a very special occasion.

The judges had returned a verdict of not guilty on all counts. It had relieved everybody. Not least of all Olivia, who felt she had done well to avoid a charge of negligence or incompetence, even though her Aunt Lisa, Jacob and George kept telling her it had been their powers of persuasion that had convinced her. Even George had got away with being so uncooperative with the court. There was a lot to celebrate, and the rebuilding of some bridges was necessary, some sore wounds needed time to heal. There was still an undercurrent of mistrust, which made Olivia feel uncomfortable, and she worried about what the future might bring.

Olivia and Ryan still held their positions. She had promoted Commander Lewis to head of the city guard, at Ryan's request. Dr Smith stayed on as a special advisor, and he and Ryan got on well.

Olivia had promoted Jacob to a special advisor, and she had compensated her Aunt Lisa with a new home and contents.

Some weeks had passed, and they could not persuade George to stay any longer. As he said, he had left the front door open and needed to do the washing up.

Everyone agreed to have a special dinner in his honour on the eve of his departure. Dr Smith pointed out that as a mercenary, they had paid him and therefore had received thanks enough, but everyone else insisted that he should have a special send off. Even George agreed, though he still hadn't quite forgiven Ryan for trying to have him killed, and he was still a little surly around Olivia, whom he still blamed for allowing the city to buy from the forced labour farms.

Despite her persistent questions he had refused to give any clues what had happened to him or his family to radicalise him so much.

Ryan had arranged everything with the pub. He knew the landlord well, and the landlord had agreed not to play any jazz that evening. Ryan remembered how much George had disliked it.

George was the last to arrive and, as he entered, he handed a parcel to Olivia.

"I guess you thought this might have got lost in all the excitement," he said.

She opened it and saw the familiar pale blue of her father's diary.

"You can give it back to him," said George. "Or read it. I've read it. It's boring. All about slaughtering goats."

Olivia laughed, and Dr Smith looked a little bit offended.

"Are you sure you won't stay?" asked Olivia. "Commander Lewis needs someone to help him rebuild the city guard."

"No," said George. "I think I might have left the oven on."

"Well, now the Northumbrians have used all our ammunition fighting the Mercians, we need someone to go to Germany to get us more," said Olivia. "Do you fancy that?"

"That all depends on how well it pays," said George with a smile.

"There you go, Lucas," Olivia said to the commander. "I told you I could talk him around."

"On one condition," said George.

"What's that?" asked Olivia.

"Jacob comes with me."

"You must ask Jacob about that," said Olivia. "Jacob?"

"It all depends on how well it pays," said Jacob, to everyone's amusement.

"You've been hanging around George too much," said Olivia.

"I've taught him well," smiled George.

Olivia made a mental note to ask Jacob about George's past.

They all sat around the large wooden table, stained black by years of varnish. Olivia, Ryan, Dr Smith, Commander Lewis, George, Jacob and Aunt Lisa.

The landlord himself came upstairs to ensure the staff served the appetisers in the right way, and also to assure Ryan that no jazz would be played for the duration of their stay in his establishment, although he expressed bemusement why anyone would object to Chet Baker. Ryan shrugged.

The appetisers were garlic bread, a speciality of the landlord since he took over the running of the pub. The garlic had been grown less than quarter of a mile away, and they had made the butter from the milk of a goat who lived even closer. Only the bread had to travel any distance.

On the orders of the Alder, the Guild had made available some of the few bottles of wine which remained from before the collapse. Everyone understood that wine quality had diminished since the collapse. Wines from France were more difficult to get hold of, and even wines from Wessex were expensive. It was still possible to get reasonable whites from Germany, but they knew the crossing through the Baltic was dangerous. There were raiders everywhere, which is why George knew the price to fetch ammunition had to be high enough.

The staff shared the wine out.

"My God!" said Dr Smith after he had taken a sip. "Where did you get wine this good? I haven't tasted wine like this since... well, I can't remember the last time I tasted wine this good."

"It's a Cabernet Sauvignon from Chile," said Olivia.

"Chile?" Dr Smith exclaimed. "I can't remember the last time I had wine from South America. Not since before the collapse."

There was a period of silence while everyone enjoyed their first sips of the wine. Even Jacob, who was not a wine drinker, could appreciate its quality.

Freshly made pasta made up the main course, with mushrooms grown in a nearby basement, and a goat's cheese sauce courtesy of the pub's goat. Accompanying the dish was a fresh rocket salad and fresh tomatoes, from Citizens' Gardens just down the road.

"I tell you what I miss," said Dr Smith. "Fish."

There was a groan of longing from around the table, except for George.

"I never liked fish," he said. "But I wouldn't eat anything that came out of that water now. That's if you can get anything out of the water these days."

"We send a boat out every so often," said Olivia. "But it's never very promising."

"More for scientific research," said Ryan. "The university has an excellent toxicology department. You should take your father for a visit."

"I will," Olivia promised.

For dessert, the pub had outdone itself with sponge pudding and custard.

"Dr Smith?" Ryan inquired. "Now that we have a shortage of supply equating to half of our vegetable requirements and 20% of our fruit needs, do you think you could make your negotiating skills available to help us source produce from farms which don't use forced labour?"

"Well, seeing as though my home was destroyed, I suppose I should earn my keep here," the doctor replied. "We should send a mission to Beverley and see what we can get. Though I can't say how receptive the Northumbrians will be after what happened."

"If you come to Germany, you might bring back some wine," said George.

"Hmm. Very tempting. Isn't it dangerous, though?" Dr Smith said.

"We don't have to go anywhere near the Baltic," said George. "We can just go straight down the River Elbe to Hamburg."

"Sounds tempting," said Dr Smith.

"The trip will be easier with the three of us," said George. "Assuming you can get me a boat."

He directed this last comment towards Ryan and Olivia.

"We might talk ethan into lending you the barge," said Aunt Lisa. "Although he still hasn't recovered from the death of his brother."

"You'd have to speak nicely," said Ryan. "The family is still mourning Muhammad."

"Well, you get me the boat," said George. "And I'll get you the ammunition...and the wine if Doctor Smith is that desperate."

"I'm sure we can organise something," said Ryan. "There are some Mercian boats to choose from now."

"Are you not concerned about reprisals from the Mercians?" asked Olivia.

There was a little bit of confusion around the table as to whom Olivia had directed her comment.

"Who are you asking?" asked George.

"Anyone," said Olivia.

"I doubt they have enough boats or men to launch much of an attack," said Commander Lewis. "George had convinced them to bring over the best of what they had left."

"I can have a look when I go over to do the washing up," said George.

"I imagine you're not very popular over there," said the commander. "If you want I can escort you with a unit to make sure everything is OK."

"If you are happy to risk it?" said George.

"I'd like to see first-hand what the situation is like over there," said Commander Lewis.

"Yes, make sure he comes back," said Olivia.

"Are you talking about Lewis or me?" asked George.

"I want both of you to come back," she said. "I need a city guard, and I need ammunition."

"And I need wine," said Doctor Smith, chuckling to himself.

"Here you go," said Olivia, passing him the bottle.

"Thank you," said Dr. Smith, refilling his glass with a smile. "What I meant was that we could do with restocking our cellar. Anyone else?"

He held up the bottle. Commander Lewis nodded. He passed the bottle to him. The commander smiled and poured himself a drink, before passing the bottle on to George.

"It's nice to know we're wanted," said George.

"Isn't it," agreed the commander.

"So, that's settled then," said Ryan. "While the commander is accompanying George to Brigg, Dr Smith and I can make a trade visit to Beverley. When George gets back, he can accompany Dr Smith and Jacob to the continent for ammunition."

"And wine," Dr Smith added.

"And wine," Ryan confirmed. "Shall we toast then? To bright futures."

"To bright futures," the gathering repeated, raising their glasses.

Epilogue

Ryan, Olivia, Aunt Lisa, Dr. Smith and Jacob all gathered at Minerva gate to watch as George steered Muhammad's barge through into the estuary. Commander Lewis stood next to him on the deck, and through the portholes, they could see a unit of city guards preparing to hide below deck.

"Good luck!" Olivia shouted as she waved them off. "Don't forget to come back."

"We won't," the commander shouted back.

"I might," said George, so that only Commander Lewis could hear him.

The group watched the barge until Minerva gate had closed behind it. Then they stepped down off the wall and walked towards a horse and cart waiting below.

"Can we offer you ladies a lift?" Ryan asked.

"No, thanks," said Olivia. "I think I'd like to walk back to the Guildhall with my aunt if that's OK with her?"

She turned to her aunt, who nodded that it was OK.

"Suit yourselves," said Ryan. "We'll head straight to Beverley then. If things go badly, we'll be back by tea time, if things go well, we might not be back for two days."

"If things go really badly," said Dr. Smith. "We may not be back at all."

"Stop it," said Olivia.

Her father approached her.

"Look," he said. "I know with the trial and everything we haven't spoken properly. I feel bad about what happened in the past and I would welcome the opportunity to make up for lost time."

"What do you have in mind?"

"When I get back from Northumberland and before I go to Germany, let's set some time aside to catch up and talk. I almost lost you once. I don't want to lose you again."

"OK," she said. "You'd better make sure you come back then."

He smiled, gave her a kiss on her forehead and then climbed onto the cart alongside Jacob.

The two women watched as Jacob steered the horse and cart around the corner and out of sight.

Olivia turned to her aunt, and they began ambling back towards the Guildhall.

"Can you trust him?" her aunt asked.

"Who?" Olivia asked.

"Ryan."

"I don't know," said Olivia. 'I hope so."

"Do you think he was in league with the Northumbrians?"

"I don't know," said Olivia. "But we've just sent him into Northumbria, so we're about to find out."

"Are you not worried about letting him go, considering we don't know what his motives are?" Aunt Lisa asked.

"Well, I don't think it matters. If we prevented him from going, he would know that we are suspicious and would find a way of making contact anyway. This way we find out without revealing our position."

"Yes, but it's risky with the commander's unit away with George."

"Yes, that is unfortunate. However, even if he were here, he wouldn't be much use against an invading Northumbrian army, given how little ammunition we have and only volunteers working as a city guard. At least this way, if anyone invades, George and Commander Lewis will be spared to fight another day and maybe find support."

"From where?"

"From the Mercians, I guess."

"That'd be impressive given everything that's happened. Well, let's hope we are wrong about Ryan."

"We'll find out soon enough," said Olivia.

The two women walked side by side, as the morning sun glistened off the boats in the marina.

*

Did you enjoy this book? You can make a big difference.

Reviews are the most powerful tools in my arsenal for getting attention for my books. Much as I'd like to, I don't have the financial muscle of a large publisher. I can't take out take out full-page ads in the newspaper or put posters on the subway.

(Not yet anyway.)

However, I have something much more powerful and effective than that, and it's something those publishers would kill to get their hands on.

A committed and loyal bunch of readers.

Honest reviews of my books help bring them to the attention of other readers.

If you've enjoyed this book, I would be very grateful if you could spend just five minutes leaving a review[1] (it can be as short as you like).

Thank you very much.

---

1.   https://www.goodreads.com/book/show/41019751-when-the-well-runs-dry?from_search=true

GET LIVING WITH SACI

Building a relationship with my readers is the best thing about writing. I occasionally send newsletters with details on new releases, special offers and other bits of news.

And if you sign up to the mailing list, you can download my first novel LIVING WITH SACI **for free**, just by signing up at https://bookhip.com/KVKVDA

ABOUT THE AUTHOR

M J Dees is the author of ***Living with Saci***, ***The Astonishing Anniversaries of James and David, Part One*** and ***When The Well Runs Dry***. He makes his online home at www.mjdees.com[1]. You can connect with M J on Twitter at @mjdeeswriter[2], on Facebook at www.facebook.com/mjdeeswriter[3] and you should send him an email at mj@mjdees.com if the mood strikes you.

---

1. http://www.mjdees.com/

2. https://twitter.com/mjdeeswriter

3. http://www.facebook.com/mjdeeswriter

<u>Living with Saci</u>[1]

Living with Saci is set in the sprawling metropolis of São Paulo, Brazil. It tells the story of Teresa da Silva, an overweight, depressed, drink dependent, and her struggles in the city. Estranged from her daughter, who lives with the ex-husband in England, life seems to constantly deal Teresa a bad hand. She begins to wonder whether the mischievous character from Brazilian folklore, Saci, might have something to do with it. Events seem to be taking a turn for the posi-

---

1. *https://bookhip.com/KVKVDA*

tive when she meets Felipe, who asks her to marry him. But when he disappears, Teresa finds that she is the object of suspicion.

The Astonishing Anniversaries of James and David, Part One[2]

How do you know if you have achieved success? No matter how successful he becomes, James doesn't feel happy. Meanwhile, his twin brother, David, seems content regardless of the dreadful, life-threatening events, which afflict him year after year. ***The Astonishing Anniversaries of James and David*** is as much a nostalgic romp through 70s, 80s and 90s England as it is a shocking and occasionally tragic comedy.

---

2. *https://dl.bookfunnel.com/4s5q5rf2un*

DEDICATION

To Transition Towns, EcoLocal, Sustainable Merton, Paul Mobbs, and everyone else in the world of sustainability and resource use, who are working very hard to avoid the scenarios alluded to in this book.

ACKNOWLEDGEMENTS

I am indebted to the following for their help: Jackie Wyant for being the first person to read the manuscript, for giving great feedback and for designing great covers. Sabrina Dees and Anna Orridge for agreeing to read yet another of my manuscripts. Mary Anglin, Bea Dees, Nicole Marie Hopkins, Leanne Pert, Kate Smillie and the rest of the Beta readers for their invaluable comments and suggestions and apologies if I ignored any of them.

I would also like to thank the Self-Publishing Community for all their support in helping me to get this book published and my Advance Reading Team for their help with last-minute feedback and, of course, those all-important reviews.

COPYRIGHT

---

1. http://www.saltandunicorns.com

www.ingramcontent.com/pod-product-compliance
Lightning Source LLC
Chambersburg PA
CBHW031957050726
47590CB00006B/1949